001

REKI KAWAHARA   ABEC   bEE-pEE

SWORD ARt ONIINE
AiNCRAd

SAO
SWORD ARt ONLINE

"Stock it cheap, sell it cheap: that's my motto."

Agil § Item Merchant in Algade, on Aincrad's 50th floor

"Strange to see you here, Asuna. Didn't think you frequented dumps like this."

Kirito § A solo player aiming to beat the top floor of Aincrad

"Kirito."

Asuna § Nicknamed "The Flash," Vice Commander of the Knights of the Blood

"I'll do a much better job of it than you."

"I will kill you... On my word, you will die by my hand... I would never leave Lady Asuna in the hands of a no-name like you!"

Kuradeel § Member of the Knights of the Blood, Asuna's bodyguard

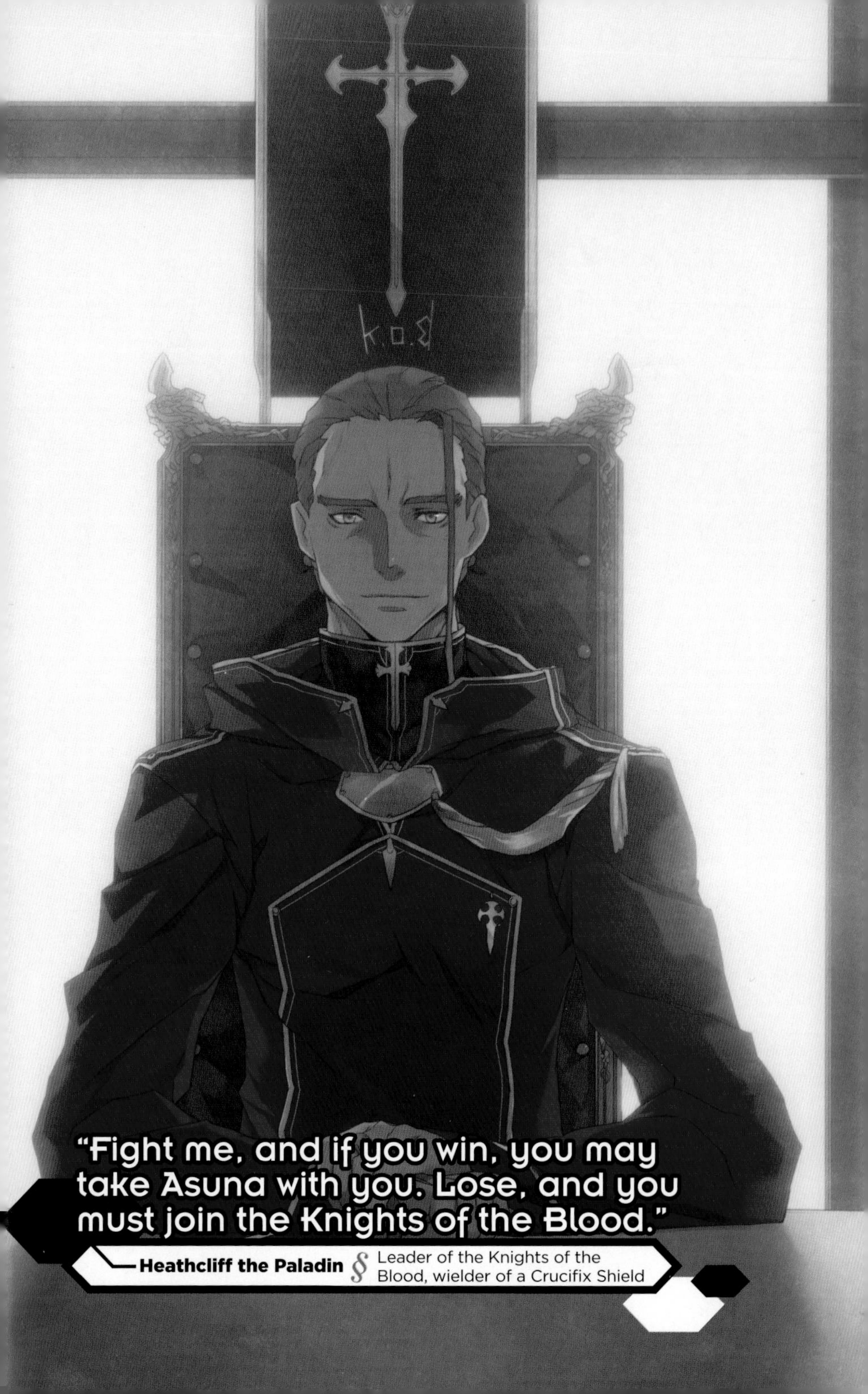
"Fight me, and if you win, you may take Asuna with you. Lose, and you must join the Knights of the Blood."
Heathcliff the Paladin
§
Leader of the Knights of the Blood, wielder of a Crucifix Shield
K.O.B

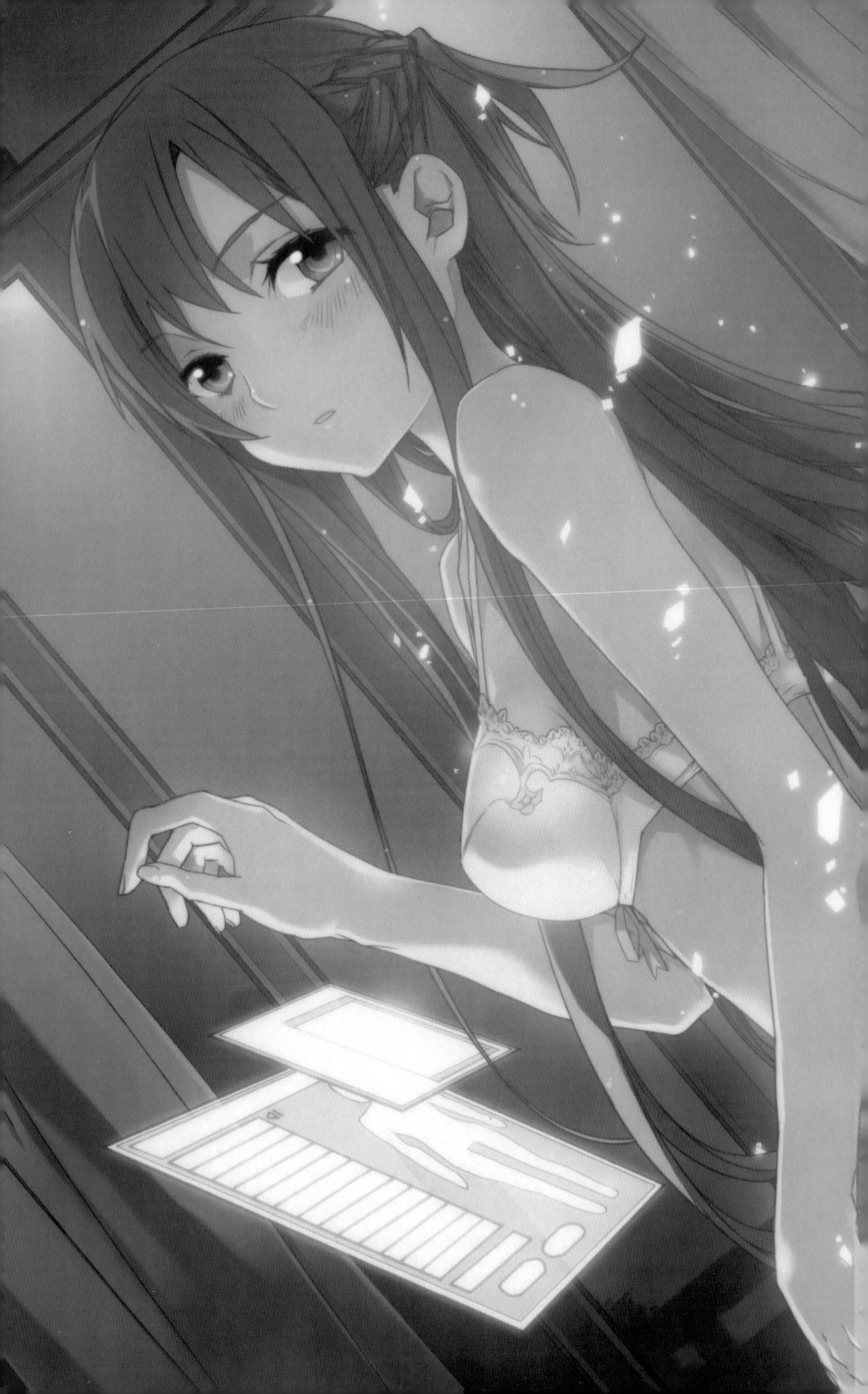

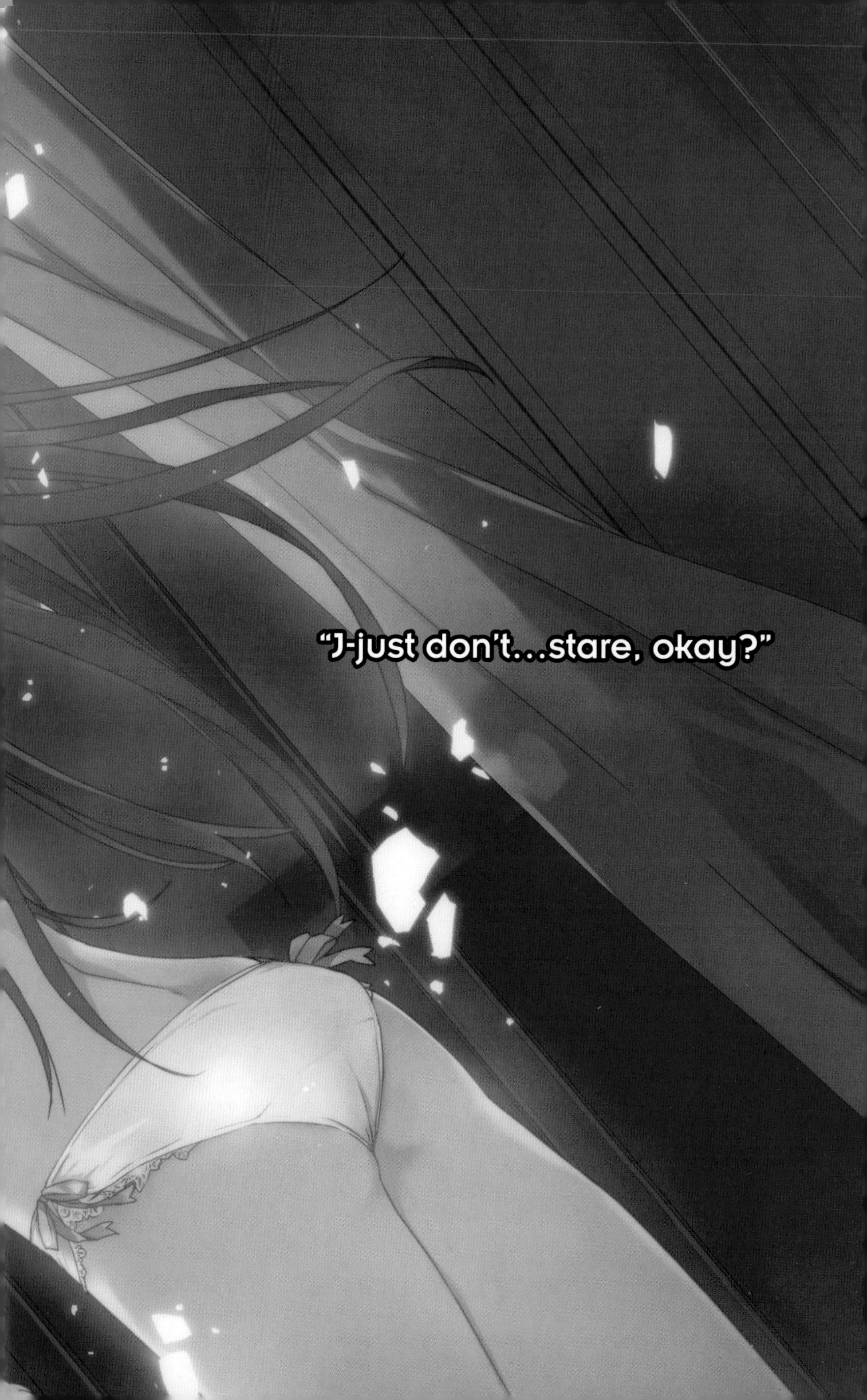
“J-just don’t…stare, okay?”

Floating Castle

Aincrad

A castle of rock and iron comprising one hundred floors. Inside are countless cities, towns, villages, forests, plains and lakes. Only one staircase connects each floor to its adjacents, and these staircases are located within dangerous mazes filled with monsters. The players within must navigate their way through these floors to the top, defeating powerful boss monsters with nothing more than the weapons in their hands. Outside of combat, there are also crafting disciplines like blacksmithing, leatherworking and tailoring; productive endeavors such as fishing and cooking; and even creative pursuits such as playing musical instruments. Players are not limited to adventuring within this vast, virtual world—they can literally choose their own lifestyles within the game.

Aincrad is the setting of *Sword Art Online*, the very first example of the VRMMO genre.

SWORD ART Online AINCRAD

VOLUME 1

Reki Kawahara

abec

Yen
Press

NEW YORK

SWORD ART ONLINE 1: Aincrad
REKI KAWAHARA

Translation: Stephen Paul

This book is a work of fiction. Names, characters, places, and incidents are the product of the author's imagination or are used fictitiously. Any resemblance to actual events, locales, or persons, living or dead, is coincidental.

SWORD ART ONLINE
© REKI KAWAHARA 2009
All rights reserved.
First published in Japan in 2009 by
KADOKAWA CORPORATION, Tokyo.
English translation rights arranged with
KADOKAWA CORPORATION, Tokyo,
through Tuttle-Mori Agency, Inc., Tokyo.

English translation © 2014 by Yen Press, LLC

Yen On
1290 Avenue of the Americas, New York, NY 10104
www.YenPress.com

Yen On is an imprint of Yen Press, LLC.
The Yen Press name and logo are trademarks of Yen Press, LLC.

First Yen On Edition: April 2014

Library of Congress Cataloging-in-Publication Data

Kawahara, Reki.
   Aincrad / Reki Kawahara ; translation: Stephen Paul. — First Yen Press edition.
      pages cm. — (Sword art online ; [1])
   "First published in Japan in 2009 by KADOKAWA CORPORATION, Tokyo."
   Summary: In the year 2022, some six thousand gamers excitedly explore the new Sword Art Online, which manipulates users' brain waves to create a wholly realistic gaming experience, but soon learn it lacks a log-out button and to escape they must conquer all one hundred floors—or die trying.
   ISBN 978-0-316-37124-7 (pbk.)
   [1. Fantasy games—Fiction.   2. Virtual reality—Fiction.
3. Internet games—Fiction.   4. Science fiction.]   I. Title.
   pz7.K1755Ain 2014
   [Fic]—dc23
                                        2014001175

14

CW

Printed in the United States of America

"THIS MIGHT BE A GAME, BUT IT'S NOT SOMETHING YOU PLAY."

—Akihiko Kayaba, *Sword Art Online* programmer

Reki Kawahara

abec

bee-pee

An impossibly huge castle of rock and iron, floating in an endless expanse of sky.

That is the entirety of this world.

A tireless, month-long survey by a team of fanatical experts found that the base floor of the fortress was more than six miles in diameter, just large enough to fit the entire Setagaya ward of Tokyo inside. And considering the one hundred floors stacked one on top of the other, the sheer vastness of the structure beggared the imagination. It was impossible to estimate the total amount of data it all represented.

Inside the castle were several bustling cities, countless smaller towns and villages, forests, plains, and lakes. Only one staircase connected each floor to those adjacent it, and these staircases were located within dangerous mazes filled with monsters. It was difficult just finding them, much less reaching them, but once someone had cleared the stairs and arrived at a major city the next floor up, a teleport gate linking the two floors would open in every city below, allowing all players instantaneous travel among the various levels of the castle.

It was thus that, over two long years, its inhabitants slowly but steadily conquered this giant fortress. The current human frontier is the seventy-fourth floor.

The castle's name is Aincrad, a floating world of blade and battle with about six thousand human beings trapped within. Otherwise known as—

Sword Art Online.

1

The dull gray point of the sword chipped my shoulder.

I felt a chilly hand squeeze deep within my chest as the thin line fixed to the corner of my vision shrank slightly.

That blue horizontal line—my HP bar—was a visualization of my remaining life force. I still had more than 80 percent of my maximum health remaining, but a wiser perspective said I was 20 percent closer to the brink of death.

Before the enemy's blade could begin its motion again, I darted backward to maintain the distance between us.

"*Huff…*"

I forcefully exhaled and took another breath. My virtual "body" in this world required no oxygen, but back on the other side, my flesh-and-blood form was no doubt panting heavily as it lay prostrate on my bed. A cold sweat would be glistening on my outstretched hands, my pulse racing without end.

It was only natural.

Everything around me was a virtual 3-D object, the only thing I'd lost being abstract, numerical hit points, but my life hung in the balance all the same.

In that sense, this battle was the ultimate injustice. The "enemy" before me—a half-man, half-beast monster covered in slick green scales with long arms, the head of a lizard, and an elongated tail—was not only inhuman, it wasn't even truly alive. It was a mass of digital data that could be rebuilt by the system endlessly, no matter how many times it was killed.

Okay, it wasn't quite that simple.

The lizardman's AI program was observing my fighting style, learning my habits, and sharpening its reactions moment by moment. But the instant this individual creature died, that information would be reset rather than carried over to the next lizardman to pop into the area.

So in a sense, this lizardman *was* alive. It was a unique individual, one of a kind.

"...Right."

It couldn't have understood what I was muttering under my breath, but the creature—a level-82 monster called the "lizardman lord"—exposed the needle fangs lining its slender jaw and hissed a laugh at me anyway.

It's real. Everything in this world is real. None of it is artificial.

I held out the long sword in a straight line, chest-high. The lizardman raised the buckler on its left arm and drew back the scimitar in its right.

As we paused, a chill breeze emanated from beyond the dim labyrinth corridor, rippling the torches along the wall. The flame light flickered off the damp stones.

"*Gruagh!!*"

With a ferocious roar, the lizardman lord leaped forward. Its scimitar darted for my stomach in a sharp arc, a brilliant orange curve flashing through the air. "Fell Crescent" was a high-level heavy attack skill for curved swords, a deadly charging blow that covered a distance of four yards in just 0.4 seconds.

But I knew it was coming.

Keeping my distance was the entire plan—I was daring the enemy AI to use it against me. The scimitar blade passed just inches from my face, my nose wrinkling at the charred odor left in its wake. I ducked, pressing up against the lizardman's belly.

"...*Seya!*"

With a cry, I slashed my weapon sideways. The blade, glowing cyan, sliced through the scales of the creature's soft underbelly, spraying beams of crimson light in place of blood as a dull *grak!* sounded from above.

But my combo continued unabated. The system automatically assisted my further assault, chaining into the next attack faster than I could have moved on my own.

This is the advantage of sword skills, the most significant and decisive feature of battle in this world.

As the sword leaped back from left to right, it found purchase in the lizardman's chest again. I followed that momentum into a full-body spin and drove my third blow even deeper into the enemy's core.

"*Urarrgh!!*"

No sooner had the lizardman regained mobility than it let out a roar of rage and fear, swinging its scimitar down from on high.

But my combo wasn't over yet. From its full extension to the right, my sword shot diagonally left and upward like a spring, directly striking the enemy's heart—its critical point.

This four-stroke combination left a square of glowing blue lines extending outward from me: Horizontal Square, a four-part sword skill.

The brilliant light reflected off the walls of the labyrinth, then faded. At the same time, the HP bar displayed above the lizard-man's head vanished without a trace. As it unleashed a long, final scream, the massive green form threw itself backward, paused at an unnatural angle—

And exploded into a mass of delicate polygons with a blast like the shattering of a huge glass structure.

This is death in the virtual world. Instantaneous and simple. Utter annihilation without a trace.

A purple font in the center of my view popped up, listing my experience and item rewards. I swiped my sword back and forth before returning it to the sheath over my shoulder. Backing up several steps to rest against the wall of the dungeon, I let myself slide to a sitting position.

When I released the breath I'd been holding and shut my eyes, my temples began to throb dully with the fatigue of the long fight. I shook my head several times to clear the pain before opening my eyes again.

The clock display in the lower right-hand corner of my vision showed that it was already past three in the afternoon. If I didn't leave the maze soon, I'd never get back to town before dark.

"...Better turn back," I muttered to no one in particular and slowly rose to my feet.

It was the end of a full day's worth of "progress." Another day of successfully eluding the Grim Reaper's grasp. But once I returned to my bed and took a short rest, the next day would bring another endless series of battles. And when the combat is endless and the stakes are fatal, all the safety nets and backup plans in the world won't prevent Lady Luck from betraying you at some point down the line.

The only real issue was whether or not the game would be "beaten" before I could draw the ace of spades.

If survival was your top priority, the smartest play would be to remain in the safety of town until the day someone else beat the game. But the fact that I spent every waking moment testing the front line on my own, risking death for ever greater statistical rewards, meant one of two things: that I was either a tried-and-true VRMMO (Virtual Reality Massive Multiplayer Online) addict...

Or a damned fool so arrogant as to honestly think he could free the world with his sword arm.

As I started making for the exit of the labyrinth, a self-deprecating grin tugging at the corner of my mouth, I thought back to that day.

Two years ago.

The moment that everything ended... and began.

2

"Ngh...arrg...hyaa!"

The strained cries were paired with desperate sword swipes, the blade swishing through nothingness.

The blue boar charged its attacker the next instant, nimbly evading his slashes despite its massive bulk. As I watched the beast's flat snout throw him skyward to roll across the field, I couldn't help laughing aloud.

"Ha-ha-ha...not like that. The important part is your very first motion, Klein."

"*Yeow*...Hairy bastard."

As the boar's attacker—my party member, Klein—rose to his feet swearing, he shot back a pitiful reply in my direction.

"Easy for you to say, Kirito...He can really move!"

I'd only met this man just a few hours earlier, his reddish hair flared back by the bandanna tied to his forehead, his lean figure clad in simple leather armor. If we'd introduced ourselves with our real names, it would have been hard not to use polite honorifics. But these were character names we'd chosen specifically for this virtual world: He was Klein; I was Kirito. Attaching -*san* to each other here would've just been weird.

Noting that Klein's legs were unsteady and his spill had

probably dizzied him, I leaned down to the grass at my feet, scooped up a rock, and held it above my shoulder. The system recognized this motion as the initiation of a sword skill, and the stone began glowing a faint green.

The rest happened nearly automatically. My left hand flashed, and the rock traced a bright arc through the air, striking the blue boar between its eyes as it prepared to charge again. The swine uttered a squeal of rage and turned to me.

"Of course it moves; it's not a training dummy. But as long as you initiate the motion and get the sword skill off properly, the system will ensure that it hits the target."

"Motion…motion…"

Klein muttered the word like a spell, waving the cutlass in his right hand.

The beast, properly known as a Frenzied Boar, was only a level-1 mob, but with all the missed strikes and painful counterattacks, Klein's HP bar was nearly half gone. Dying wasn't a big deal, since he'd simply revive at the nearby starting town, but we'd have to trek all the way back here to the hunting grounds again. This fight could only last one more round.

I tilted my head in hesitation as I deflected the boar's charge with my sword.

"How do I explain this…? You don't just hold it up, swing it, and cut the enemy like one, two, three. You have to pause just enough in your first motion to feel the skill cue up, then *kapow*! You blast it into him…"

"Kapow, huh?"

Klein held his curved sword at mid-level as his handsome features crumbled into a pathetic grimace beneath the tasteless bandanna.

He took one deep breath in and out, lowered his waist, then lifted the sword as though to cradle it on his right shoulder. This time, the system recognized the required motion and his arched blade glinted orange.

"*Raah!*"

He roared and, in a much smoother motion than before, bounded forward with his left foot. A satisfying *shgeen!* sound effect rang out as his blade carved a path the color of fire. Reaver, a single-handed scimitar skill, caught the charging boar squarely on the head, wiping out its remaining HP.

The enormous bulk shattered like glass with a pitiable squeal, and purple experience numbers floated before our eyes.

"Hell yeah!"

Klein struck a victory pose, turning to me with a huge smile, his hand held high. I returned the high five and cracked a smile of my own.

"Congrats on your first kill. Just remember, that boar was basically the wimpiest little slime in any other game."

"Are you serious? I was convinced he was a mid-level boss."

"Not a chance."

I returned my sword to the sheath on my back, my smile fading to a wry grin.

Behind the friendly teasing, I understood Klein's euphoria. With my extra two months of experience and leveling, I'd been singlehandedly responsible for all of our battles so far, making this the first time Klein had truly tasted the pleasure of dispatching a foe with his own sword.

As if to practice his lesson, Klein repeated the same skill several times, hooting and cackling, while I turned to survey our surroundings.

The field around us was brilliantly illuminated by sunlight just beginning to take on a tinge of red. Far to the north lay the silhouette of a forest, while a lake sparkled to the south, and the walls of a town could be faintly glimpsed to the east. To the west was nothing but endless sky and golden clouds.

We were standing in a field to the west of the Town of Beginnings, the starting area at the south edge of the very first floor of Aincrad. Countless other players were no doubt fighting monsters of their own in our vicinity, but the scale of this space was so vast that none were within eyeshot.

Finally satisfied, Klein returned the cutlass to the scabbard on his waist and approached, scanning the horizon with me.

"Man...no matter how many times I see this, I just can't bring myself to believe that it's all inside a game."

"Just because we're 'inside' it doesn't mean the game world has absorbed our souls or whatever. All our brains are doing is bypassing our eyes and ears, taking in the information directly through the NerveGear." I spoke through pursed lips like a pouting child, my shoulders hunched.

"Yeah, well, you're already used to it. This is my first full dive into the game! It's unbelievable. What a time to be alive!!"

"You act like it's such a big deal."

I laughed it off but secretly agreed.

NerveGear.

The name of the hardware that runs Sword Art Online, this VRMMORPG—a Virtual Reality Massively Multiplayer Online Role-Playing Game. But this machine is fundamentally different from the home TV gaming consoles of the past.

Unlike previous hardware featuring two points of man-machine interface on a flat monitor and a handheld controller, the NerveGear has just a single interface: a streamlined piece of headgear that entirely covers the head and face.

Countless transmitters embedded within the unit generate a multilayer electric field that connects directly to the user's brain. Information is sent not to the eyes and ears but to the visual and auditory centers of the brain itself. And not just vision and hearing. Touch, taste, smell—the NerveGear is capable of accessing all the senses.

With the headgear on and the chin-arm locked in place, a simple "link start" spoken command instantly causes all external noise to fade out and plunges your vision into darkness. Pass through a floating rainbow ring materializing out of the emptiness, and you're in a different world composed entirely of digital data.

In other words, this machine, released to the public in May of 2022, finally succeeded in creating a perfect virtual reality. The major electronics manufacturer that developed the NerveGear coined the term "full dive" to describe the act of connecting to the VR world.

It was an all-encompassing isolation from reality, more than worthy of the term.

After all, the machine didn't just provide virtual stimuli to all five senses; it also intercepted and collected the brain's commands to the body.

This was a vital function in providing full control within the virtual world. In other words, if your mental commands to your real body were allowed to pass, you might run within the virtual world during a full dive, but your real body would quickly slam into the wall of your room.

It was only because the NerveGear intercepted the signals from the spine to the body and converted them to digital information that Klein and I could race around the virtual battlefield, swinging our swords with abandon.

You leap into the game.

The sheer impact of this experience profoundly enchanted many gamers, myself included. Once you tasted a full dive, there was no going back to the world of touch pens and movement sensors.

I turned to Klein, his eyes watering as he stared out at the rippling fields and distant city walls.

"So is SAO your first NerveGear game, period?"

"Yeah." Klein nodded, turning his gallant face to me, like some proud samurai from the distant past.

When he maintained a serious expression, he could have been the lead actor in a period piece, but this did not reflect his real-life appearance. It was nothing more than a virtual avatar created from scratch out of a robust list of finely tuned parameters.

Naturally, I had also chosen a look befitting the hero of a fantasy anime, almost embarrassing in its shameless elegance.

Klein continued in a strong and clear voice, also likely to be falsified.

"Actually, I got SAO first, so I needed to buy the hardware just to play it. I mean, the first shipment was only ten thousand copies, right? I'm one of the lucky ones. Although, since you've been playing SAO since the beta test, that makes you ten times as lucky. There were only around a thousand testers!"

"I guess you could say that." I scratched my head as he stared holes into me.

I could remember as though it were yesterday the excitement and enthusiasm that swept through the media when Sword Art Online was announced.

The NerveGear and its revolutionary new full-dive format were so novel that the actual software to take advantage of it lagged in response. Initial offerings were simple puzzle and educational titles, a source of serious disappointment to full-blown game addicts like me.

The NerveGear creates a true virtual world. But the effect of such freedom is entirely lost when the world you inhabit is so small that an impassable wall can be found within a hundred yards in any direction. Hardcore gamers like me were initially entranced by the experience of truly being inside a game, but it was only a matter of time before we sought a killer title in one very specific genre.

We wanted an MMORPG—an online game that hosted thousands of players in the same vast world together, living, fighting, and adventuring.

Just when desire and expectations had reached their peak came the announcement of Sword Art Online, the first-ever entry in the VRMMO genre.

The game took place in a massive floating fortress made up of a hundred expansive levels. Armed with nothing but the weapons in their hands, players explored each floor, packed with fields, forests, and towns, looking for the staircase upward and defeating terrifying guardian monsters in their quest to reach the top.

Unlike typical fantasy-themed MMOs, the concept of magic spells had been largely excised from the setting, making way for a nearly limitless combination of special attacks called "sword skills." This was an intentional move to maximize the full-dive experience, forcing players to use their own bodies and swords to fight.

Skills applied not just to combat but also to crafting disciplines like blacksmithing, leatherworking, and tailoring; productive endeavors such as fishing and cooking; and even creative pursuits such as playing musical instruments. Therefore, players weren't limited to adventuring within the vast virtual world—they could literally choose their own lifestyle within the game. With enough hard work, a player could buy a home, till fields, and raise sheep if he chose.

As details of these features trickled out in stages, enthusiasm among the gaming public rose to a fever pitch. A beta test was announced, in which a thousand players would be granted access to the game before release to help stress test the system and isolate software bugs. The developer was quickly swamped with more than 100,000 applicants, which represented nearly half of all NerveGear units sold at that point. That I somehow managed to slip through the crowd into one of those valuable slots was nothing short of a miracle. Not only that, being a beta tester gave me priority access to the retail edition of the game when it hit the market.

The two months of the beta test were like a fever dream. Even at school, my head was swimming with thoughts of my skill loadout and equipment, and once I got home, I dove into the game until dawn. In no time at all, the beta test ended, and when my character data was erased, it felt like I had lost a part of myself.

The day was Sunday, November 6, 2022.

At 1:00 PM, Sword Art Online would finally go live to the public.

I was ready a full thirty minutes early, of course, logging in without a second's hesitation and checking the server status to confirm that more than 9,500 lucky purchasers were brimming with anticipation just as I was. The major online retailers had sold out of their initial shipments in seconds, and brick-and-mortar shops had made the news with crowds lining up three days early to get copies of the game. In other words, everyone who managed to secure a copy of SAO was almost certainly a serious gaming addict.

My first interaction with Klein seemed to support that assumption.

As I logged in to SAO and marched down the familiar cobble-stones of the Town of Beginnings, I ducked into a back alley heading for a particularly cheap weapons dealer. He must have noticed my lack of hesitation and pegged me for a beta tester. "Hey, spare some advice?" Klein hailed me.

Impressed by his utter lack of restraint, I tried to pass myself off as a helpful town guide NPC with a feeble, "H-hello...Are you looking for the weapon shop?" Soon we were grouped together into a party, followed by some hands-on combat lessons outside of town—and here we were.

Frankly speaking, I was at least as antisocial in the game as I was in real life, if not more so. I grew familiar with many other gamers during the beta test, but there wasn't a single one of them I'd have called a friend.

But this Klein fellow had a mysterious ability to slip past one's defenses and latch on, and to my surprise, I didn't really mind. Thinking that I might actually be able to stick around with him, I opened my mouth again.

"So, what now? Want to keep hunting until you get the hang of it?"

"You bet your ass I do! Or...normally I would..."

Klein's shapely eyes darted to the right—he was checking the time readout displayed in the corner of his vision.

"But I need to log out for a bit to eat dinner. I scheduled a pizza delivery for five thirty."

"Now there's a guy who comes prepared." I sighed.

Klein straightened up and continued as though he'd just thought of something. "Um, so, I'm gonna go back to the Town of Beginnings after this and meet up with some friends I made in another game. If I introduce you, would you want to add them to your friends list? It makes it easy to send messages to each other."

"Uh, hmm…" I stammered.

I found it easy to get along with Klein, but there was no guarantee I'd hit it off with his friends. In fact, it seemed all too easy to envision feeling uncomfortable around them, which might make things awkward with Klein himself.

"Yeah, well…"

As I failed to give a clear response, Klein quickly shook his head in understanding.

"I mean, I'm not saying you have to. There'll be other chances to meet them."

"…Sure. Thanks for asking, though," I apologized, as Klein shook his head again.

"None of that! I'm the one who should be thanking you! You helped me out a ton; I'll make it up to you sometime. Y'know, mentally."

He grinned and checked the time again.

"All right, man, I'm gonna log out for now. Thanks again, Kirito. We gotta hang out sometime."

As I reached out and grasped his extended hand, it occurred to me that this man was probably an excellent leader in that "other game" he'd played.

"Sure thing. If you ever have any questions, just ask."

"Yeah. Will do."

We released the handshake.

This was the instant that Aincrad, the world of Sword Art Online, stopped simply being a fun game, a pleasant diversion.

*   *   *

Klein took one step backward, held out the index and middle fingers on his right hand, and swung them downward—the action that called up the game's main menu screen. With a sound like bells jingling, a translucent purple rectangle materialized in midair.

I took a few steps backward myself, sitting down on a nearby rock to open my own window. My fingers traced the display as I sorted the items I'd earned from fighting boars.

The next instant—

"Huh?" Klein muttered, perplexed. "What the heck? There's *no log-out button.*"

At those last words, I stopped moving my hand and looked up.

"No button? That can't be true. Look closer," I said, exasperated. The tall scimitar-wielding hero leaned over, his eyes wide beneath the ugly bandanna as he stared at the window.

In its default state, the elongated horizontal window featured several menu tabs on the left and a human silhouette on the right detailing the user's inventory and equipment. At the very bottom of that menu was a LOG OUT button that enabled the player to leave the world—or at least, there should have been.

As I returned my gaze to the list of items I'd earned over the last few hours of battle, Klein repeated himself, louder this time.

"No. It's just gone. You should see for yourself, Kirito."

"I'm telling you, it has to be there..." I sighed, then tapped the button in the upper left of the screen that led back to the main menu.

My item storage display closed smoothly, returning the window to its default state. The silhouette reappeared, several equipment slots still empty, and the list of menu tabs materialized again on the left.

With a familiar motion, I slid my finger down to the bottom button...

And all of my muscles froze solid.

It was gone.

During the beta test—in fact, just after logging in at one o'clock today—the log-out button was right in the corner, but as Klein noted, it had simply disappeared.

I stared at the blank space for several seconds, then moved my eyes upward, carefully scanning the menu tabs to ensure that it hadn't simply changed positions when I wasn't paying attention. Klein tilted his head at me as though to say, *See?*

"...Gone, right?"

"Yep. Gone," I reluctantly agreed.

He raised his cheeks in a grimace and stroked his shapely chin.

"Well, it is launch day. Bugs happen. I bet tech support is getting drowned in calls. They're probably tearing their hair out right now," he said nonchalantly, to which I gave a barbed retort.

"Is that all you have to say about it? Weren't you just talking about getting a pizza delivery at five thirty?"

"Oh crap, that's right!"

I grinned despite myself at the sight of him bolting upright, wide-eyed with alarm.

The red glow of my inventory screen subsided as I discarded enough junk items to squeeze back under the weight limit. Standing up, I walked over to Klein, who wailed on about lost anchovy pizzas and ginger ale.

"Look, you should try opening a support ticket with the GMs. They might be able to boot you off from the system side," I suggested.

"I tried that, but there was no response. Man, it's already five twenty-five! Kirito, was there any other way to log out of the game?" he pleaded pathetically, his hands outstretched.

My lazy grin stiffened. A vague sense of anxiety began to chill my spine.

"Let's see... Logging out, logging out...," I muttered.

To leave the game and return to my room back in the real world was simply a matter of opening the menu window, hitting the log-out button, then confirming the action when a safety prompt appeared. It was quite easy—but I didn't actually know of any other way to leave.

I looked up at Klein's face above me and slowly shook my head.

"Nope. There's no way to manually log out other than through the menu."

"But that's crazy. There has to be a way out of this!" Klein wailed, as though denying my answer would make it untrue. "Go back! Log out! Exit!!"

But nothing happened. SAO did not respond to voice commands.

He continued shouting and chanting, eventually growing agitated enough to leap about, until I called out in a low voice.

"It won't work, Klein. The manual doesn't say anything about an emergency termination method, either."

"But...but that's crazy! I know games have bugs, but not the kind where you can't even get back to your own home, your own body, your own free will!"

Klein turned around to me, his face aghast. I agreed with him. This was crazy. It was absurd. But it was the reality we were facing.

"You've gotta be kidding me...This can't be happening. We're trapped inside the stupid game!" Klein ranted, breaking into a panicked laugh. "I know—I'll just power off the machine. Or rip the NerveGear off my head."

Klein rubbed his hands over his head as though removing an invisible hat, but I felt the cold anxiety return.

"We can't do either of those things. We can't move our actual bodies. The NerveGear intercepts all the commands going from our brains to the rest of our limbs."

I tapped the back of my neck with my fingers.

"The system translates those commands into actions within the game. It's the only way we're able to move our avatars like this."

Klein fell silent and slowly lowered his arms.

We remained locked in place for a moment, our minds racing.

In order for the NerveGear to successfully create the full-dive experience, it has to read the movement signals going from the brain to the spine, cancel them out, and translate them into digital actions within the game world. No matter how desperately I waved my arms inside the game, my real body would remain motionless on my bed, ensuring that I wouldn't bruise myself hitting the corner of my desk by accident.

But it was that very feature that now physically prevented me from disengaging the dive.

"So does this mean we either have to wait for the bug to be fixed or for someone to pull the headgear off of our bodies?" Klein muttered, still dumbfounded.

I gave him a silent nod.

"But I live by myself. You?"

I hesitated, then answered honestly. "I live with my mom and little sister. I bet that if I don't come down for dinner, they'll eventually force me out of the dive."

"Oh? H-how old's your sister?" Klein leaned forward, his eyes suddenly sparkling. I pushed his head away.

"That sure got you to take your mind off the situation, didn't it? Look, she's on a sports club at school and she hates video games. She has nothing in common with people like us. Besides"—I waved my hand, trying to change the subject—"don't you think this is weird?"

"Sure it is. The game is buggy."

"This isn't just any old bug. Not being able to log out is a huge deal. It could spell disaster for the game's future. Even as we speak, your pizza is getting colder by the second. That represents a real monetary loss for you, doesn't it?"

"Cold pizza is worse than nattō that doesn't get sticky," Klein muttered cryptically. I continued.

"A situation like this means the programmers have to shut down the servers and force all the players offline. And yet, even though it's been at least fifteen minutes since we discovered this bug, not only are we still online, there hasn't even been an official announcement within the game. It makes no sense."

"Yeah, that's a good point." Klein rubbed his chin, finally looking suitably serious. His slender eyes glinted beneath the bandanna stretched over the high bridge of his nose.

I listened to Klein continue, struck by how odd it was that I was discussing such real-world affairs with a person I'd only met by sheer chance and would likely never see again if I simply deleted my game account.

"Argus, the developers of SAO, made a name for themselves based on their customer outreach. The fact that their first online game was so highly anticipated is a sign of how much trust the community has in them. How could they ruin that reputation with such a stunning screwup on their very first day?"

"Exactly. Not only that, SAO is the very first example of a VRMMO. If this turns into a huge controversy, the entire genre could get regulated out of existence."

Klein and I sighed slowly at the same time, our virtual faces turned to each other.

Aincrad's climate was attuned to the real-life season, meaning that it was early winter in the game, just as it was outside.

I breathed in the chilly air deeply, filling my lungs with virtual oxygen, and looked skyward.

More than a hundred yards above, the bottom of the second floor glowed a faint purple. As I followed the flat, rocky surface toward the horizon, my eyes finally rested on a vast tower far in the distance—the labyrinth that would lead to the next level of the castle. Beyond that, I could even see the aperture on the far side of the floor.

It was now past 5:30, and the sliver of sky to be seen over the vast distance was glowing crimson. The setting sun shone through, lighting the rippling fields in a dazzling gold, and I found myself at a loss for words despite the gravity of our situation.

In the next instant...

The world changed forever.

3

Klein and I jumped to our feet, startled by a sudden ringing sound, blaring like an alarm at full volume.

"Wha...?"

"What's that?"

We shouted simultaneously, then noticed each other's bodies, our eyes wide.

Both Klein and I were enveloped in pillars of brilliant blue light. The scenery of the fields faded out behind the colored film.

I'd experienced this phenomenon multiple times during the beta test. It was the teleport effect that took place when you used an item to travel instantaneously across the game. But I didn't have the right item, nor had I given the system any such command. If it was a system-side forced teleportation, why was it happening without any announcement?

As my mind raced, the light surrounding me pulsed stronger, blocking my vision.

The blue light faded, and the environment returned but was no longer the evening field in which we had been standing. I was greeted by wide paving stones, trees lining the street, and a cleanly elegant medieval town. In the far distance straight ahead, a massive palace gleamed darkly.

I recognized it instantly as the central square of the Town of Beginnings, the game's starting point. I turned to face Klein next to me, his mouth agape. We stared out at the sea of humanity pressed in around us.

It was a teeming mass of beautiful men and women, a clash of bristling equipment and hair in every color of the rainbow. These were all fellow SAO players. There had to be several thousand people here—nearly ten thousand, in fact. It seemed likely that every single player who was logged in to the game had been forcibly teleported to this square.

For a few seconds, there was a tense silence as everyone took in their surroundings. Mutters and murmurs broke out everywhere, steadily rising in volume. Shards of conversation could be made out above the din.

"What's going on?"

"Can we log out now?"

"Hurry it up!"

The murmuring took on a distinct tone of anger and frustration, raised voices demanding the GMs come out to explain themselves.

Abruptly, someone screamed, cutting through the noise.

"Hey...look up!!"

Klein and I instinctively raised our eyes, which were met with an unnatural sight.

The bottom of the second floor hanging a hundred yards above us was bathed in a red checkerboard pattern. Looking closer, I could see that the pattern was made of two pieces of English text. I could make out WARNING and SYSTEM ANNOUNCEMENT in the red font.

After my fleeting initial shock, the tension in my shoulders relaxed. Finally, the developers were going to give us an explanation. The roar in the square died down as the crowd strained its ears.

But what happened next was nothing like what I expected.

The center of the crimson pattern that covered the entire sky above suddenly sagged in the middle, pooling like an enormous drop of blood. The viscous drop slowly extended downward, but rather than breaking off and falling, it abruptly changed shape in midair.

What emerged was the form of a giant person at least sixty feet tall, clad in a robe with a crimson hood.

But this wasn't quite correct. We were staring up at it from the ground, at an angle that should have given us a glimpse underneath the hood—but there was no face. It was an empty space, the underside of the hood and the stitching of the seam clearly visible. The long, dangling sleeves also contained nothing but a faint darkness.

I recognized the shape of that robe. It was the signature outfit of official Argus GMs during the beta test. But at the time, the male GMs were depicted as elderly magicians with long white beards, and female GMs were bespectacled young women. Perhaps some technical issue had prevented them from creating an avatar, with the robe being the best that could be managed, but the sight of that empty void beneath the hood filled me with a wordless dread.

The mass of players around me must have shared that apprehension. Mutters of confusion arose in waves: "Is that a GM? Why doesn't he have a face?"

As if to quiet the murmuring, the right arm of the enormous robe suddenly shifted. A white glove peeked out of the pendulous sleeve, but once again, there was a stark separation between robe and glove with no flesh to be seen connecting them.

Now the other sleeve rose in turn. The empty white gloves spread apart, looming over ten thousand heads, and the faceless being opened an invisible mouth—or so it seemed. From above the crowd, a man's calm, deep voice cut through the din.

"Welcome to my world, dear players."

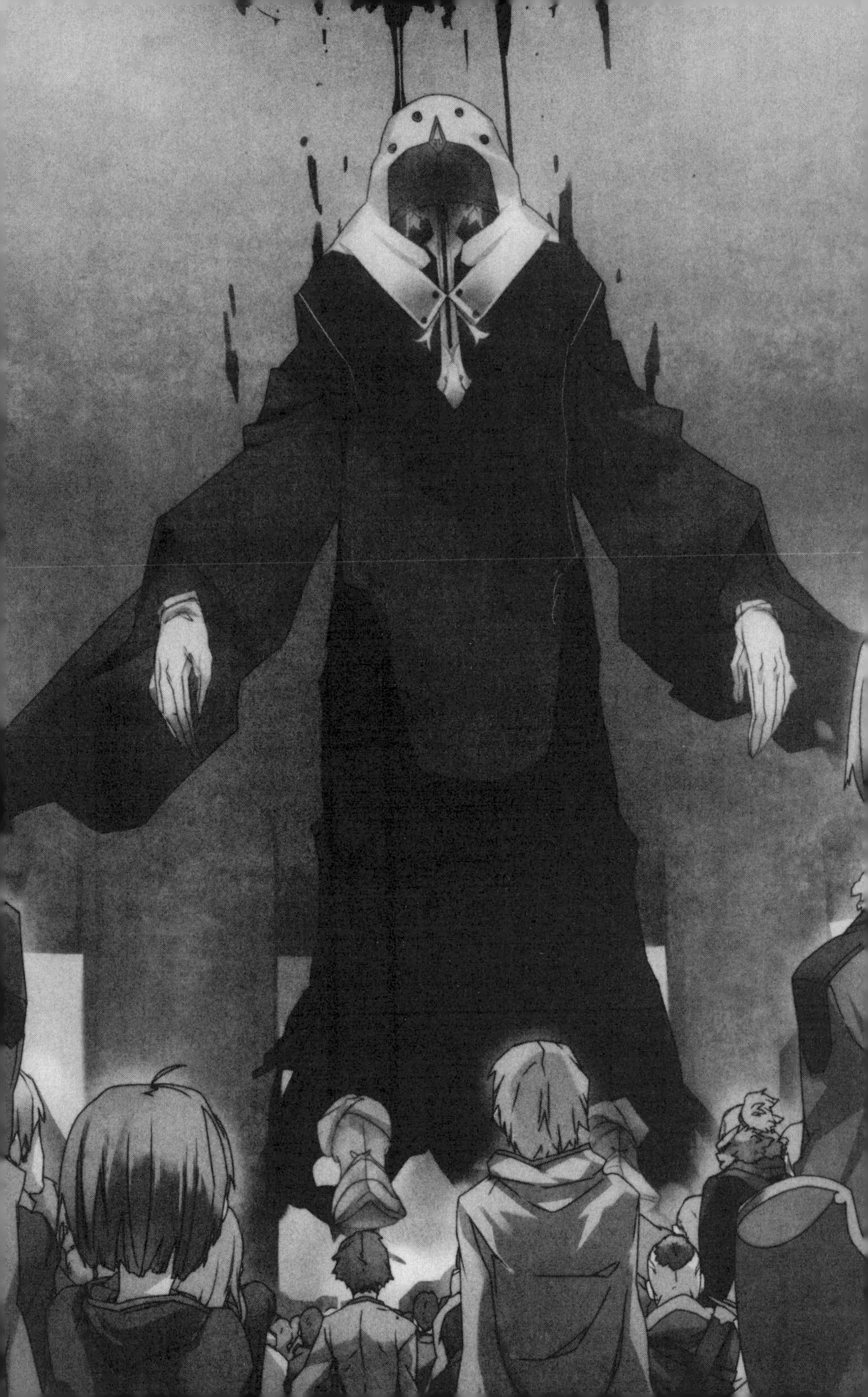

* * *

I didn't immediately register his meaning.

My world? The red GM robe meant that he possessed the ability to manipulate the world as he saw fit. If he was already a god, why the need to announce it to everyone?

As Klein and I stared at each other in disbelief, the robed figure lowered its arms and continued speaking.

"My name is Akihiko Kayaba. As of this moment, I am the only human being alive with control over this world."

"Wha...?" I was so shocked that not only did my avatar's breath catch in its throat, the same likely happened to my real body.

Akihiko Kayaba!!

I knew that name. I couldn't *not* know it.

He was the brilliant young game designer and quantum physicist who transformed niche game studio Argus into one of the foremost developers in the business. Not only was he the executive director of SAO, he also designed the basic foundation of the NerveGear unit itself.

Like most other hardcore gamers, I held a deep reverence for Kayaba. I bought every magazine profile and reread his precious few interviews until I could practically quote them from memory. Just the brief sound of that voice conjured my mental image of Kayaba, looking smart in his ever-present white lab coat.

But he'd always preferred to stay out of the spotlight, avoiding media attention wherever possible, and he'd certainly never stepped into an active GM role within a game like this—so why now?

I stood stock-still, urging my mind back into motion, trying to grasp the situation. But try as I might, the words that followed from the empty hood mocked my feeble attempts at comprehension.

"You have likely noticed by now that the log-out button has disappeared from the main menu. This is not a bug. I repeat, this is not a bug—it is a feature of Sword Art Online."

"F-feature...?" Klein muttered, his voice cracking.

The smooth baritone continued, overlapping the end of his question.

"From this point onward, you will be unable to freely log out of the game until the summit of this castle is conquered."

The word *castle* snagged on the inside of my brain. Where was there a castle in the Town of Beginnings? But my momentary confusion was instantly wiped away by his next statement.

"Furthermore, the NerveGear cannot be removed or shut down via external means. If forceful means of exit are attempted..."

A pause.

A palpably heavy silence filled the air, ten thousand breaths held in apprehension. The next words came with a slow, awful finality.

"...the high-powered microwaves emitted by the NerveGear will scramble your brain and shut down your vital processes."

Klein and I stared at each other for several seconds, our faces blank masks. It was as though our brains themselves refused to process the words. But Kayaba's simple ultimatum shot through my body from head to toe with a palpable impact.

Scramble our brains.

In other words, it would kill us. Turning off the NerveGear's power or attempting to remove it from the user's head would prove fatal, according to Kayaba.

Murmurs rippled through the crowd, but no one screamed or raged. Everyone present, including me, either couldn't or wouldn't process the implications of his declaration.

Klein's hand slowly rose to his head, attempting to grasp the NerveGear that existed only in the outside world. He let out a dry, quick laugh.

"Ha-ha...what's he talking about? Is he crazy? That's not possible. The NerveGear's just a game system. It can't possibly, like... destroy our brains or whatever. Right, Kirito?" he finished in a rasping shout. Despite his pleading glare, I couldn't bring myself to nod in agreement.

The underside of the NerveGear helmet is embedded with countless transmitters that emit faint electromagnetic waves, sending false sensations directly to the brain cells. It's a piece of ultra-sophisticated, cutting-edge tech, but it also works on the same fundamental principles as a home appliance that has been around for decades: the kitchen microwave.

With enough power, the NerveGear could potentially vibrate the moisture in the brain cells, causing frictional heat strong enough to steam the brain from the inside out. But...

"...In principle, it's not impossible...but he has to be bluffing. I mean, if you just pull the plug on the NerveGear, how can it produce enough juice to do that? Unless it's packing some massive... batteries..."

Klein understood exactly why I trailed off. He moaned, a desperate expression plastered across his face. "But...it *is*. I heard that a third of the unit's weight is battery cells. But still, this is ridiculous! What if there's a blackout?"

As though he heard Klein's roar, Kayaba continued his proclamation.

"To be more specific, the brain-frying sequence will commence upon any of the following circumstances: ten minutes of no external power; two hours of network disconnection; removal, dismantling, or destruction of the NerveGear. The authorities and media in the outside world have already announced the details of these conditions to the general public. At present, the friends and family of several players have already ignored these warnings and attempted to forcefully remove their NerveGears, the result being..."

The echoing, metallic voice paused for a breath.

"...that sadly, two hundred and thirteen players have already been permanently retired from both Aincrad and the real world."

A single shrill scream rang out from somewhere in the crowd. But the majority of players were stock-still, either unable or refusing to believe, their faces displaying absentminded smiles. Like them, my mind resisted Kayaba's words, but my body was more honest, my legs beginning to quaver. I hobbled backward several steps on buckling knees, trying not to fall. Klein simply fell straight onto his rear, his face still empty.

Two hundred and thirteen players.

The words reverberated over and over in my ears.

Was Kayaba telling the truth? Were more than two hundred people who had been playing this game just minutes ago already dead?

Some of them must have been beta testers like me. Possibly even people whose faces or names I recognized from my time playing. And now Kayaba said their NerveGears had fried their brains and killed them?

"I won't believe it...I refuse to believe it," Klein muttered from the paving stones, his voice hoarse. "It's just a threat. He can't do this. Quit dicking us around and let us out already. I've got better things to do than sit around while your little stunt plays out. That's all this is, right? A stunt. A bit of excitement to juice up the game's grand opening, yeah?"

The same thoughts had been racing through my mind at the exact same time. But Kayaba's dry, practical announcement continued, disregarding the wishes of his captive audience.

"There is no need to worry about your physical bodies back in the real world. The current state of the game and today's fatalities have been covered far and wide on television, radio, and the Internet. The danger that someone will forcefully remove your NerveGear is already much diminished. The two-hour offline leeway period should provide enough time for your physical bodies to be transported to hospitals and other long-term care facilities with proper security, eliminating concerns over your physical well-being. You may rest assured...and focus on conquering the game."

"Wha—?" A scream finally ripped out from my throat. "What do you mean? Conquer the game? You expect us to just sit back and enjoy the game when we can't even log out?"

I glared at the headless crimson robe stretching up to nearly the upper floor and continued bellowing.

"This isn't even a game anymore!"

And again, as though he heard my voice, Akihiko Kayaba's monotone continued.

"However, please proceed with caution. As of this moment, Sword Art Online is no longer a game to you. It is another reality. The standard means of player resurrection will no longer function as they did previously. When your hit points dwindle to zero, your avatar will be permanently deleted..."

I knew what he was about to say before the words even came.

"...and the NerveGear will destroy your brain."

I felt an instant urge to burst into a high-pitched laughter bubbling up from my gut and had to stifle the impulse. In the upper left-hand corner of my vision sat a thin bar, glowing blue. When I trained my eyes on the bar, the numbers 342/342 popped up next to it.

My hit points. My remaining life.

If that number hit zero, I would *actually* die—the game console would fry my brain with microwaves and kill me on the spot, according to Kayaba.

Yes, this was a game. A game in which my life hung on the line. A game of death.

During the two-month beta test, I must have died a hundred times. When that happened, you popped back to life with a cackle in Blackiron Palace to the north of the square, free to rush back out to the battlefield.

That's how RPGs work. You die and die, learning lessons each time and honing your skills. But now we couldn't do that? Die once, and we were dead forever? Without even the option of quitting the game?

"This is ridiculous," I muttered.

Who would possibly venture out into the dangers of the wilderness under those circumstances? Everyone was bound to stay within the safety of town.

But as though anticipating the skepticism of all players present, Kayaba issued his next challenge.

"There is only one condition through which you can be freed from this game. Simply reach the hundredth floor at the pinnacle of Aincrad and defeat the final boss who awaits you there. In that instant, all surviving players will be able to safely log out once again."

A moment of sheer silence.

I finally realized the meaning of his earlier phrase, "Conquer the summit of this castle." He wasn't referring to just any castle; he was referring to Aincrad itself, the mammoth floating fortress on whose very bottom floor we now stood, ninety-nine floors stacked above our heads.

"Clear the hundredth floor?" Klein shouted abruptly. He clambered to his feet and shook his fist in the air. "W-we can't possibly do that! I heard the entire group of beta testers barely got through the very start of the game!"

He was right. A thousand players took part in SAO's beta test, and when the two-month period was over, we'd only cleared the sixth floor. True, there were nearly ten times that number taking part in the game now, but how long would it take to reach a full hundred floors?

My guess was that the entire square was wrestling with the same apprehension. The silent tension shifted into low rumblings. But I wasn't hearing sounds of fear or despair. Most likely, the majority of players here couldn't make up their minds whether this was true danger or simply a flashy opening ceremony held in poor taste. Kayaba's statements were so bizarre and dreadful to comprehend that the story lacked credibility.

I tilted my head upward, glaring at the empty robe, desperately trying to adjust to this new reality.

I couldn't log out. I couldn't get back to my real room, my real life. The only way that could happen was if someone reached the top of this castle and defeated the final boss. And if at any point my HP reached zero, I would die. Real death. I would cease to exist.

But…

No matter how hard I tried to accept this information as truth, I simply couldn't. Just five or six hours ago, I'd eaten my mother's home-cooked lunch, spoken to my sister, and climbed the stairs to my room. And now I couldn't go back? Could this actually be happening?

The red robe once again preempted the thoughts of all present, sweeping its white glove and continuing in a voice devoid of emotion.

"Finally, let me prove to you that this world is now your one and only reality. I've prepared a gift for all of you. You may find it in your item storage."

Without thinking, I made the two-fingered downward swipe to pull open the menu. Others around me made the same motion, the square filling with electronic chiming sounds. When I hit the inventory tab on the menu screen, I noticed something new at the top of the list.

It was labeled HAND MIRROR. Curious, I tapped the name and selected the MATERIALIZE button from the list of options. With a sparkling sound effect, a small square mirror popped into being.

I reluctantly picked up the mirror, but nothing happened. All I saw reflected in the surface was the painstakingly crafted face of my virtual avatar. Tilting my neck, I glanced at Klein. Like me, the chiseled samurai stood staring into his own mirror.

Then…

A brilliant white light enveloped Klein and several other characters nearby. In the next instant, my vision went blank as the same light surrounded me. A few seconds later, it faded, returning the same old sights.

Except…

This wasn't the Klein I recognized. The mismatched plate armor, ugly bandanna, and spiky red hair were the same as before. It was the face that had changed. The slender eyes were now bulging and round. The slender bridge of his nose was a beak. And his fine cheeks and chin were now covered in scraggly facial hair. If his former avatar was a gallant young samurai, the new Klein was a wandering ronin—or worse yet, a bandit.

Forgetting everything for an instant, I muttered, "Who... are you?"

The man before me returned the question. "Me? Who are *you*?"

And in a flash of enlightenment, I understood the meaning of Kayaba's "gift." Raising my own mirror again, I stared at the reflection within.

Black hair in an inoffensive style. Gentle eyes set beneath long bangs. A soft, rounded face that still got me confused for a sister instead of a brother when strangers saw me side by side with my sister.

There was none of Kirito's previous heroic look. The face I saw in the mirror...

...was the real-life face I'd been trying to escape.

"Whoa...it's me..." Klein murmured into his mirror, flabbergasted. We faced each other again and shouted in unison.

"*You're* Klein?"

"*You're* Kirito?"

The voice-filtering function had apparently stopped working, shifting the sound of our voices as well, but that was the least of our concerns.

Both mirrors slipped through our fingers, hitting the ground simultaneously with a faint *crack*. A quick glance around showed that the prior gathering of wildly colored, beautiful fantasy characters had changed dramatically. It was as though someone had taken the crowd of a real video game convention and given them swords and armor to wear. Even the ratio of men to women had gone frightfully askance.

How was this possible? We had all gone from our virtual avatars to our real-life appearances. It was still presented in polygonal form with a few slight details felt out, but the degree

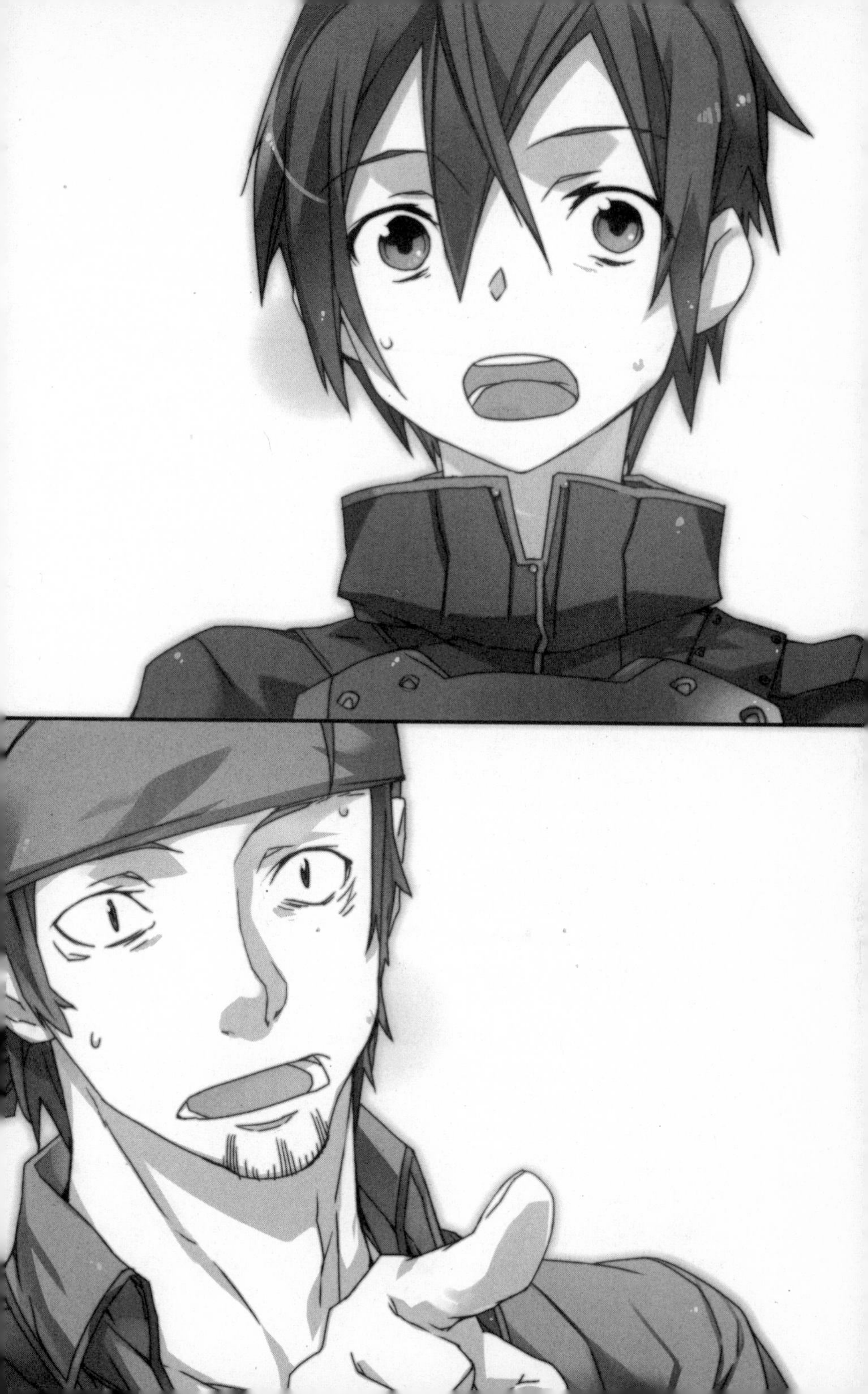

of accuracy was startling. It was like I'd undergone a full-body scan.

A scan.

"...Of course!" I muttered, looking up at Klein. "The Nerve-Gear's got those transmitters all over the underside of the helmet, including the part that covers your face. So not only can it read your brain, it also recreates your facial details..."

"But what about my height...and my weight?" Klein peered around, his voice uncharacteristically quiet.

The crowd of players, still staring about in amazement, had clearly lost a few inches in average height after the "adjustment." Both Klein and I had set our avatars' heights to be about the same as our own, hoping to avoid throwing off our physical coordination during full dive due to any changes in eye-level. But judging from the crowd, the majority of players had given themselves an extra six inches, if not more.

And that wasn't all. The average girth of the crowd had swollen considerably as well. But the NerveGear could only scan our heads. How could it have gauged our body size?

Klein had the answer.

"Wait a sec. I remember this 'cos I just bought my NerveGear yesterday. It did that thing during the set-up phase...What was it, calibration? It asked me to touch my body in all these different spots. Could that have been it?"

"Oh...right, of course..."

The calibration process was a measurement of how far the user needed to move to touch his or her body, such that the system could recreate the proper surface area digitally. In essence, it was enlisting the user's help to build an internal measurement of the user's body.

It clearly worked. Every player in the world of SAO at this moment had been turned into a virtually perfect polygonal replica of themselves. The intent was obvious.

"It's reality," I muttered. "He just said so. My avatar and my hit points are now my real body and life. Kayaba recreated our faces and figures to force us to recognize the truth."

"B-but, Kirito," Klein wailed, scratching his head as his eyes bulged beneath the bandanna. "Why? Why would he do something like this...?"

I couldn't answer that. Instead, I pointed upward.

"Just wait. He's about to answer that, I'm sure."

Kayaba did not disappoint. The solemn voice continued a few seconds later, ringing out from the bloodred sky.

"You are likely asking yourselves, why? Why would Akihiko Kayaba, developer of SAO and the NerveGear unit, do such a thing? Is it an act of terrorism? An elaborate kidnapping to extract ransom money?"

And for the first time, Kayaba's emotionless voice began to take on the faintest signs of color. Despite the situation, I felt a hint of longing in his voice. But that couldn't be right.

"What I seek is neither of these things. I have no goals or justifications at this moment. In fact, this very situation *was* my ultimate goal. I created the NerveGear and SAO precisely in order to build this world and observe it. I have now achieved that aim."

After a short pause, Kayaba's voice was back to its usual monotone.

"This concludes the tutorial phase of Sword Art Online. I wish you the best of luck, dear players."

His last word echoed briefly before dying out.

The crimson robe silently ascended, the tip of the hood melting into the system warnings still displayed in midair. The shoulders, chest, arms, and legs followed into the bloodred surface, leaving a single outward ripple behind. The next instant, the giant wall of messages plastered across the sky disappeared as abruptly as it came.

The wind blew over the top of the square, and the BGM from a band of NPC musicians slowly approached from afar, bringing life back to my ears. The game had returned to its original state. The only difference lay in a few very crucial rules.

Finally, at long last, the throng of players exhibited the proper reaction.

The square exploded into noise, convulsing with the sound of ten thousand voices all at once.

"This can't be happening... You've gotta be kidding me!"

"Screw this! Let me out! I want out of here!"

"You can't do this to me! I'm supposed to meet someone tonight!"

"No! Let me leave, let me leave!"

Screams. Rage. Shrieks. Insults. Pleading. And roars.

In the span of several minutes, we'd been turned from players to prisoners. We held our heads, sunk to our knees, shook fists in the air, grabbed others, and turned on one another.

Oddly enough, the more the screaming continued, the clearer my thoughts became.

This is reality. Everything that Akihiko Kayaba said was the truth. He, of all people, would be capable of this. That destructive, unpredictable genius was part of his allure.

I would not be back in the real world for quite some time—months, if not longer. I wouldn't be able to see or speak to my mother or sister. I might never do so again. If I died here...

I was really dead.

The NerveGear—game console, shackles, and guillotine blade all in one—would fry my brain and kill me.

I took a slow, measured breath and opened my mouth.

"Come with me, Klein."

I grabbed his arm, his figure still imposingly tall even after the shift to our actual body types, and quickly led him out through the hysterical mob. We must have been placed near the outside of the group, as it took little time to escape the crowd. I marched down one of the town streets radiating out from the square and stepped behind a stationary carriage.

"Klein," I snapped at the dazed man in the most sober tone I could manage. "Listen up. I'm leaving this city right now and heading for the next village. Come with me."

I pushed on, my voice low, as Klein stared at me from beneath his hideous bandanna.

"If what he said is true, then we have to get stronger and stronger in order to survive. I'm sure you already know that MMOR-PGs are a battle over system resources. There's only so much gold, loot, and experience to go around, so the more you win, the stronger you get. Everyone's going to have the same idea, so the fields around the Town of Beginnings will be bled dry in no time. You'll be forced to wander around, endlessly waiting for mobs to repop. We need to take this opportunity to set up base in the next town. I know the way, and I know which spots are dangerous. I can get us there safely, even at level one."

By my standards, it was a marathon speech, but Klein listened to every word. A few seconds later, he grimaced slightly.

"But...remember what I said earlier? I stayed in line all night with some friends from another game just to buy this. They were logged in. They must still be back in the square. I can't just leave them behind."

"..."

I held my breath and bit my lip. The intention behind Klein's pensive stare was as plain as day. The jovial, faithful man couldn't leave his friends behind. He wanted to bring them with us.

And I just couldn't agree to that.

Even at level one, I was confident that I could protect Klein alone from the more aggressive monsters along the route to the next village. But any more than that would make the risks too great. What if someone died en route and, as Kayaba said, had his actual brain fried? The responsibility would lie with me: the guy who wanted to leave our initial haven and failed to keep everyone safe.

I couldn't handle that unbearable pressure. It was impossible.

Klein seemed to pick up on my momentary hesitation once again. A stiff but broad smile cracked his stubbly cheeks, and he shook his head slowly.

"Nah...I can't ask for more of your help than you've already given. Hell, I was a guild leader myself back in the last game. Don't worry, I'll get by with the techniques you taught me. Besides, there's always the possibility that this really was just a bad prank, and we'll be able to log out in no time. So go on, jump ahead and don't mind me."

"..."

For a few seconds, I stayed silent, grappling with a conflict the likes of which I'd never faced before.

And then I spoke the simple words that I would grow to regret over the following two years.

"...Okay." I nodded, taking a step back. In a hoarse voice, I continued. "We'll part ways here, then. Shoot me a message if anything comes up. Well...see ya, Klein."

As I averted my eyes and tried to turn away, Klein barked out.

"Kirito!"

"..."

His glance said he wanted to ask something, but his cheekbones only twitched, and no words came out. I waved and turned northwest, the general direction of the village I sought to go next.

After five steps, I heard his voice call out behind me again.

"Hey, Kirito! Turns out you look pretty cute after all! Just my type!"

I grimaced and called back over my shoulder. "And you look ten times better now that you're a mountain bandit!"

And having turned my back on the first friend I ever made in this world, I started walking forward. After a few minutes traveling down the twisted back alleys of the city, I turned around to look. There was no one there, of course.

Gritting my teeth and swallowing the strange sensation that seemed to block my windpipe, I picked up my heels and ran.

First the northwest gate of the Town of Beginnings, then a vast field and deep forest, and finally a little village. I raced onward toward what lay beyond, headlong into a lonely battle for survival without end.

4

Two thousand players were dead within a month.

In that time, we never received a single message from outside, much less any kind of resolution to our crisis.

I didn't stick around to see it for myself, but tales of the panic that erupted when it finally sank in that there was no escape told of sheer madness and chaos. The crowd wailed, cried, and raged. Some even claimed they would destroy the game world, making futile attempts to dig up the cobblestones of the city square. Needless to say, the structures were permanent, immovable pieces of the game environment, and the demolition didn't last long. It took several days for full acceptance of the status quo to sink in and new plans to emerge.

The players split up into four rough categories.

First and largest of those groups, at nearly half the game's population, were those who chose not to believe Akihiko Kayaba's conditions for release and simply waited for help. Their reasons were painfully understandable. Our bodies were sitting on chairs or beds in real life, living and breathing. Those were our real selves, and what happened here was just temporary. One simple little change of circumstances and we could go back. Not through the log-out button in the menu, perhaps, but surely there was *something* if we just figured out what it was . . .

The other source of hope was that the game's developer, Argus (to say nothing of the government itself), was most certainly making every effort possible to rescue us. If we were simply calm and patient, we would eventually wake up in our beds, surrounded by our loving families. We might even be temporary celebrities at school or work.

It was hard not to fall into this line of thinking. Part of me was hoping for the same thing. This group of players chose to "wait." They stayed within the first city, using their initial allotment of money—measured in a currency known as *col*—bit by bit to buy food and cheap lodgings, grouping together in loose cliques.

Fortunately, the Town of Beginnings took up nearly a fifth of the first floor, as large as one of the smaller wards of Tokyo. This meant there was more than enough capacity for five thousand players to settle in without feeling cramped.

But as time dragged on, there was no sign of help. Every waking moment brought the same scenery outside the window: not a blue sky, but the gloomy cover of rock and metal looming overhead like a giant lid. Their initial allotment of money wouldn't last forever, and the waiters would eventually have to do something.

The second group made up about 30 percent. These three thousand players decided that cooperation was the best chance of survival. The leader of the group was the manager of one of Japan's biggest websites about online gaming.

Under his supervision, players were grouped together into smaller bands, sharing items and col, and trading information about the labyrinths that housed the staircases to the next floor. The leader's group claimed Blackiron Palace, the castle that loomed over the central square of the Town of Beginnings, from which they sent instructions to smaller parties and accumulated supplies.

This massive gathering was without a proper title for some time, but once they all started wearing the same uniform, the "Army" label stopped being just a cute nickname.

The third category, of which there were about a thousand people, were the ones who wasted their col early, didn't feel like braving the monsters in the wilderness, and began to get desperate.

Incidentally, even in the virtual world of SAO, there are inescapable natural urges—hunger and sleep. It made sense that you needed to sleep. Regardless of whether the stimuli received are real or virtual, the brain needs to turn off and recharge at some point. When players get tired, they find inns, rent rooms that suit their pocketbooks, and sink into their beds. With enough col, it's possible to buy a residence in the town of your choice, but it's a monumental task.

The hunger was more of a mystery. Though we don't like to imagine it, presumably our real bodies are being kept alive through some means of force-feeding. Eating food in SAO doesn't actually fill our bellies in real life. Yet stuffing virtual bread or meat into your face will get rid of the hunger and make you feel sated. You'll have to ask a neurologist to explain how that works.

On the other hand, once you start feeling hungry, it'll never go away until you eat. I don't think fasting could actually end in starvation, but it's still a natural urge that is incredibly hard to resist. So every day, players rush into pubs and restaurants run by NPCs, stuffing their bellies with food made of pure data. And that's where the digestive process ends, by the way. No use dwelling on the less pleasant aspects.

But enough about that.

Most of the players who'd wasted their initial earnings and started going hungry wound up with no other choice but to join the Army. After all, orders were easy to follow if they were the only way you got fed at the end of the day.

But even in virtual worlds, there are those to whom cooperation is anathema. The ones who resisted joining any groups or got kicked out for causing trouble wound up inhabiting the slums of the Town of Beginnings, living a life of crime.

Town interiors were a protected zone where the system prevented players from harming each other, but there were no rules outside of town. Vagabonds teamed up with their own kind, avoiding monsters for the easier and more rewarding prey of unsuspecting adventurers.

At least they didn't stoop to killing—for the first year. This group of players grew over time until it reached my estimated count of around a thousand.

The fourth and final category might as well be titled "miscellaneous."

Around five hundred players who wanted to help conquer the game but didn't want to join the Army formed roughly fifty smaller groups known as guilds. They were a positive force in our advancement through the game, using their limited resources more nimbly than the Army's massive bureaucracy could manage.

There was also the extreme minority of crafters and traders. These two to three hundred players formed guilds of their own, focusing on the skills that would enable them to raise col and make a living without fighting.

The remaining several dozen adventurers, myself included, were the solo players. We were the individualists who chose to act alone rather than join any group, either out of self-interest or because we felt it was the most effective means of survival. Most of the solos were former beta testers. We'd called upon our prior experiences to fly out of the gate at the game's start, but once we were powerful enough to handle monsters and robbers on our own, we found little reason to work with others.

On top of that, SAO was a game without magic (i.e., easy long-range attacks), which meant that enemies were fairly easy to manage single-handedly, even when they came in groups. With proper skill, a good solo player could earn experience much faster than he could with a group.

Not that this was without risks. For example, contracting paralysis while in a party just meant that someone else had to heal you. On your own, it could be a death sentence. The fatality rate among solo players was easily the highest of any category.

But with enough knowledge and experience to properly avoid danger, the returns easily outweighed the risks. And we beta testers had an advantage over the others in those categories. As the solos used their knowledge to far outpace the new players, serious friction developed between the two groups, and when the initial chaos eventually settled, the solo players all left the first floor to settle in towns higher up.

Within Blackiron Palace was a room formally known as the Chamber of Resurrection. Since the beta test, a massive metallic epitaph had appeared there, etched with the names of all ten thousand players. It had been thoughtfully designed such that when a player died, his or her name was very clearly crossed out, with the time and cause of death printed next to it.

It only took three hours for someone to earn the honor of being the first. The cause of death was not monsters, but suicide.

The unfortunate victim claimed that due to the structure of the NerveGear, if we simply removed ourselves from the game system, we would automatically leave the program and regain consciousness on the other side. He climbed over the tall railing of the terrace on the south edge of town, the very outer border of Aincrad itself, and threw himself overboard.

No matter how hard you peered down, there was never the slightest hint of land or any other surface beneath Aincrad. Nothing but endless sky and layer upon layer of clouds. With the crowd at the terrace watching, the man's scream grew steadily fainter as he plummeted, until he finally disappeared through the cloud layer.

Two minutes later, his name was unceremoniously, mercilessly crossed out on the monument. His cause of death: *fell from a great height*. I don't want to think about what he experienced on that fall. Whether he reawoke in the real world or got brain-fried, as Kayaba claimed, was impossible to determine from within the game. But most players agreed that if it were that easy to escape, we'd all have been detached from the outside and rescued by now.

Still, there were others here and there who also succumbed to the temptation of such a simple conclusion. It was extremely difficult to fully appreciate the concept of death within SAO.

That still hasn't changed. The visual effect of polygons breaking apart when HP reaches zero is just too close to the GAME OVER screen, a harmless phenomenon familiar to all gamers. The only way to fully understand death in SAO is to experience it for oneself. I have no doubt that the mental distance from our supposed mortality was a major contributing factor to the decline in population.

When the Army, the other minor guilds, and the wait-and-see types clogging the Town of Beginnings finally started tackling the game itself, we started losing people to the monsters.

Experience and instincts are necessary to win battles in SAO. The trick is to not try doing everything on your own—you have to "ride" the system's automatic support.

Take a simple, single-handed uppercut slice. If you've learned the One-Handed Sword category and "Upward Slice" is equipped in your list of sword skills, all you need to do is perform the proper motion, and the system will move your body automatically. If you don't have the skill equipped and try to mimic the movements on your own, the result will be so much slower and weaker that there's no point even trying it. In essence, the knack to combat in SAO was a bit like pulling off combos in a fighting game.

Those who couldn't get the grasp of the system just swung their swords back and forth lamely, scuffling against even the weakest boars and wolves, enemies that were easily defeated with the most basic of initial skills. And even if your health was dwindling and the fight was proving difficult, there was always the option of disengaging and retreating to avoid death...

Except that unlike fighting 2-D monsters on a simple TV screen, the incredible realism of SAO's world brought forth a kind of primal fear in its players. In every encounter, you were faced with actual monsters bearing wicked fangs, ready to charge and kill.

Plenty of beta testers felt an initial panic when they first experienced the combat of SAO, but that was nothing compared to fighting with the specter of actual death overhead. When the grips of fear took over, players forgot even the most basic of skills or dodges, becoming helpless targets as their hit points were torn from them.

Suicide. Defeat in combat. The lines on the epitaph proliferated, unstoppable and uncaring.

When the number of dead topped two thousand in just the first month, the remaining population was plunged into black despair. If that mortality rate continued, we'd all have been dead within half a year. Clearing all hundred floors was just a pipe dream.

The thing about human beings is, we learn.

After just over a month, we had finally conquered the first floor of Aincrad. It took only ten days for the second to fall, and by then the death rate was plummeting. As survival tips spread throughout the population, people began to realize that as long as they earned experience and gained levels, the monsters weren't so frightening after all.

Maybe we *can* beat this game. Maybe we *can* get back to the real world. Confidence and optimism dared to peek their heads out once again.

The top floor of Aincrad was impossibly far away, but that hope was enough to jump-start us into motion. The world began ticking away again.

It's been two years. There are twenty-six floors left to conquer and six thousand survivors. Such is the present state of Aincrad.

5

My battle with the powerful lizardman lord in the seventy-fourth-floor labyrinth concluded, I traveled the route back, tracing distant memories in my head. At long last, the light of the exit came into sight, and I heaved a sigh of relief.

I cast aside the stuffy memories and rushed out of the corridor, breathing the fresh, crisp air deeply. Before me was a dark forest path, the sides overgrown. Behind me loomed the labyrinth, its mammoth spire stretching upward in the evening light to the bottom of the floor above.

Given that the objective of the game was to reach the top of the castle, the dungeons of this game took the form of massive towers rather than underground catacombs or caves. They still held fast to the basic tenets of a dungeon, though: more dangerous foes than you found elsewhere, winding corridors, and a terrible boss at the very end.

The seventy-fourth-floor labyrinth was 80 percent mapped out at this point. Within a few days, we'd find the boss's lair, and a raiding party would be arranged. Even as a solo, I'd play a part in the battle.

Grimacing at my equal measures of anticipation and anxiety, I walked out of the doorway.

My current home is in Algade on the fiftieth floor, the de facto largest city in Aincrad. In terms of scale, the Town of Beginnings is bigger, but given that the Army controlled it entirely now, it was best to give that place a wide berth.

As I passed through the field, darkening with the onset of evening, I came to a forest of gnarled, ancient oaks. A thirty-minute walk would bring me to the residential area of the seventy-fourth floor, from which I could use the teleport gate to reach Algade instantly.

I could have used a teleportation item to return to Algade from any point in Aincrad, but they were pricey and best saved for emergencies. There was still time left before the light was fully gone, so I plunged into the forest, resisting the temptation to teleport and plop onto my bed immediately.

Outside of a few load-bearing structures, the outer edge of each floor of Aincrad was essentially open to the sky. The sunlight tilting through the distant opening set the trees aflame with a reddish glow. Thick mist flowing through the branches glinted eerily as it reflected the dying light. The raucous daytime birdcalls grew sparse, and the rustling of the breeze through the branches seemed to echo louder than before.

Despite knowing that I could handle the monsters in this area while half asleep, it was hard to repress an instinctual fear of this hour of darkening. It resembled the sensation of being lost on the way home at a young age, frozen with anxiety.

I didn't dislike the feeling, however. I'd forgotten this kind of primal emotion back in the real world. And after all, wasn't a solitary march across the wilderness without a soul in sight one of the great pleasures of an RPG?

A faint, unfamiliar cry broke me out of my nostalgic reverie. It was a single high note, brief and clear, like a leaf whistle. I stopped in my tracks, trying to discern the direction of the call. Unfamiliar sights and sounds in this world meant the advent of fortune—good or bad.

As a solo player, I'd put lots of work into my Search skill. It was designed to help you protect against ambushes, and as it rose in level, it enabled you to spot foes and players hidden in stealth mode. Pretty soon, the form of a monster came into view in the shadows of a large tree, about ten yards away.

It wasn't very big. I could see gray-green fur suited to blending in with leaves and elongated ears longer than the animal's body. By focusing my vision, I prompted the game to automatically target the monster for me, bringing up a yellow cursor and the target's name.

When I saw the words that appeared, I held my breath. It was a Ragout Rabbit, an ultra-rare creature. It was certainly the first I'd ever seen. The fluffy little things lived in trees, weren't particularly strong, nor rewarding in terms of experience points. Their value came from something else.

Silently, I slipped a narrow throwing pick out of my belt. My Throwing Knife skill was only active in a skill slot to round out the bunch, and my proficiency was modest. But I'd heard that the Ragout Rabbit had the highest escape speed of any monster yet discovered, so I didn't think I could actually get close enough to use my normal sword.

At least I had the opportunity for a first strike, given that the rabbit hadn't noticed me yet. The pick in my right hand, I said a silent prayer and queued up the motion for the basic throwing knife skill, "Single Shot."

My proficiency in Throwing Knives might have been weak, but the skill's chances were adjusted based on my agility stat, which was through the roof. The pick flashed like lightning in my hand and shot into the shadows of the branches, leaving a momentary trail of light behind it. The instant I initiated the skill, the targeting cursor went from yellow to hostile red, bringing up the rabbit's HP bar below.

As I watched the trail of the pick, I heard an even higher-pitched scream, and the HP bar immediately dropped to zero. When the sound effect of disintegrating polygons rang out, I clenched my fist in triumph.

I called up my menu and switched to the inventory, my

fingers fumbling. There it was, right at the top of the new items list: "Ragout Rabbit meat." An absolute gold mine, worth at least six figures on the open market. It was valuable enough to buy me the highest-class custom-made weapons with change to spare. The reason was simple: Out of all the limitless ingredients in the game, it had the very highest flavor rating.

Eating was about the only pleasure to be found in the world of SAO. Most of the available food seemed to be in a rustic European style—simple breads and soups. The tiny minority of crafters who chose to utilize the cooking skill could create other dishes in order to expand our options, but given how few of those cooks there actually were, and the surprising difficulty of obtaining good cooking ingredients, nearly all the players in the game were perpetually starving for quality food.

Count me among them. I didn't mind the soup and black bread at my favorite NPC restaurant, but it was hard to resist the craving to sink my teeth into a hot, juicy piece of meat. A soft moan left my lips as I stared at the name of the item.

It was incredibly unlikely that I'd ever find another top-ranked food ingredient like this again. I desperately wanted to eat it for myself, but the finer the item, the higher the skill rank required to cook it. I'd have to ask a master chef to do it for me.

I'd be lying if I claimed that I didn't know anyone who fit the bill, but tracking that person down would be a pain, and I'd been needing a new set of armor, so I made up my mind to sell the meat for col.

Closing the status screen was a painful act of will. I engaged my Search skill to scan the surroundings. Chances that any thieving players would be hanging out in the deadly frontier looking to make a score were absurdly slim, but when you're sitting on an S-rank gold mine, you tend to err on the side of caution.

I opened the pouch on my waist to rummage for a teleportation crystal to return straight to Algade, operating under the assumption that I could buy all the crystals I wanted with the money I'd make selling the meat.

The crystal was elongated and eight-sided, sparkling deep blue. With the absence of any kind of magic spells in SAO, the few magical items to be found all took the form of these crystals. The blue ones were for teleporting, the pink ones for healing, the green for curing poison—it was all pretty self-explanatory. They worked instantaneously, but given the price, it made more sense to simply retreat from battle and use a cheap potion if you needed to regain HP.

Telling myself that this was a worthy emergency, I gripped the blue fragment and shouted, "Teleport: Algade!"

A beautiful chiming like the ringing of many bells sounded, and the little crystal crumbled in my hand. A blue light enveloped my body, the sights and sounds of the forest vanishing. The light pulsed brighter, then disappeared, and the transition was complete. The rustling of leaves had been replaced with clanging blacksmith mallets and the lively roar of many voices.

I was at the teleport gate in the center of Algade.

The enormous metal gate towered over the rest of the city square, at least sixteen feet tall. The interior space beneath the frame shimmered like a mirage, and people streamed through the gate in a steady flow, teleporting to and from other cities in Aincrad.

Four wide avenues stretched out from the central square with countless tiny shops crammed into the margins. For those seeking solace after a hard day of adventure, there were carts selling food and pubs full of lively chatter.

If there was one word to sum up the city of Algade, it was *chaos*.

There were no singular large structures such as in the Town of Beginnings, but rather a vast space crisscrossed with cramped alleys, suspicious workshops selling unknown wares, and sketchy taverns that promised a way in but probably not out.

This wasn't just hyperbole—players told horror stories of getting lost in the byzantine alleys of Algade for several days at a time. I'd set up residence in this city almost a year ago, and I still didn't know half the streets in it. Even the NPCs of Algade didn't seem to fit into the standard roles, and any human players who spent too much time here developed an eccentricity or two during their stay.

But for all that, I liked the vibe. It was often the case that sipping oddly scented tea in my favorite back-back-back-alley establishment was the only moment of tranquility I had in a day. I couldn't deny that part of the attraction came from Algade's nostalgic resemblance to the notable electronics district I liked to visit back in the real world.

I decided to take care of business before returning to my hideout and set off for a familiar item merchant. After several minutes of weaving through the crowds on the western boulevard, I reached the shop. It had all the hallmarks of a player-run establishment: a cramped interior that could fit no more than five people, a chaotic jumble of merchandise on display, and racks full of weapons, tools, and food. The proprietor was in the midst of a deal right out front.

There are two main methods of selling items in the game. One is to sell to an NPC—in other words, to the system itself. There's no danger of being ripped off, but you're only going to get one fixed price for your goods, and the prices are automatically set to be lower than the market purchase value to prevent inflation.

The other method is dealing directly with another player. It's possible to get a much better price for your wares this way, but first you have to actually find someone to buy them, then you have to deal with finicky buyers, people who come back wanting a refund, or plain old scam artists. This is where traders making a living in the secondhand market come in.

Of course, that's not the only reason they exist.

As with item crafters, merchants have to fill the majority of their skill slots with non-combat skills, but they still have to venture out into the wilderness. Merchants need items to sell and crafters need ingredients, which means farming monsters for goods is necessary. As you might imagine, battle is a lot tougher when you aren't playing a traditional warrior class. There is nothing glamorous or enjoyable about fighting as a merchant.

This all means that their class identity is rooted in a pure and admirable desire to assist those adventurers who are working their damnedest on the front lines to beat the game. I held a deep and secret admiration for merchants and crafters.

...But the shopkeeper I stared at now was about as far from the definition of self-sacrificing as anyone could be.

"You got yourself a deal! Five hundred col for twenty Dusklizard hides!"

Agil the pawnbroker swung his burly arm, whacking his victim, a weak-willed spearman, on the shoulder. He popped open the trading window and entered the gold amount on his side without waiting for an answer.

The seller still appeared hesitant, but with a powerful glare from Agil's imposing face—not only was he a merchant, he was also an excellent ax warrior—the man quickly transferred his materials to the trade window and hit the accept button.

"Thanks for your business! Come again!" Agil boomed a laugh as he slapped his mark's back one last time. Dusklizard hide was a valuable crafting ingredient in making armor. Five hundred col seemed to be a steal for that many of them, but I held my tongue and watched the spearman trudge away. I told myself that he'd just learned a valuable lesson: Never let your guard down around a secondhand buyer.

"Another day making a living ripping off honest folks, Agil?"

The bald head craned around to see who'd called to him, and Agil beamed.

"Good to see you, Kirito. Stock it cheap; sell it cheap: That's my motto," he lied without a trace of irony.

"Not sure about the latter part, but whatever. Got some more stuff to sell you."

"You're a regular, Kirito. You know I won't do you wrong. Let's see..." He trailed off, leaning over to peer at my trade window.

Our avatars within Sword Art Online were accurate recreations of our faces and bodies, thanks to the NerveGear's scanners and the initial calibration process. But I had to admit that I hadn't seen anyone who appeared to fit the role they played quite like Agil did.

He stood nearly six feet tall, with a hefty frame of muscle and fat, topped off by a face like a wrestling heel, practically carved out of a boulder. The one customizable option we had was hairstyle, and he chose to go as bald as a cue ball. He was as imposing as any barbarian foe to be found in the game.

But when a grin cracked his face, that craggy scowl became lovable and comforting. He appeared to be in his late twenties, but it was impossible to guess what he did back in the real world. It was an unspoken rule that no one in SAO discussed the other side.

When Agil saw the contents of the trade window, the eyes under his thick brows grew wide.

"Wait a second, that's an S-rank item, man. Ragout Rabbit meat...never actually seen one for myself. You aren't that hard up for cash, are you? You thought about eating it yourself?"

"I have. But it's hard to find folks with a cooking skill high enough to handle this sort of—"

Someone poked my shoulder from behind.

"Kirito."

It was a woman's voice. There weren't many female players who would call my name. In this situation, there was only one. I didn't need to turn around to know who it was. Instead, I quickly grabbed the hand over my shoulder and spoke as I swiveled around.

"Caught me a chef."

"Wh-what do you mean?" she asked, trying to retreat with her hand still clutched in mine.

She had a small oval face framed by long chestnut hair on either side and hazel-colored eyes that flashed brightly. Under her petite, slender nose was a set of bright pink lips. Her graceful body was clad in a knight's uniform of red and white, and an elegant silver rapier sat in a scabbard of white leather at her waist.

Her name was Asuna, and she was familiar to virtually everyone inside the game. The reasons were plentiful. First, there were her undeniably stunning good looks in a game with an extremely low ratio of female players.

Though it pains me to be so frank, SAO recreates its players' bodies and—in particular—faces with nearly perfect detail, and it was extremely rare to come across a truly attractive female player. You could probably count on your fingers the number of beauties at her level in the entire game.

Another reason for her fame was the white-and-crimson outfit she wore—the uniform of the Knights of the Blood. Abbreviated "KoB," they were unanimously considered the most talented and powerful player guild in Aincrad.

At thirty members, the KoB was modestly sized, but they were all high-level swordsmen, and their leader was a legendary figure held by many to be the most powerful man in SAO. Behind her winsome looks, Asuna was the vice commander of the guild. Her skill and speed with the rapier had earned her the moniker "The Flash."

In short, she stood atop all six thousand players in Sword Art Online in the combination of appearance and skill. It would've been crazy if she *wasn't* famous. Naturally, she had gained many fans, including some who took their appreciation to the depths of obsession, and others who felt a fiery antagonism. It couldn't have been easy for her.

Very few people were foolish enough to take on one of the best warriors in the game, but the guild intended to ensure the safety of its officers, so multiple bodyguards always attended her. Sure enough, two men in metallic armor and white capes stood a few steps behind her. The one on the left, a thin man with longer hair pulled back behind his head, was staring daggers at me as I held Asuna's hand.

I let go, my fingers drifting a sardonic greeting to the man as

I responded to her question. "Strange to see you here, Asuna. Didn't think you frequented dumps like this."

Veins throbbed on the foreheads of both the long-haired man at my casual address and the shopkeeper at my appraisal of his establishment. But when Asuna gave Agil a friendly greeting, his scowl melted into a sappy beam. She turned back to me, her lips pursed.

"What was that for? We're about to tackle the next boss, so I'm only checking in on you to make sure you're still alive."

"You're already on my friends list, so you can see my status anytime. Besides, the only reason you're even here is because you tracked me down on your map."

She turned her face away from me in a huff. Despite only being a sub-leader in her own guild, Asuna was a principal figure in the game's progress. It was part of her responsibility to round up solo players like me when arranging raid parties on the latest floor's boss, but coming out to personally check up on me was getting ridiculous.

She put her hands on her hips and jutted her chin out at my gaze of half astonishment and half admiration.

"Look, the only thing that matters is that you're alive. And... what was that about a chef?"

"Oh, right. What's your Cooking skill at now?" I remembered that she had been putting time into building up her Cooking skill on a whim between all of the usual combat practice. She let a gloating smile cross her lips.

"Are you ready for this? I mastered it last week."

"What?!"

That's...idiotic. (I didn't verbalize the thought.)

Skill proficiency increases the more you use that skill, but the pace is glacial, and the skill isn't fully mastered until you get it all the way to a full 1,000. It's a separate process from the character level that goes up as you earn experience points. A level-up increases HP, strength, agility, and the number of skill slots available.

I had twelve skill slots at this point but had only mastered three of them: One-Handed Swords, Search, and Weapon Defense. In other words, she had poured an unfathomable amount of time and energy into a skill that had absolutely no use in battle.

"Well, I could use your help." I beckoned her over and enabled visible mode on my window so she could see it. She squinted doubtfully at first, but her eyes grew wide when she saw the item I had highlighted.

"Wow! Is that...an S-rank ingredient?"

"Let's make a deal. If you cook this thing for me, I'll let you have a bite."

Almost before I could finish the sentence, Asuna the Flash's hand darted over and seized my shirt. She pulled my face down until it was just inches from her own.

"*H-a-l-f!*"

Stunned by this unexpected menace, I nodded my head automatically. By the time I realized what I'd done, she was already pumping her other fist in triumph. I tried to convince myself that it was a price worth paying for the point-blank view of such a pretty face.

I closed the window and turned to Agil. "Sorry, man. The deal's off."

"It's cool, I understand. But we're bros, right? Right? You'd let me take a little taste..."

"I'll write you an eight-hundred-word review."

"You can't do this to me, man!" Agil wailed as though the world itself were ending. I turned my back on him, and Asuna tugged on my coat sleeve.

"I'll cook it for you, but where is that supposed to happen?"

"Uh..."

In order to utilize the Cooking skill, you need ingredients, utensils, and some kind of oven or stove, at the very least. Technically, I did have the bare minimum of supplies at my home, but such a filthy hovel was no place for the exalted vice commander of the KoB.

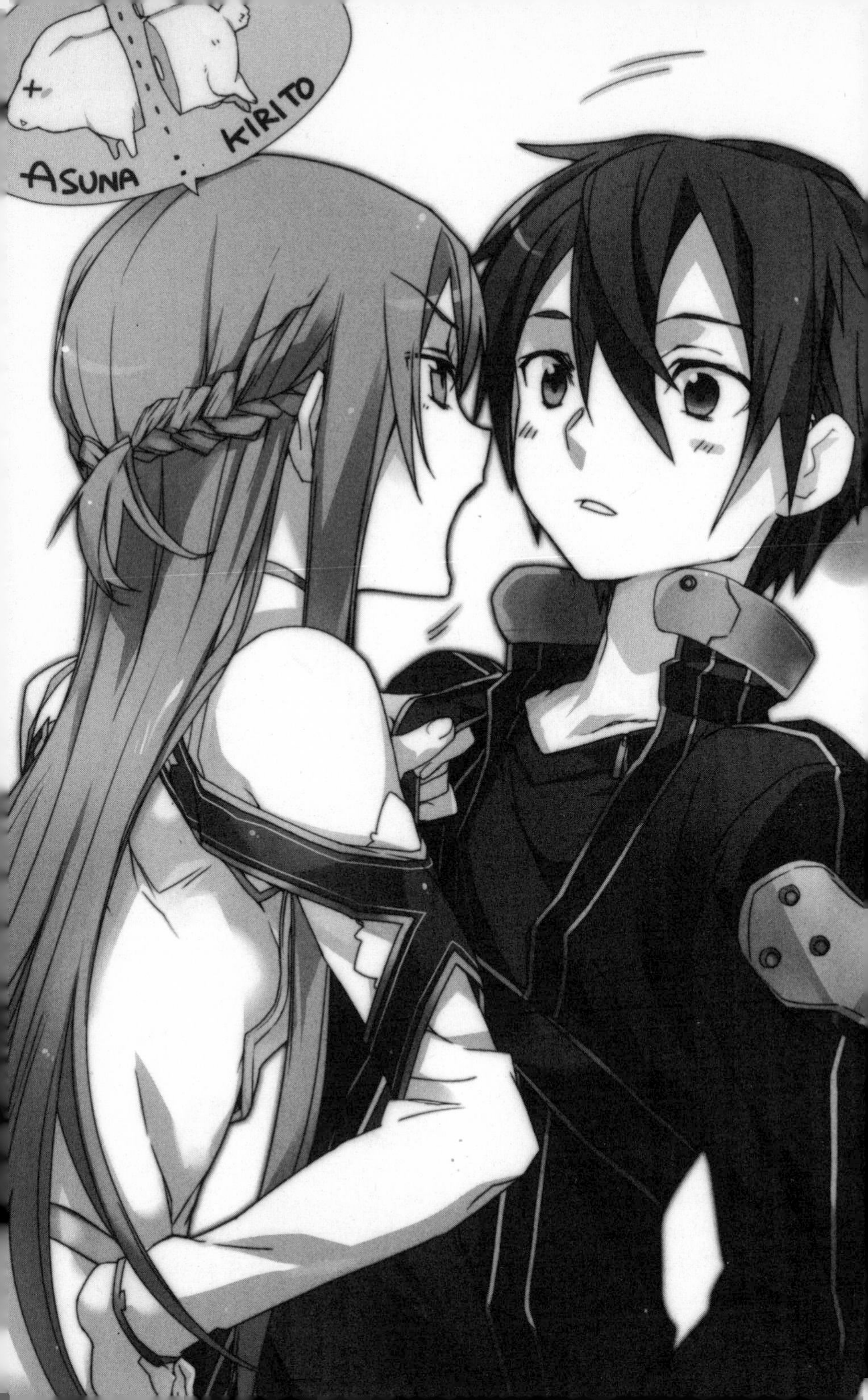
ASUNA
KIRITO

She turned an exasperated eye to me as I stammered.

"I'm assuming you don't have any of the necessary tools. But given the value of your ingredients, I might be willing to let you use my room," she offered, shockingly enough.

My brain lagged as it struggled to comprehend her meaning. Asuna turned to the two guardsmen who made up her escort. "I'm going to teleport straight to Selmburg. I won't need my guard for the rest of the day. You may go."

The long-haired man exploded as though he'd been holding in his rage for quite a while. If the fidelity on SAO's facial expressions were finer, he'd have had two or three purple veins bulging out of his forehead.

"L-Lady Asuna! It's bad enough that you're visiting this slum, but I cannot allow you to bring such a suspect individual into your home!"

His exaggerated mannerisms made me wince. "Lady" Asuna? He was probably no better than her obsessed stalker fans. I noticed that she seemed just as exasperated as I was.

"His character aside, he's a worthy fighter. He's probably got at least ten levels on you, Kuradeel."

"Th-that's preposterous! How could I possibly be inferior to..."

The high-pitched protest echoed off the alley walls. His sunken, glaring eyes fixed on me, then widened with comprehension.

"That's it! You're a beater, aren't you?"

Beater was an epithet unique to SAO, a portmanteau of *beta tester* and *cheater*. I'd heard the slur time and time again, but it always caused a certain level of pain. The image of someone I'd once called a friend flashed through my mind—the first person to ever say the word to my face.

"Yeah, that's right," I said without expression, but he continued more forcefully than before.

"Lady Asuna, he doesn't care for anyone but himself! Nothing good can come from fraternizing with his kind!"

Asuna had been playing it cool, but now her brows knitted together in displeasure. A crowd was starting to gather around us, and I could hear the words *KoB* and *Asuna* being murmured. She took note of the increased interest and turned on Kuradeel, who showed no signs of regaining his composure.

"I told you to leave. That's an order from your vice commander," she growled, grabbing the rear belt of my coat and pulling me backward. She began tugging us toward the main square.

"H-hang on, are you sure about this?"

"I'm sure!"

Well, who was I to argue? We left the two guardsmen and the crestfallen Agil behind and slipped into the throng. I took one last backward glance. The picture of Kuradeel glaring with fury stuck in my mind like an afterimage.

6

Selmburg was a beautiful castle town on the sixty-first floor.

The city itself wasn't particularly large. An old castle with fragile minarets loomed over the center of town, but the buildings were painstakingly built of chalk-white granite with copious greenery placed to great effect. The selection of shops was rich as well. Many players coveted the chance to live in Selmburg, but the cost was exorbitant—at least three times that of Algade. Residence was a pipe dream for all but the highest-level players.

It was well past sunset when we arrived through the teleport gate, the last remaining traces of sunlight reflecting purple on the town.

Most of the sixty-first floor consisted of lakes, and Selmburg itself sat on a small island surrounded by water. The view of the sun shining through the outer aperture of Aincrad and reflecting off the lake was worthy of a painting, at least. The sparkling scenery of dark blue and red set atop that massive lake was so breathtaking, I couldn't help but be bewitched. The only thing that could take away from the sight was the knowledge that it was just child's play to the NerveGear's diamond-semiconductor CPU.

Selmburg's teleport gate was located in the square before the old castle. The town's main street stretched south, lined with leafy trees. Shops and homes both quaint and elegant stood along the boulevard, and the NPCs and players who walked the city seemed to carry themselves with more class than elsewhere. Even the air seemed to taste different than in Algade; I couldn't help but stretch my arms and inhale deeply.

"It's so big and spacious here. Feels liberating."

"You should move, then."

"Don't have nearly enough money," I mumbled, shoulders slumped. I gathered myself and cast her a concerned look. "Seriously, are you sure this won't cause trouble with your folks?"

"..."

Asuna seemed to catch my meaning and turned around, hanging her head and kicking the heel of her boot on the ground.

"It's true that I've had some unpleasant encounters while alone, but my own personal guard? It's too much. I keep telling them I don't want this, but it's guild protocol, the chief of staff tells me..."

She continued in a downcast mutter.

"In the past, we were just a small guild. The commander picked every member himself. But we just keep taking on more members, and people come and go... Things started to get crazy when they began calling us the most powerful guild here."

She stopped talking and twisted her torso around. Something in her eyes seemed to plead for help, and the breath caught in my throat. *I have to say something*, I thought, but as a solo who did everything out of self-interest, what could I say? Several seconds of silence passed.

Asuna broke the eye contact first. She looked at the deep blue of the lake and piped up in a much higher pitch, sounding eager to change the mood.

"But it's not that big a deal! Better hurry before it gets dark."

I started walking after her through the town. We passed no small number of players, but none of them stopped to stare at Asuna's face.

I spent a few days in Selmburg about a half year back, when it represented the frontier of our advancement through the game, but I couldn't remember ever stopping to take in the sights. Gazing at the exquisite sculptures on display, I felt a momentary desire to live here permanently, but then thought better of it, deciding it was better suited to the occasional holiday trip.

Asuna's residence was on the third floor of an attractive little maisonette, immediately to the east of the main street. It was my first visit, of course. Thinking back on it, the most I'd ever interacted with Asuna before was at boss strategy meetings. I'd never even stopped at an NPC-run restaurant with her. I couldn't help but hesitate at the entrance of the building.

"So, uh...are you sure this is okay with you?"

"It was your idea, wasn't it? Besides, there's nowhere else to do the cooking."

She turned her head with a huff and trotted up the stairs. I steeled my willpower and followed her.

"W-well, pardon the intrusion."

I stopped stock-still when I passed through the door, my mouth agape.

I'd never seen such a neat and orderly player home. The spacious living room and adjacent kitchen were filled with lightly colored wooden furniture, and accents of moss-green cloth tied together the visual style. It was all likely custom-made of the highest quality by other players.

Despite the emphasis on looks, there was no ostentatious decoration, which made the whole place seem inviting and comfortable. It was a stark contrast to the lair I called a home. I was glad I'd chosen not to invite her there.

"H-how much did all of this cost?" I asked bluntly.

"Hmm, about four M for the room and furnishings together, I think? Sit wherever you like; I'm just going to change." She disappeared through the door on the other side of the living room. The letter *M* was shorthand for million, just like *K* for thousand. I spent my days adventuring on the front line, so I'd probably earned that much in total during my time in SAO, but with my penchant for spending money on whatever swords and equipment caught my eye, there was no way I'd save up a lump sum like that. Indulging in a rare moment of self-reflection, I sank into a soft couch.

Eventually, Asuna emerged from the back room wearing a simple white tunic and skirt that stopped above the knee. Changing clothes in the game didn't involve actually removing or putting on anything—it was as simple as dragging items onto the character mannequin in the equipment screen. But because there were a few seconds during the shift in which a player was temporarily reduced to his or her underwear, female players made certain not to change in public, though the men didn't seem to mind doing it. Our bodies were just 3-D models made of ones and zeros, but when you'd lived in this world for two years, you tended to take things at face value. My eyes naturally traveled to the newly exposed skin on Asuna's limbs.

Unaware of my inner conflict, she shot back a look at me. "How long are you going to wear that gear?"

I hastily brought up the menu and removed my leather coat and scabbard. I switched to my item window and materialized the Ragout Rabbit meat into a ceramic pot, placing it on the table.

Asuna picked up the container and peered into it with a reverent expression.

"So this is what an S-rank ingredient looks like! What dish are we having, then?"

"Um, I'll have the chef's choice."

"Okay...how about a stew? They don't call it a 'Ragout' Rabbit for nothing."

I followed Asuna into the other room. The kitchen was spacious, with pricey-looking cooking tools hanging next to a large, wood-fired oven. Asuna tapped the front of the oven twice as though double-clicking, and a menu popped open. She set a cooking time and pulled a metal pot out of the cupboard, transferred the meat from its container, added some herbs and water, then placed a lid on top.

"Normally there'd be many more steps in the process, but

SAO's cooking system is really simplified and boring," she complained.

Asuna placed the pot in the oven and hit the start button on the menu. The timer was set to three hundred seconds, during which she hummed about quickly, pulling ingredients out of a seemingly unlimited larder and arranging dishes with the efficiency of familiarity. I couldn't help but admire her flawless speed without a single mistake.

Five minutes later, there was a gourmet feast on the table, and Asuna and I sat facing each other. The plate in front was piled high with a piping-hot brown stew that stimulated my nose with every waft of steam. Rich chunks of meat wallowed in a thick, shining sauce marbled with white streaks of cream. It was bewitching.

Barely stopping to say thanks before the meal, I grabbed my spoon and shoveled up a mouthful of the most delicious food in the entirety of Sword Art Online. The savory heat and flavor filled my mouth as I sank my teeth into the soft meat, letting the juice spill out.

Eating in SAO isn't a realistic simulation of every single sensation that should occur from chewing in-game objects. Argus utilized a "Taste Recreation Engine" contracted from an environmental software developer.

The engine is designed to send "eating" sensory input to the brain of the user based on certain pre-set variables, originally for the sake of those on a diet or who would otherwise need to observe a period of limited food intake. It sends false signals of flavor, scent, and heat to the sensory areas of the brain to fool the user. Our real bodies aren't receiving any nutrition from this act of eating—the system is simply stimulating our brains.

But there was no use dwelling on this fact. What I felt in that moment, all that mattered, was that I was eating the greatest meal I'd had in the two years since I first logged in to the game. We didn't share a word, silently shoveling spoonfuls of the stew into our mouths.

Finally, after we had literally cleaned every last trace of stew from our plates and the cooking pot, Asuna let out a contented sigh.

"Ahhh...I'm glad to still be alive..."

I had to agree. I sat back, sipping a strangely scented tea, reveling in the fulfillment of a primal urge satisfied to completion. Were the meat and tea programmed to resemble some real-life ingredients, or were those flavors just the fictional product of a number of finely tuned parameters?

After several minutes of silent contentment, Asuna began to speak, a mug of tea cupped in her hands.

"It's so strange...It feels like I was born here. Like I've always lived in this world."

"There are days that I don't even remember about my life over there. And I'm not the only one. You don't see as many players desperate to beat the game and escape these days."

"The rate of our conquest is slowing down. There aren't even five hundred players fighting at the front line at this point. It's not just the danger...we're all getting used to this life..."

I gazed at her beautiful, pensive face, lit by the warm orange light of the lamp. It wasn't the face of a living, breathing human being. The skin was too smooth, the hair too lustrous to be real. But it didn't even look like a polygonal model to me at this point. It was easy to accept her as a living being inhabiting this space. In fact, if I went back to the real world now, I would probably find true reality off-putting.

Do I even really want to go back?

I was startled by the thought. Were all the early mornings, dungeon adventures, mapping expeditions, and level-ups really for the purpose of escaping the game? It must have been that way once. The game was deadly, and I wanted out. But now that I'd gotten used to life within SAO...

"I still want to go back," Asuna said clearly, as though to drown out my indecision. I raised my head with a start. She flashed me a rare grin and continued. "There are so many things left to do back there."

I had to nod in agreement.

"Good point. And it's not fair to the crafters working for our benefit if we don't give it our best…"

I tilted my cup and took a deep swig, trying to swallow my hesitation. The top floor was a long ways off. I could think about this when the time came.

Feeling bold, I gazed at Asuna as I tried to formulate the right words to properly thank her. Instead, she grimaced and started waving a hand in front of her face.

"Wh-whoa…stop."

"Huh? What?"

"I've gotten too many marriage proposals from players giving me that look."

"Wha…"

Despite my mastery of battle skills, I had far less experience when it came to delicate matters like this. My mouth opened and closed repeatedly with no sound. I must have looked like an idiot. Asuna smiled.

"Let me guess—you're not that close to anyone else, either."

"Well, sorry for being a solo player."

"You're in an MMORPG—making friends is the point."

Her smile disappeared, and she asked me a question in the tone of an older sister or teacher. "Have you ever thought about joining a guild?"

"Huh…?"

"I know you beta testers don't like to work in groups." Her expression grew even more serious. "But it feels like the monster activity patterns have been increasingly irregular since we hit the seventieth floor."

I'd noticed that, too. It wasn't clear if the drop in CPU predictability was planned from the start or the result of the system itself learning. If it was the latter, we'd have our work cut out for us.

"And playing solo leaves you much less capable of handling unexpected situations. You can't always make an emergency escape. You're much, much safer forming a party."

"I'm always cautious enough to leave myself a safety margin. Thanks for the warning...but guilds just aren't my thing. Besides..."

My mind screamed at me to stop, but my mouth barreled onward.

"Party members usually end up being more of a hindrance than a help for me."

"Oh?"

A silver flash of light passed before my eyes.

It was Asuna's knife, held motionless at the end of my nose.

This was a basic rapier skill called Linear. Basic, but scaled in effectiveness based on one's agility stat. She'd moved so fast, I hadn't even seen the skill's telltale movement trail. With a grin frozen on my face, I assumed the hands-up position of surrender.

"Fine, fine...you're an exception."

"Good."

She pulled back the knife, unamused. As she twirled the blade around her fingers, her next words were completely unexpected.

"In that case, I want you to partner up with me. Being in charge of arranging boss raid parties, I've always wanted to see if you're as good as they say. Plus, I want to show you just how tough I really am. And lastly, black is my lucky color this week."

"What's that supposed to mean?!" Shocked by the absurdity of her demand, I weakly grasped for some kind of counterargument. "B-besides, what about your guild?"

"We don't have a leveling quota to meet."

"Y-your personal guards, then?"

"I'll leave them behind."

I raised the teacup to my lips in a bid to buy time, then realized that it was empty. Gloating, Asuna snatched it from my hands and served more of the steaming liquid.

To be honest, the invitation was tempting. Who wouldn't

want to team up with the most beautiful woman in Aincrad? But the more enticing the offer, the more my hesitation and suspicion grew. Why would she want to be with me?

Perhaps she felt pity for a gloomy, introverted solo player. Stuck in a negative thought process, I uttered the words that sealed my fate.

"The frontier's dangerous, you know."

The knife in her hand rose again, and when I saw an even stronger glow envelop the blade, I hurriedly nodded. Even among the "clearers," as those who fought on the front line to advance the game's progress were known, I was hardly notable. Hesitantly, I pushed on.

"F-fine, fine...I'll see you at the seventy-fourth-floor gate tomorrow at nine o'clock."

Asuna lowered her hand and chuckled confidently.

I wasn't sure how long etiquette dictated it was acceptable to stay in a single woman's apartment, so I hastily pardoned myself once we finished eating. Asuna escorted me down the stairs of the building and inclined her head slightly.

"Anyway...I should thank you for the food."

"Me, too. We should do this again sometime...though I doubt I'll ever get that particular ingredient again."

"Oh, even normal ingredients will work. You just need the skill to do it."

She turned her head to look upward. The sky was dark with night, but there were no stars to be seen. The only object overhead was the giant gloomy lid of rock and metal, several hundred feet above.

"I wonder if what we're in right now really is the world Kayaba wanted to create," I muttered, looking up as well.

There was no answer to this query, of course.

Kayaba must be taking refuge somewhere, observing his creation. What was he feeling now? We had passed through the initial period of blood and chaos, reaching the current stasis of relative peace and order. Did this satisfy or disappoint Kayaba? I had no idea.

Asuna silently took a step closer. I felt a faint glow of warmth on my arm. Was that an illusion or a subtle temperature simulation?

The game of death began on November 6, 2022. It was now late October 2024. Almost two years later, there was still no sign of rescue, no messages from outside. All we could do was survive day by day, getting closer to the top, one step at a time.

It was the end of another day in Aincrad. Where we were going and what waited for us at the end of the game were still a mystery. The road ahead was long and arduous, and the light at the end was faint. But even then, it wasn't worth giving up.

I stared up at the metal lid, letting my mind wander through the unknown worlds left to conquer.

7

9:00 AM

The weather was set to "lightly cloudy." The morning fog enshrouding the city still hung thick, refracting the sunlight from the aperture into fine particles and dyeing the sights in lemon yellow.

According to Aincrad's calendar, this was the Month of the Ash Tree, deeper into autumn. The air was cool on the skin, the most refreshing of all the seasons, but my mood was downcast.

I stood in the teleport gate square on the seventy-fourth floor, waiting for Asuna. For once, I'd struggled to sleep, tossing and turning in my bed back in Algade. I don't think I finally passed out until after three in the morning. SAO has a number of useful features to assist players, but a button that would instantly put you to sleep was sadly not one of them.

But for some reason, it *can* do the opposite. The main menu has a "forced alarm" option that will automatically wake you up to the music of your choice, though it can't prevent you from falling back asleep. I'd set my alarm to 8:50 and successfully managed to roll out of bed.

It was gospel to the great unwashed hordes of SAO that there was no need to bathe or change clothes—you could take a bath if you wanted, but the liquid simulation was rather taxing on the NerveGear, and it just wasn't quite up to the standards of a real bath. So a mere twenty seconds after waking up, I was in my armor, shuffling off to Algade's teleport gate and struggling with my lack of sleep, because I was supposed to be meeting Asuna. And yet...

"She's not coming..."

It was already ten past the hour. Diligent clearers were popping out of the gate one after the other and heading off to the labyrinth. Since I didn't have anything better to do, I opened my menu to pore over the already memorized labyrinth map and check on my skill progress. I was briefly disgusted when I caught myself hoping for a handheld game console of some kind to kill time.

Itching to play a video game inside a video game? It was enough to make me want to crawl back into bed... when the blue light of the teleport gate flashed again. I automatically flicked my eyes over, not expecting much, when—

"Aaaah! L-look out!"

"Whaaa?!"

Normally, you pop out of a teleport gate with your boots firmly on the ground, but for some reason, this person materialized several feet in the air—and flying directly at me.

"Wh...what the...?"

There was no time to duck or brace myself for the impact. We collided at full force and sprawled onto the paving stones, the back of my head smacking hard. If we weren't in the safety of town, I'd have easily lost a few ticks off my HP bar.

I was piecing it all together in my head. Whoever this idiot was had probably jumped directly into the teleport gate, emerging on the other side with the same balance and momentum as before. Grappling with wooziness, I lifted my right hand up to shove the moron off me and squeezed.

"...?"

The sensation on my hand was not at all unpleasant. Trying to identify the soft but resilient material, I squeezed a few more times.

"Aaaah!!"

A piercing scream erupted directly in my ear, and the back of my head was slammed into the pavement again. The weight finally lifted off. Back to my senses from this new impact, I bolted upright.

Before me was a female player, sitting on the ground. She wore a knight's uniform with red stitching on a white background, a miniskirt, a silver rapier hung in a scabbard, and for some reason, a vicious glare of pure murder. The emotion simulator plastered her face red from ear to ear, and her arms were crossed tightly over her...chest...?

Suddenly I realized what I'd been squeezing. And with that came the belated recognition of my present danger. All of my finely honed escape instincts forgotten, I sat frozen with my mouth an open circle, my hand helplessly closing and opening.

"H-hey...morning, Asuna."

It seemed as though the malice in her eyes grew hotter. They were the eyes of someone debating whether or not to draw her weapon.

Just as I began to seriously consider the option of dropping everything and fleeing for my life, the teleport gate flashed again. Asuna spun around with a start, hastily getting to her feet and circling around behind me.

"Wha...?"

I stood there, confused. The gate grew brighter and brighter until a new figure emerged. This one had the good sense to be standing upright.

When the light faded, a familiar face came into view. Another ostentatious white cape with red insignia—it was the Knights of the Blood uniform. He was clad in loud plate armor, just a bit too ornamental for its own good, and a large double-handed sword. It was the long-haired guard who'd attended to Asuna yesterday. Kuradeel, if I recalled his name correctly.

As Kuradeel walked out of the gate and spotted us standing together, the furrows between his eyebrows grew deeper. He couldn't have been that old, probably in his early twenties, but the wrinkles made him look much older. He clenched his teeth so hard it was practically audible and spoke with barely suppressed rage.

"L...Lady Asuna, this willful behavior will not do!"

The hysterical tone to his high-pitched voice told me this was nothing but trouble. Kuradeel continued, his beady eyes flashing white.

"Come, Lady Asuna, let us return to the guild."

"No way, I'm not on guild duty today! Besides, why were you camping out in front of my house this morning?" She sounded plenty angry herself, behind my back.

"*Hah!* I had a premonition this might happen. As a matter of fact, I've been performing early-morning guard duties here in Selmburg for the past month."

It was hard not to be taken aback by Kuradeel's arrogant response. Asuna was equally frozen with shock. She spoke after a long pause, her voice hard.

"That...wasn't on the commander's orders, was it...?"

"My orders are to guard you, end of story! Naturally, that includes home observation..."

"N-no, it doesn't, you idiot!"

Kuradeel's expression instantly flashed with greater irritation. He stormed over, muscled me out of the way, and grabbed Asuna's arm.

"Please, my lady, see reason. Come back to headquarters."

Asuna momentarily shrank back at the barely controlled force in his voice. She cast a pleading glance in my direction.

Until that moment, I'd been grappling with my typical instinct to flee and avoid trouble. But the look in her eyes caused my hand to move of its own accord. It closed around the wrist of Kuradeel's offending hand, just soft enough not to set off the anti-criminal code within the safe limits of town.

"Sorry, pal. I'm renting out your vice commander for the day."

It was a groaner of a line, but there was no turning back now.

Forced to acknowledge my existence at last, Kuradeel swung his arm away, his face a mask of rage.

"Insolent brat!" he gnashed. Even accounting for SAO's tendency to exaggerate facial expressions, something in his face seemed to have gone off the rails.

"I'll take responsibility for Asuna's safety. We're not running off to fight a boss today. You can go back to your HQ."

"N-nonsense! I would never leave Lady Asuna in the hands of a no-name like you! I am a full member of the Knights of the Blood—"

"I'll do a much better job of it than you."

Honestly, I shouldn't have said that one.

"Why, you snotty little... If you're going to talk the talk, then let's see you walk the walk."

His face pale, Kuradeel pulled open his window with a trembling hand. A translucent system message appeared before me, but I didn't need to read it to know what it was.

Kuradeel has challenged you to a one-on-one duel. Do you accept?

Beside the clinical words were buttons for YES and NO and a few options. I glanced at Asuna next to me. She couldn't see the prompt, but she seemed to understand what was happening. I assumed that she'd tell us to knock it off, but to my surprise, she gave a curt nod, her face hard.

"Are you sure? Is this going to cause trouble within the guild?" I muttered. She responded in the same low tone.

"Don't worry, I'll report to the commander."

I nodded and pressed the YES button, selecting FIRST STRIKE out of the list of victory conditions. This meant that whoever inflicted a heavy blow first or got his opponent down to 50 percent HP would win the duel. The message changed to read, *You have agreed to a one-on-one duel with Kuradeel*, accompanied by a minute-long countdown. When that clock reached zero, the HP protections afforded us by the town would disappear, and we'd battle until a winner emerged.

Kuradeel seemed to have found his own unique interpretation of Asuna's consent.

"Watch closely, Lady Asuna! You'll see that no one else is fit to stand guard for you!" he cried in a tone that suggested madness, noisily unsheathing his massive sword in a theatrical display.

Once I'd seen Asuna take several steps back to give us room, I pulled out my own weapon. True to his status as a member of an elite guild, his blade was certainly more impressive than mine. Not only was his two-handed sword much larger than my weapon, it was also augmented with some of the finest decorative craftwork you could see in the game. In comparison, my sword was simple, unadorned, and of average size.

We took positions about five yards apart. The countdown hadn't finished, but an audience was already forming. This wasn't a surprise—we were right next to the teleport gate in the middle of town, and both of us were reasonably well-known players.

"Look, Kirito the solo and someone from the KoB are starting a duel!" someone cried out, and the crowd raised a cheer. Duels were normally between friends testing their skills, so the gallery roared, hooting and whistling, unaware of the ugly dispute that had led to this moment.

As the count dwindled, the din of the crowd faded. Much like when I faced a monster, I could feel frozen cords of pure concentration piercing my body. My entire focus was trained on Kuradeel, who was clearly annoyed by the onlookers. I watched the way he held his sword, the opening of his stance.

The tricks and tells of what skill you were about to use were much more important when fighting another human being than when fighting the AI-controlled monsters of SAO. Giving away too much information—whether your next move was to charge or defend, going high or ducking low—could be the difference between victory and defeat in a duel against another player.

Kuradeel held his sword at mid-level, balancing the weight of the blade, his waist slightly crouched forward—clear signs of an upper-thrust attack. This could have been a feint, of course.

I myself was loosely holding my sword downward, giving off the appearance that I'd strike low and fast to begin. Only instinct and experience could help you win a game of bluffs.

The count reached single digits, and I closed the window. I couldn't even hear the crowd anymore.

Kuradeel's eyes bounced back and forth between the countdown and me until he finally tensed up, his entire body still. A purple sign flashing DUEL!! blinked into the space between us, and I leaped forward in the same instant. Sparks flew from the soles of my boots, and the air growled as I sliced through it.

Kuradeel burst into motion as well, just the faintest moment after I did, but a look of shock was plastered across his face. Instead of pouncing low to receive his attack, I was charging full-speed.

As I suspected, Kuradeel's initial move was Avalanche, a greatsword upward dash skill. It was an excellent attack—even if you managed to block it, the impact was too strong to transition to an effective counterattack, and if you dodged, the lengthy charge distance gave the attacker plenty of time to turn around and prepare for you. If you were a monster, that is.

Knowing that it was coming, I'd chosen Sonic Leap, another upward charge attack. Our skills would be intersecting in midair.

His attack was more powerful than mine. Furthermore, when two attacks collide, the heavier one is given the advantage. Under normal circumstances, my sword would be jolted aside, and although the impact would weaken his blow, it'd probably still be enough to win the duel. But I wasn't trying to hit Kuradeel himself.

We closed simultaneously at blinding speed, but my senses were accelerated, slowing down my perception of time. Whether this was the SAO system giving me a boost or just my natural human instincts was unclear. At any rate, I could easily see every little movement he made as he unleashed his attack.

The greatsword held far behind his back came rushing up at me, trailing orange light. He was apparently a worthy member of that elite guild, as his skill came faster than I was expecting. If that glowing blade hit me, it could inflict critical damage, duel or not. Kuradeel's face was flush with mad excitement, his victory all but assured. Except…

My sword was faster. It flew in a diagonal arc, its own light yellow-green, intersecting with the side of the greatsword just as it was about to connect with me. Sparks exploded from the collision.

It was the other possible outcome when two blades meet: weapon destruction.

This rarely ever happens, of course. It's only possible when a skill is just beginning or ending, no hit detection has occurred yet, and a powerful outside force strikes the weakest structural point or angle of the weapon.

But I knew it would break. The most finely ornamental swords didn't stand up to rigorous combat.

And with an earsplitting metallic *crack*, Kuradeel's two-handed sword split apart, right along the side. Glowing lights burst in every direction like a bomb exploding. Our bodies continued through the air, and we each landed on the other's launching point. The half of his sword that fractured off flew through the air, flashing in the sunlight, then clattered on the pavement between us. Soon after, both the broken edge and the hilt still clutched in Kuradeel's hand crumbled into countless tiny polygons.

The square was silent for several moments. All stood stock-still, mouths agape. I rose from my landing position, swung my sword left and right out of habit, and a cheer rose all around us.

I could hear individual voices picking apart our exchange, wondering if I really meant to do that. I had to bottle up a sigh—it didn't feel right to have to show off a secret trick like that before a crowd of onlookers.

My sword still in hand, I turned and walked slowly to Kuradeel, still slumped on the ground. His back was trembling beneath the white cape. I audibly pushed my sword back into its scabbard to draw his attention and then spoke in a low voice.

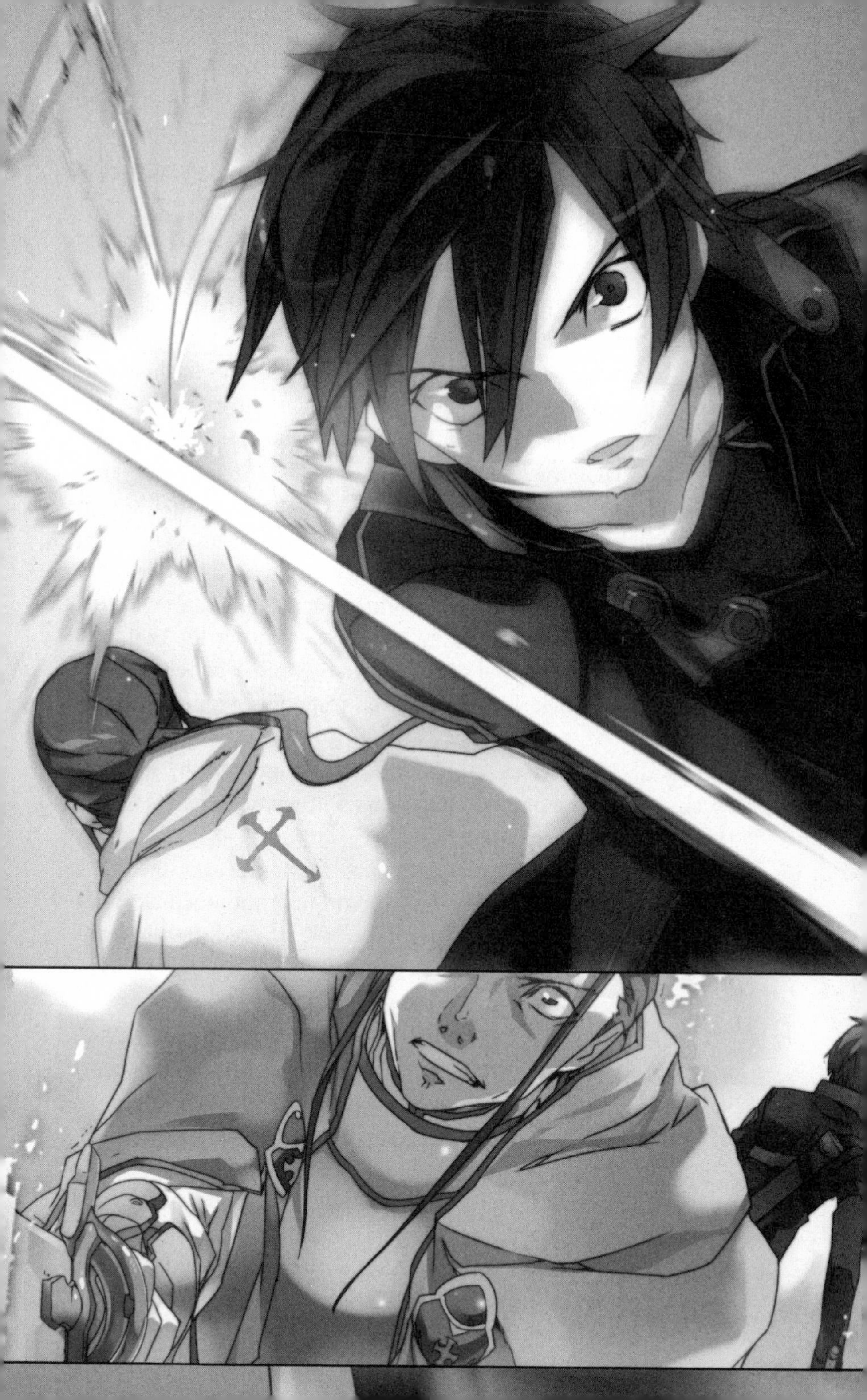

"I'll wait if you want to switch weapons...but I think we've settled this."

Kuradeel did not look at me, but he scraped his nails into the stones with apparent rage, his frame quivering. Finally, his voice grating, he said, "I resign," in English. It would have been perfectly valid to say it in Japanese, though.

The purple text flashed again in the same location, this time marking the end of the duel and announcing the winner. Another cheer rose from the throng. Kuradeel lurched to his feet and screamed at the onlookers.

"This isn't a sideshow! Move along!" He slowly turned to face me. "I will kill you...On my word, you will die by my hand."

I couldn't deny that the look in his eyes sent a shiver down my spine. SAO's emotion display engine may have had a penchant for being overly expressive, but even accounting for that, the sheer hatred in Kuradeel's beady eyes was more ferocious than any monster. I held back silently as someone stepped forward beside me.

"Kuradeel, as vice commander of the Knights of the Blood, I hereby relieve you of your guard duty. Return to guild headquarters to await further orders."

Asuna's voice was even frostier than her look suggested, but I could sense the note of suppressed pain in it and unconsciously put a hand on her shoulder. Her tense body shifted slightly, leaning some of its weight on me.

"...Wh...wha...? You...little..."

I heard it faintly. Kuradeel glared at us, a hundred foul curses and epithets spilling out under his breath. I could see the gears working in his head, a plot forming to equip his backup weapon and attack us, anti-crime limitations be damned.

But he controlled himself and pulled a teleport crystal from the underside of his cape. Gripping it so tightly he could have crushed the stone, he sputtered, "T-teleport: Grandzam." Kuradeel continued glaring at us with sheer loathing until the blue light subsided and he disappeared for good.

The square hung with an uncomfortable silence. The onlookers all appeared as shocked as though Kuradeel had directed his vitriol directly at them, and bit by bit, they broke off and wandered away. Finally, only Asuna and I remained.

My mind screamed at me to say something, anything, but I'd spent the last two years honing my skills in combat, not mingling in society. I didn't have anything clever or considerate to say. I wasn't even sure if it was a good thing that I'd accepted the duel and won.

Asuna finally took a step away and said, without any of her usual vigor, "I'm sorry. You didn't need to be dragged into that."

"Uh, I'm fine. How are you doing?"

The vice commander of the most powerful guild in the game shook her head slowly, flashing a brave but frail smile.

"Well, I suppose I'm partially responsible for pushing the guild to follow rules in order to prioritize beating the game…"

"I don't think you can be blamed for that. I mean, if it wasn't for people like you, we'd be way further behind on conquering the castle. I know that means nothing coming from a solo player like me. But…what I mean is…"

I'd totally lost sight of what I wanted to say and grasped for the right words.

"If you feel like you need to take a breather by partying up with someone irresponsible like me, I don't think anyone has a right to blame you for it."

Asuna looked stunned. She blinked several times, then broke into a halfhearted grin.

"Well…thanks for saying that. Maybe I will accept your offer and take it easy for a day. Thanks for taking forward position!"

She spun around and headed toward the town gate.

"Uh, hey, you're supposed to trade off at forward!" I complained, breathed a sigh of relief, and followed the swaying chestnut hair.

8

The forest path leading to the labyrinth was enveloped in a comforting warmth that was a far cry from the previous night's eeriness. Morning light fell through the branches in golden pillars, and delicate butterflies flitted in and out of the gaps. Unfortunately, they were only a visual effect, not actual material creatures, so there was no use trying to catch them.

The soft, thick undergrowth made pleasant rustling noises as we marched through it.

"I've noticed you're always dressed the same way," Asuna teased. I looked down at my outfit with a start. An aging black leather coat, black shirt, and black pants. Hardly a sign of any metallic armor.

"Uh, I don't mind. If I have money for clothes, I'd rather spend it on good food..."

"Is there a logical reason for all that black? Or is it just for style?"

"W-well, speak for yourself. What's up with that stupid red and white?"

As we chatted, I ran a Search scan out of habit. No sign of any monsters. But...

"What else am I going to wear? It's my guild uniform...Hmm? What's up—"

"Hang on." I cut her off, raising my hand. There was a player presence right at the edge of my Search radius. I focused on the distance behind us, and a number of green cursors that represented human players sprang into sight.

It couldn't be a gang of criminals. They preferred targets that were clearly weaker than themselves, so they virtually never ventured to the front lines, where the strongest players gathered. On top of that, any player who committed even a single crime was marked as a criminal for a lengthy period, their green cursor automatically displaying orange as a warning to all. No, what concerned me was the number and formation of these players.

I called up the map screen and set it to be visible so that Asuna could see as well. The map displayed our forest surroundings, and in combination with my Search scan, a series of green dots represented these new visitors. There were twelve in total.

"That's a lot…"

I agreed. Parties were harder to manage when the number grew too high, so five or six was considered ideal.

"And look at the way they're lined up."

The grouping of dots at the edge of the map was coming this way at considerable speed, arranged in two orderly columns. Dungeons were one thing, but I'd never seen such precision out in the open, where there was little danger to worry about.

Had I been able to at least see the levels of the members, I might have discerned their identities, but the cursor didn't display names or levels of absolute strangers. It was designed that way by default to protect against PKing—player killing—which meant that in this case, I'd have to see them for myself and make an educated guess based on their equipment.

I closed the map and looked at Asuna.

"I just want to be sure. Let's find a hiding spot and watch them pass."

"Good idea." She nodded nervously. We left the path and climbed up an embankment, hiding in the shadows of a clump of bushes about our height. It was the perfect position for watching the road.

"Ah…"

Asuna was looking down at her outfit. Red and white wasn't the greatest combination for blending in with the undergrowth.

"What should I do? I don't have a change of clothes…"

The lights on the map were bearing down. They'd be coming into range any second now.

"Pardon me."

I opened up the front of my leather coat and swung my arm around Asuna, who was crouching at my side. She glared at me for an instant but let herself be covered by the protection of the coat. It might not look great, but it had an excellent hiding bonus. With as many concealing factors as we had, they wouldn't find us without an exceedingly high-rank Search skill.

"See? Sometimes it helps to wear a one-color outfit."

"Oh, shut up! Here they come."

She put a finger to her lips. We crouched lower and heard the first signs of rhythmic, diligent footsteps. Finally, the group appeared around the bend in the path ahead.

They were all swordsmen, outfitted in matching gunmetal armor and dark green battlewear. It was designed to be practical rather than ornamental, but the front six did carry large shields emblazoned with the image of a familiar castle.

The front line bore one-handed swords, the rear line halberds. All wore long helmet visors that hid their faces from view. Their progress was so clean and mechanical that it gave the impression that the system had cloned a dozen copies of the same NPC and set them marching across the map together.

There was no mistaking it: They were from the Army, the mega-guild based out of the bottom floor of Aincrad. Asuna had realized this as well; she froze next to me, her breath held.

They didn't antagonize ordinary players. In fact, they were the most proactive, player-run source upholding any kind of justice

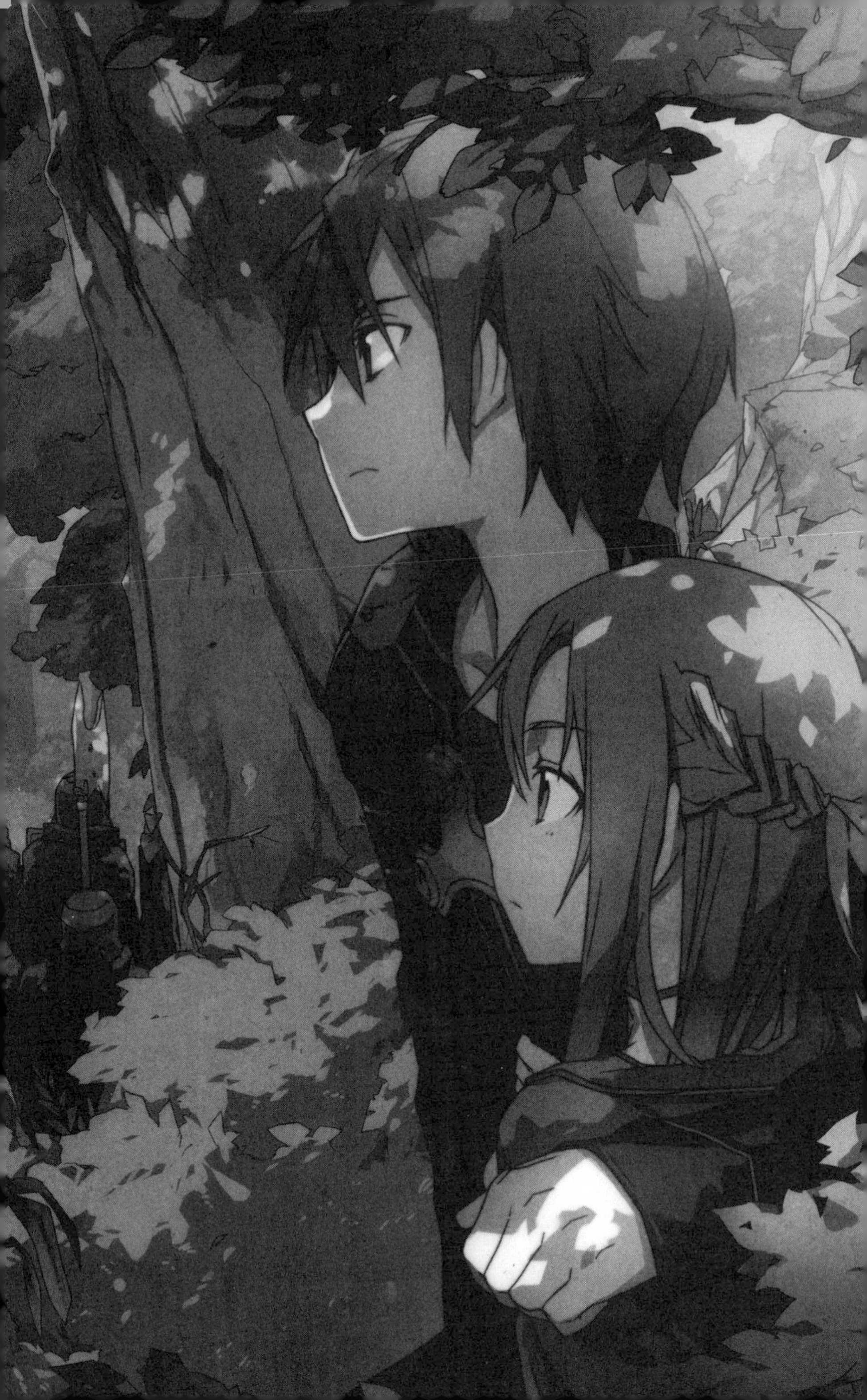

in the game. But their methods could be extreme. They immediately attacked without hesitation when they spotted a marked
criminal—nicknamed "orange players" for the color of their
cursors—and disarmed those who surrendered, imprisoning
them in the jail beneath their base at Blackiron Palace. Rumor
also spoke of more unsavory ends for those who did not surrender and failed to escape the fight.

Their large parties and lengthy control of hunting areas led to
an understanding among other players to avoid the Army when-
ever possible. Then again, since they preferred to keep the peace
and expand control in the weaker areas beneath the fiftieth floor,
you didn't have to worry about running into them on the front
lines.

The twelve warriors marched down the path before us, their
heavy boots and armor grinding loudly as they passed by. We
held our breath until they disappeared farther into the forest.

Given the difficulties of simply procuring a first-day copy of
Sword Art Online, every player currently held prisoner inside the
game was presumably a hardcore gamer. And if any species of
human being is allergic to rules and regulations, it's a gamer. It
was abnormal that any group of gamers could achieve that rigid
discipline, even after two years' time. They had to be an elite
squad within the Army.

After confirming that they'd left the radius of my Search skill
on the map, we both let out a long breath, still crouched over.

"So the rumor was true," Asuna muttered, wrapped up in my
coat.

"What rumor?"

"I heard it at a guild meeting. The Army's changing focus and
coming to the upper floors. Remember, they were formed to
beat the game, just like we were. But after they got burned clearing the twenty-fifth floor, they stopped pushing upward and
concentrated on strengthening their organization instead. Well,
apparently there's been some unrest from within about that.
So they decided that rather than just sending chaotic waves of

players into the labyrinth, they'd arrange smaller, elite parties to show their dedication to clearing the game. The report said they were just about to send out their first group."

"So it's mostly just a bit of propaganda for their organization? Still, do they know what they're doing, charging into unfamiliar territory like that? I mean, they did look pretty tough, but…"

"Maybe they're looking to head straight for the boss."

Every floor had a boss monster deep in its labyrinth that guarded the staircase up to the next level. They only appeared once and were frightfully strong, but there was always a buzz after the latest boss fell. If they wanted good publicity, this was one way to get it.

"So that explains their numbers… Still, this is insane. No one's even seen the seventy-fourth-floor boss yet. Normally, you send out numerous scouting parties to learn the boss's power and patterns, then put together a huge raid group."

"And it's always a cooperative effort between multiple guilds. Are they planning to join in the effort, too?"

"We'll see. Anyway, they can't be reckless enough to challenge the boss blind like that. C'mon, let's go and hope we don't run into them inside."

Reluctantly, I stood up and pulled my coat off of Asuna. She shivered in the open air.

"Brr, it's almost winter… I'll need a coat soon. Where'd you get that one?"

"Um… I think it was at a player shop in West Algade."

"You'll have to show me where when we're done."

She lithely leaped down to the path nearly ten feet below. I followed her—when your stats adjusted your fall damage, drops like this were nothing.

The sun was just about to reach the apex of its daily arc. We rushed ahead toward the labyrinth, paying close attention to our maps. We made it through the forest without running into a single monster and emerged in a field of sky-blue flowers. The path cut straight through to the west, and the ominous presence of the labyrinth tower loomed beyond.

Most labyrinth towers had an especially large room at the top where a boss monster would guard the staircase to the next level of Aincrad—in this case, the seventy-fifth floor. Once you defeated the boss, climbed the stairs, and made your way to the town on the next floor, a simple activation of the teleport gate there would officially mark the conquest of another floor.

"Town opening" was always a rowdy and exciting time, when players from lower floors would flood into the new outpost in search of fresh goods and shops. Today was the ninth day since reaching the seventy-fourth floor, which meant it was about the right time for the boss's lair to be discovered.

The labyrinth beyond the field was a cylindrical, sandstone structure colored reddish brown. Asuna and I had visited it multiple times between the two of us, but the closer you approached and the more it seemed to blot out the sky, the more imposing it became. It was only one hundredth the height of Aincrad itself. Despite knowing it was impossible, I harbored a secret desire to one day see the entirety of Aincrad from the outside.

The Army was nowhere in sight—they were likely inside already. Our footsteps quickened as we grew closer and closer to the mouth of the tower.

9

It was more than a year ago that the Knights of the Blood earned their reputation as the strongest guild in Aincrad. Tales spread throughout the populace of the "Man of Legend," who led the guild, and its vice commander, "Asuna the Flash." Now, her level much higher and her skill with the rapier at its peak, I was getting a front-row view of Asuna fighting a monster one-on-one for the very first time.

We were in the center of a long corridor flanked by rows of pillars near the top of the seventy-fourth-floor labyrinth. The enemy was a skeletal warrior known as a Demonic Servant. It stood nearly seven feet tall, wreathed in eerie blue light, a long sword in its right hand and a circular metal shield in its left. Despite the absence of any kind of muscle, it was a powerful foe that struck hard, and yet Asuna stood her ground, unafraid.

"Frrrurrrgh!"

It unleashed a bizarre guttural cry and swung the sword downward repeatedly, trailing blue light: Vertical Square, a four-part combo. I stood a few steps back from the action, watching restlessly, but Asuna neatly sidestepped each of the blows in turn.

Just because it was a two-on-one battle didn't mean that we could simply gang up on the enemy together. It was possible, of course, but when you had two people unleashing blindingly fast skills, it was more likely that you'd end up accidentally sabotaging each other's attacks. That's where the switching tactic came into play for parties.

After Asuna avoided the last and largest of the Demonic Servant's four attacks, it was left slightly off-balance. Asuna didn't miss her opportunity to counterattack. She thrust her flashing rapier several times at its midsection. Every one of them struck true, shortening the skeleton's HP bar. Each individual thrust did only minor damage, but the frequency was relentless.

After a three-part mid-level thrust combo, the skeleton was about to recover and guard, but Asuna spun around and slashed at its legs. She tore diagonally upward and connected powerfully on two more thrusts up high, her blade spraying white light.

It was an eight-part combination named Star Splash, if I recalled correctly. Rapiers and their thrusting strength weren't the best against skeletons, but her skill in connecting with the enemy each and every time was considerable.

The sheer beauty of it all had me completely entranced, to say nothing of its power in knocking out a third of the skeleton's health. This was a true sword dance.

Asuna jolted me out of my reverie, shouting as though she had eyes in the back of her head.

"Kirito, time to switch!"

"Y-yeah!"

I hurriedly readied my sword as she unleashed a powerful single strike. The tip struck the skeleton's shield with a gaudy shower of sparks. This was part of the plan, though. An enemy that blocks a heavy blow is left immobile for an instant and cannot attack right away. Asuna was frozen by the clash as well, of course, but it was the pause that we wanted.

I charged in front of the enemy in her place. The switch tactic was an intentional use of a break point in mid-combat to allow an ally to step in.

I glanced at Asuna out of the corner of my eye to ensure that she'd retreated to an adequate distance, and then I leaped at the enemy. Asuna was a true expert of the game and could hold her own, but in most cases, slashing attacks were far preferable to thrusts against skeletal foes like the Demonic Servant. All those skinny bones weren't easy to hit with jabs. Bludgeoning weapons like maces were best of all, but I didn't think either of us had learned that skill.

Unlike the enemy's ill-fated attempt, my Vertical Square hit right on the money all four times, huge chunks flying off its HP bar. The skeleton was slow to react. Monster AI in Sword Art Online did not handle sudden changes in attack tactics very well.

The day before, it had taken long minutes coaxing the lizardman's AI to allow me to recreate this effect, but with a partner, one switch is all it takes. This is one of the greater advantages of adventuring with a party.

I parried the foe's attack with my blade and initiated a powerful skill that would finish the battle. I slashed hard downward and right, then flicked my wrists backward like a golf swing, spinning the sword through the same trajectory in reverse. Each time the blade edge struck bone, it made a percussive *chunk* and spilled orange beams of light.

The skeleton tried to raise its shield to block a high swipe, but I caught it by surprise with a left-shoulder body blow. It faltered backward, helpless to stop my horizontal right slash. Another shoulder, this time the right. Tackling the foe to keep him from maintaining balance was a rare strategy, and Meteor Break was a combo skill that required Martial Arts proficiency to learn.

This string of attacks had wiped out most of the enemy's health; it was nearly defeated. I put all of my strength into the high horizontal slash that finished the seven-hit combination. The sword left a trail of light in its wake as it struck true, deep beneath the skeleton's lower jaw. With a dry *crack*, the skull flew off, and the rest of the body clattered into a lifeless pile of bones like a puppet with its strings cut.

"Nice job!" Asuna smacked me on the back as I put away my sword.

We hurried onward, saving the distribution of spoils for later. This was our fourth monster encounter inside the labyrinth, and we'd barely taken any damage at all. I preferred to string together massive blows, while Asuna specialized in quicker, varied combinations. When it came to seizing the advantage by overloading the enemy AI—not in sheer computational power, of course, but within the limits of the game's programmed algorithms—our two styles were actually quite complementary. It seemed as though our levels were close as well.

We carefully proceeded down the long, pillared hallway. Thanks to my Search skill, there was little fear of ambush, but I couldn't help but pay attention to the footsteps echoing off the hard stone walls. There was no direct source of light within the labyrinth, but the surroundings were bathed in a mysterious bluish glow that provided us with visibility.

I carefully scanned the hallway, watching for signs of danger. The lower portions of the tower were made of that dusky red sandstone, but as we climbed higher, the material gradually shifted to a type of stone with green highlights, as though the walls were running with moisture. The pillars were finely etched with eerie images, and their bases were submerged in a lowered canal. All in all, the decorative detail of the dungeon was growing finer and denser. There was little blank space left on the map. If my hunch was right, we were nearly there.

At the end of the hallway stood large, gray-blue double doors. They were covered with the same creepy reliefs of monsters as the pillars. It was all digital data, of course, but I couldn't help but feel an eerie, unnatural evil emanating from it.

We stopped in front of the door and looked at each other.

"Is it just me, or is this…?"

"Yeah, I agree…this must be the boss's lair."

Asuna grabbed the sleeve of my coat.

"What should we do? Just take a quick look inside?"

The words were confident, but her voice carried an anxious

tone. Even the most powerful warrior would be fearful in this situation. I didn't blame her—I was scared, too.

"Remember, the boss monster never steps outside its lair. I'm guessing that if we just open the door and look…we'll be fine…" I trailed off uncertainly. She looked exasperated.

"Keep a teleportation item on hand, just in case."

"Okay."

She nodded and pulled a blue crystal out of the pocket of her skirt. I readied one of my own.

"Ready? Here goes…"

Asuna hanging on my right arm, I placed my left hand against the door, clutching the escape crystal. If this had been happening in real life, my palm would be slick with sweat.

I pushed slowly, and the door gave way with a surprising ease for being nearly twice my height. Once put in motion, both doors opened simultaneously with almost alarming speed. As Asuna and I held our breath, they reached full extension with a heavy *thud*, exposing the contents of the room.

Which at this point was nothing but sheer darkness. The light that filled the hallway apparently did not extend to the chamber beyond. It was a thick blackness brimming with cold, and no amount of squinting revealed any details.

"…"

Just as I was about to open my mouth, two pale blue flames softly popped into existence along the floor just past the doorway. We both jumped despite ourselves.

Soon after, another two flames appeared a bit farther away. Then another pair. And another.

Bof-bof-bof-bof-bof…The flames sounded off consecutively, picking up speed as they created a path straight for the center of the chamber. Finally, a much larger flame burst into life, lighting the contours of the long, rectangular room in a blue haze. It was large. Large enough to fill the remaining blank space on my map by itself.

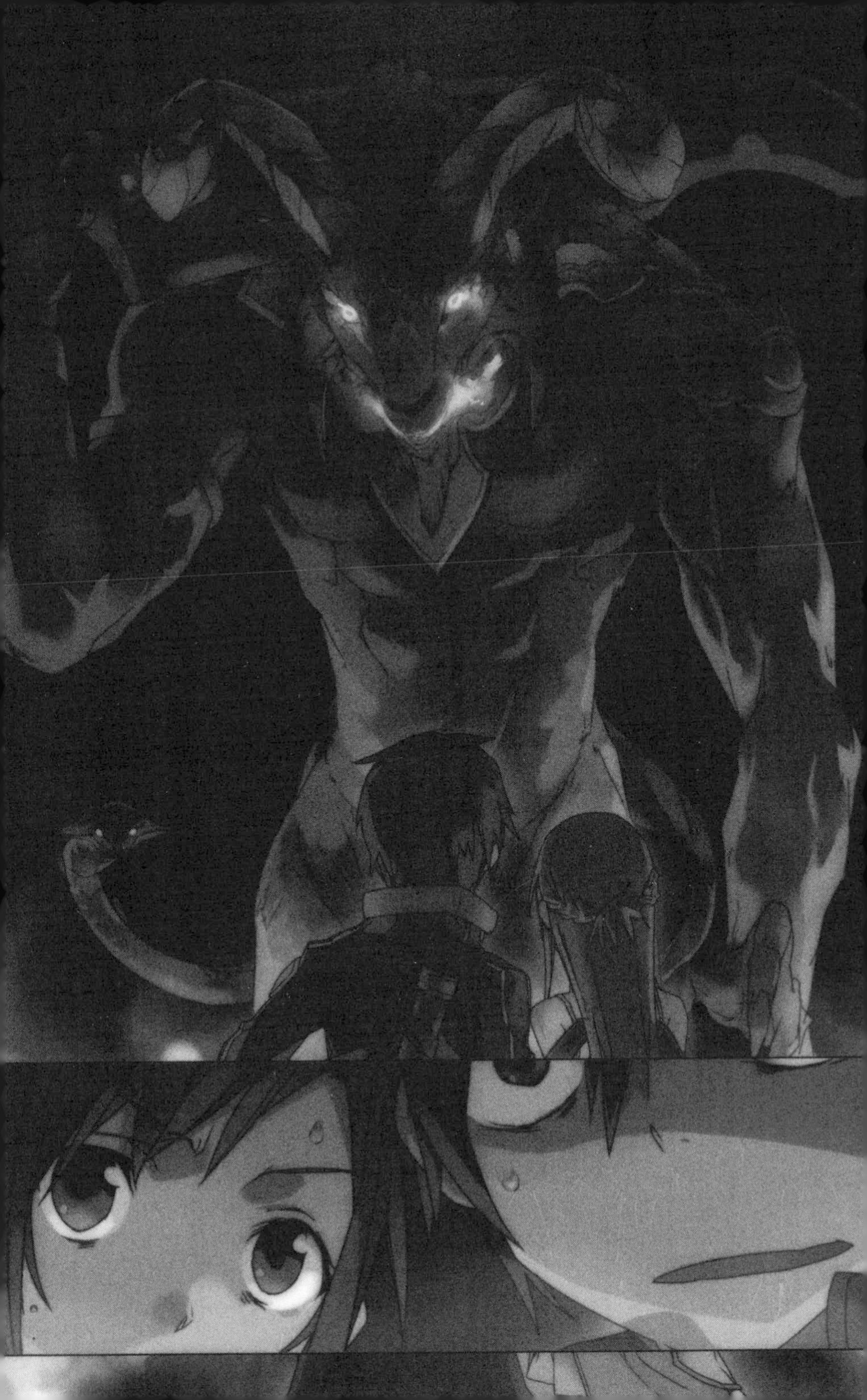

Asuna gave in to her nerves and grasped my entire arm, but I didn't have the presence of mind to enjoy it. A massive shape was steadily approaching from behind the thrashing dance of fire.

Muscles taut as ropes rippled up its towering form. Its skin was a deep blue to match the tint of the flames, and the head that rested atop the thick chest was not a human's but a goat's. Thick, twisted horns stretched backward from the sides of its head. The eyes glinted with the same blue-white hue but were clearly trained directly at us. Its lower half was covered in long navy hair, and although it was hard to see behind the flame, the legs looked bestial as well. In short, it matched the classic description of a demon.

There was a considerable distance from the center of the chamber to the door, and yet we stood immobilized, as though it were nearly upon us. I'd fought countless creatures during my two years in SAO, but I'd never seen a demon. Sure, they appeared in plenty of RPGs, but face-to-face with the real thing, it was impossible to stifle a primal terror from emerging.

I timidly focused my eyes and read the name off of the cursor that appeared. "The Gleameyes"—this was most definitely the boss of the labyrinth. Every named boss was preceded by a definitive "the" that marked it as unique. This one was named for its shining eyes.

As soon as I put it all together, the blue demon raised its elongated snout and let out a rumbling bellow. The columns of fire rippled, and the ground vibrated beneath my feet. It snorted pale blue breath, raised the massive sword in its right hand…and charged for us with stunning speed, the ground rattling.

"Aaaaah!"

"Kyaaaa!"

We screamed together, turned, and sprinted at full speed. I knew on principle that boss monsters couldn't leave their chambers, but I couldn't force myself to rely on that now. I let my significant agility stat do the work, speeding down the long hallway like a burst of wind.

10

Asuna and I ran pell-mell for the safe area established about midway through the labyrinth. I felt like we drew the attention of more than a few monsters during our dash, but I didn't have the wherewithal to care.

We leaped into the safe room and collapsed to the floor, our backs against the wall. After catching our breaths, we turned to each other, and...

"Pfft!"

A laugh came bubbling up from my chest. It would have only taken a second to check my map and confirm that the giant demon never left its lair, but I couldn't stay still long enough to bother.

"Ha-ha! Wow, that was quite an escape!" Asuna laughed, sprawled out on the floor. "I don't think I've run that hard in years. And that was nothing compared to you!"

"..."

I couldn't deny it. She giggled at the consternation and embarrassment on my face for several moments, until eventually her mirth subsided.

"This doesn't look like it'll be easy," she murmured pensively.

"I agree. It's only got the one greatsword, but I bet it has all kinds of special attacks at its disposal."

"We'll need plenty of tanks for the forward line so we can just keep switching members."

"I'd want at least ten fighters good with a shield...but for now, all we can do is observe its style and plan a strategy around that."

"Shields, huh?" She cast a meaningful glance at me.

"Wh-what about it?"

"Are you hiding something from me?"

"What do you mean...?"

"It doesn't make any sense. The greatest advantage of using a one-handed sword is the ability to pair it with a shield. But I've never seen you put one on. In my case, it slows down my rapier, and some people refuse to equip them for style reasons, but your case is different. It's suspicious."

She was correct—I *was* hiding something. But I'd never shown it off in front of others before. Not only was skill information an important lifeline, but the revelation of my secret was likely to further isolate me from everyone else in the game.

But, I thought, *maybe it wouldn't be the end of the world if she knew...*

Just as I was about to open my mouth, she spoke.

"Well, whatever. Prodding someone about his skills is impolite, after all." She laughed. My window of opportunity closed, I shut my mouth. Asuna's gaze flicked to her clock and her eyes went wide.

"Oh my gosh, it's already three. Ready for a late lunch?"

"What?" I perked up. "Is it homemade?"

She shot me a smug look, opened her menu, removed her white leather gloves, and materialized a small picnic basket. There was at least one excellent advantage to teaming up with her, I thought, but she stopped me short with a glare.

"...What are you thinking?"

"N-nothing. Can we eat now?"

She pursed her lips but took out two large paper wrappings from the basket anyway, handing one to me. I hastily unwrapped it to find a circular sandwich crammed with cooked meat and vegetables. It smelled fragrant, a bit like pepper. Suddenly I felt ravenous and stuffed it into my mouth without a word.

"Mm...that's good," I said honestly, after a few more bites. It looked similar to the foreign-seeming food that the NPCs served in Aincrad's restaurants, but the flavoring was different. The thick, sweet-and-salty taste reminded me of the Japanese-style fast food I'd eaten constantly before my two-year stay in SAO. I continued silently scarfing down the sandwich, tears of nostalgia threatening to spill down my cheeks.

I swallowed the last bite, gulped down in one go the cold tea Asuna handed me, and heaved a sigh of satisfaction.

"How'd you make this flavor?"

"A year of training and study, and a full analysis of all seasoning ingredients available in Aincrad. This one's gurogwa seeds, chèvre leaves, and calim water."

She pulled two small bottles out of the basket, pulled the plug out of one, and stuck her finger inside. It emerged covered in a truly bizarre thick purple substance.

"Open your mouth."

Nonplussed, I obediently opened my mouth, and Asuna flicked the tip of her finger. The tiny drop that landed in my mouth was stunning.

"It's...mayonnaise!"

"Now, this one is avilpa beans, sagu leaves, and wula fish bones."

I suspected that last one was used as an ingredient in antidote potions, but the droplet landed on my tongue before I had time to confirm it. This one was an even greater revelation than the previous. It was pure soy sauce flavor. In a fit of joy, I grabbed Asuna's extended finger and jammed it in my mouth.

"Aaack!" she shrieked. Asuna glared at me as she pulled her hand away, then laughed when she saw my slack-faced expression of bliss.

"That's the sauce I used for the sandwich."

"Incredible. It's perfect. You could make a fortune selling this stuff!"

To be honest, I felt like these sandwiches were even better than last night's Ragout Rabbit stew.

"Y-you think so?" She smiled shyly.

"Wait, don't do that. There'd be none left for me."

"Oh, don't be so greedy! There'll be plenty for you if I feel like it…" She trailed off. She leaned just enough that our shoulders brushed. There was a pleasant silence, and for a moment it almost felt like we weren't in the middle of a perilous dungeon.

If I could eat this food every day, I might just change my mind and move to Selmburg…right next to Asuna. I was nearly about to say this out loud when a troop of players in rattling armor walked through the door from the lower floor. We instantly sat up and separated.

The moment I saw the leader of the six-man group, I sighed with relief. It was a familiar katana-wielder, the person in Aincrad I'd known the longest.

"Hey, Kirito! Long time no see." The lanky fellow noticed me and strolled over for a greeting. I stood up and faced him.

"Oh, it's you, Klein."

"Geez, don't act so glad to see me! And you're actually with someone for…once…?"

When he saw Asuna, who had quickly arranged her belongings and stood up, his eyes went wide beneath the ugly bandanna.

"Well, I'm guessing you've already met at the boss strategy meetings, but I'll introduce you anyway. This is Klein, from the Furinkazan guild. And this is Asuna from the Knights of the Blood."

Asuna gave a little nod, but Klein stood frozen, his mouth now as wide as his eyes.

"Hello? Say something. Are you lagging?" I elbowed him in the ribs, and he finally shut his maw, giving her an extremely courteous bow.

"H-hello, miss! I'm K-K-Klein, age twenty-four, single!"

I elbowed him in the guts harder this time. But before Klein had gotten all the words out of his mouth, the other five members of his party shuffled over and began introducing themselves all at once.

The members of Furinkazan knew one another from before SAO. Klein had seen to it that they all survived their trials and had raised them into one of the more important forces advancing player progress through the game. He had shouldered the weight that I shrank away from two years ago and bore it splendidly.

I swallowed the lump of self-disgust that rose in my chest, turned to Asuna, and said, "A-anyway, they're not half bad, as long as you ignore their leader's villainous looks."

Now it was Klein's turn to stomp on my foot. Asuna bent over, chuckling at our bickering. Klein gave her a sloppy, flushed grin, then grabbed my arm and pulled me aside, speaking in a low but murderous tone.

"Wh-wh-what does this mean, Kirito?"

I struggled to come up with an answer, so Asuna sidled up with one prepared.

"I'll be partnering up with him for a while, so it's nice to meet you," she said in a clear voice. I was stunned. *It isn't just for today?* Klein and his friends vacillated between disappointment and jealous rage. Finally, Klein cast a beady eye on me and growled through gnashing teeth.

"Kirito, you rat…"

Just as I was slumping my shoulders with the resignation that I wasn't going to get out of this easily, a new set of rattling and footsteps from the same doorway told of a new set of visitors. Hearing the rigid discipline of their march, Asuna brushed my arm, worried.

"It's the Army, Kirito!"

I turned to the entranceway with a start to see the same squad of heavily armored soldiers that we witnessed earlier in the forest. Klein raised a hand, and his comrades retreated to the wall. The soldiers entered in the same two-row formation, but it was not as crisp as before. They looked sluggish, and the bits of their faces that could be seen beneath the helmets were heavily fatigued.

The squad came to a halt on the other side of the safety zone. The man in front gave the command to be at ease, and the other eleven clattered to the floor with an incredible din. He turned to us without a second glance at his subordinates.

Upon closer look, his equipment was slightly different from the others'. The plate armor was of finer make, and his breast-plate was the only one that contained a crest meant to symbolize the full shape of Aincrad.

The man stopped in front of us and removed his helmet. He was quite tall. I'd put him in his early thirties, with short hair and a square face; thick eyebrows; small and sharp eyes; and a thin, disapproving mouth. After an imposing gaze, he turned and spoke to me, as I stood the farthest forward.

"I am Lieutenant Colonel Corvatz of the Aincrad Liberation Army."

That last part came as a surprise to me. I'd thought "The Army" was just a nickname that others used. When did it get appropriated into their official title? And he was a lieutenant colonel, to boot. I gave him a brief, "Kirito, solo."

The man nodded, then continued imperiously. "Have you already cleared the area?"

"Yeah, we've mapped out everything up to the boss's lair."

"Good. I'd like your map data."

I was momentarily taken aback by his matter-of-fact tone, but Klein lost it altogether.

"Wh-wha...? You think we're just gonna hand it over? Do you have any idea how much work it takes to map a labyrinth?" he bellowed. Maps of unfinished areas were a valuable resource. Treasure hunters who sought unopened chests would pay a fine price for that information.

The man raised an eyebrow at Klein's outburst and jutted out his chin.

"We are fighting for the liberation of all players, including you!" he barked. "It should be your duty to share your information with us!"

It was sheer arrogance. The Army had barely bothered to help clear floors in the past year.

"Wait just a second…"

"Why, you shameless…"

I had to hold out both hands to stop Asuna and Klein from converging on the man.

"I don't mind. I was going to release the data once I got back to town anyway."

"Oh, c'mon, man! You're being too generous!"

"I don't treat map data like a business opportunity."

I opened a trading window and sent the man named Corvatz my map. He accepted it stone-faced, said, "Your cooperation is appreciated," without a shred of appreciation, and turned on his heel. I called out to his back.

"I wouldn't bother the boss right now if I were you."

Corvatz barely turned his head.

"…That decision is at my discretion, not yours."

"We just took a look at it earlier, and it's not the kind that a half-size raid can tackle. Besides, your soldiers look pretty wasted to me."

"My men aren't weaklings, to complain about a simple march!"

Corvatz put extra weight on *my men*, but the exhausted warriors sprawled out on the floor didn't seem to share his camaraderie.

"Back on your feet!"

They slowly climbed up and re-formed into two rows. Corvatz took his spot at the fore without sparing us a second glance. He raised and lowered his arm, and the twelve readied their weapons and resumed the march.

While their HP appeared full, the tense battles of SAO left invisible strain on its players. Our real bodies weren't budging an inch back on the other side, but the fatigue we felt here would not disappear without sleep or relaxation. From what I could tell, the

Army soldiers weren't used to battle on the front line, and they were at their limit.

"Do they know what they're doing...?"

The Army squad disappeared through the exit farther up the tower, and the measured footsteps faded out. Klein was too concerned for his own good.

"I mean, they're not just going to charge right into the boss lair..."

Asuna looked worried. Something in Corvatz's attitude suggested that they were taking a risk that was downright reckless.

"Should we at least check on them first?" I suggested. Even Klein's party nodded in agreement. "Who's too concerned for his own good now?" I grimaced to myself, but my mind was made up. I wouldn't sleep well that night if we left now and found out later that the group never returned.

I checked my equipment and was preparing to leave when I heard Klein whispering to Asuna behind my back. At first I was exasperated, but that turned to surprise when I listened to what he was saying.

"So, um...Asuna? Er...how should I say this? I know he might not deserve it, but be good to Kirito, will you? Even if he is a introverted, grumpy, battle-obsessed idiot."

I spun around and yanked hard on Klein's bandanna.

"Wh-what are you talking about?"

"Oh, come on." He rubbed his stubbled chin, head tilted. "I mean, you're actually teaming up with someone now. Ensnared by feminine wiles or not, it's still progress."

"I-I'm not being seduced!"

I noticed that Klein, his party, and even Asuna were all grinning at me, so I had no choice but to clamp my mouth shut and turn around. I even heard Asuna assure Klein, "I'll take good care of him."

I beat a hasty retreat through the doorway, my boots clacking on the stones.

11

We were unlucky enough to run into a group of lizardmen, so by the time the eight of us reached the hallway at the top of the tower, it had already been thirty minutes. We never caught up to the Army squadron.

"Maybe they used some items to return already?" Klein offered in an attempt to break the tension, but none of us believed it. Our pace quickened as we headed down the hallway. About halfway to the door, we heard the echoing sounds that confirmed our fears. I stopped abruptly and focused my ears.

"*Aaaahh...*"

It was soft, but undeniably a scream.

And not from a monster. We looked at one another and raced forward. Asuna and I pulled away from Klein's group due to our agility, but this was no time for playing nice. We sped over the slick stones shining blue, this time in the opposite direction of our last, panicked sprint.

Finally, we came to the massive chamber doors. They were already wide open, the flickering blue flames visible amid the darkness within. And behind them, a massive shadow, writhing. Periodic metallic clanging. Screams.

"Those idiots!" Asuna shrieked, dashing even faster. I strained to keep up. We were going about as fast as the system could allow us. It felt like my feet weren't even touching the floor. The pillars that lined the hallway were a blur.

We screeched to a halt right before the doorway, the hobnails of our boots raising sparks.

"Hey! Anyone okay in there?" I shouted, leaning my upper half through the doorway.

The interior of the room was a picture of hell.

The blue-white flames were flickering across the floor in a lattice pattern. At the center, its back to us, loomed a gigantic form gleaming with metal—the blue demon, the Gleameyes.

The wicked goat head emitted burning breath, and it swung around a gargantuan blade like a zanbato—a sword more suited for dicing horses than human beings. It hadn't even lost a third of its HP. All around it, miniscule shadows leaped and fled. It was the Army.

Their prior discipline was entirely gone. I tried to do a quick head count and came up two short. Hopefully they'd used teleport crystals to escape.

One of the men took a tremendous swipe from the zanbato to his side and went sprawling across the floor. His HP was down in the red zone. Somehow, the Army had managed to get trapped, with the Gleameyes standing between them and the doorway where we stood now. I shouted to one of the collapsed players.

"What are you doing? Teleport out of here!"

His face, lit blue with the room's eerie flames, was a rictus of terror and despair.

"It won't work...We can't...use any crystals!"

"Wha..."

My breath caught in my throat. The chamber was an anti-crystal zone. It was a rare trap that you occasionally saw in labyrinths, but none of the boss lairs had been this way before.

"They can't teleport out...?"

Asuna swallowed. This meant that it would be much harder to save them. On the other side of the demon, one of the players raised his sword and gave a battle cry.

"Nonsense! Retreat is not an option for the Liberation Army! Fight, you scoundrels, fight!!" It was clearly Corvatz.

"You fools!" I screamed. The fact that there were two people missing in an anti-crystal zone meant they were dead, gone forever. The unthinkable had already occurred, and he wanted them to keep going? I could feel all the blood in my body boiling.

Klein's party finally caught up to us. "What's going on here?!" I explained as briefly as I could. Klein grimaced.

"Isn't there anything we can do for them?"

If we leaped into the fray, it was possible that we could clear a path for the soldiers to escape. But without a quick and easy way to teleport out, there was no guarantee we wouldn't suffer casualties in the process. We just didn't have enough people. As I hesitated over what to do, Corvatz had rallied his men to their feet across the room and was bellowing orders.

"All units...charge!"

Out of the ten survivors, two were slumped on the floor in critical condition. The other eight formed two lines of four, with Corvatz brandishing his sword in the lead.

"No! Stop!!" But my scream didn't reach them.

It was sheer madness. Eight warriors attacking all at once wouldn't do a thing but cause chaos and limit their individual strengths. They ought to be taking a defensive stance, doing bits of damage one at a time, and switching out constantly.

The beast stood upright, hands on hips, and let out an earth-shaking roar, spewing bright steam from its mouth. The exhaust must have had a damaging effect, because the soldiers who came into contact with it slowed their attack. Out came the demon's giant sword again. One man was flipped straight over the demon's head by the blade, crumpling in a heap on the floor right before us.

It was Corvatz.

His HP bar was empty. He wore an expression of utter disbelief, his mouth moving slowly.

Impossible.

As soon as he mouthed the words, Corvatz's body shattered into countless tiny shards with a nerve-grating crackle. Asuna gave a brief shriek at his disintegration, so sudden and unceremonious.

Their leader gone, the Army squad was completely lost. They fled and screamed, all discipline gone. None of the men had even half his health remaining.

"No...no...you can't..."

Asuna seemed to be wringing the words out of herself. I tried to reach out and grab her arm, but I was an instant too late.

"You can't do this!" she cried, leaping forward like a burst of wind. She pulled out her rapier in midair and plunged into the Gleameyes, a beam of light.

"Asuna!" I shouted, forced to follow in her footsteps.

"Whatever happens, happens!" Klein's party brought up the rear.

Asuna's desperation attack struck the demon directly in the back. Sadly, its effect on the monster's health was nearly imperceptible. The Gleameyes spun around with a bellow of rage, swinging its zanbato with fearful speed. Asuna darted out of the way, but the blade's shock wave threw her to the ground. It swung around mercilessly for a follow-up.

"Asunaaa!!"

Sheer terror chilled my spine, and I desperately lunged for the space between Asuna and the sword. At the last possible instant, I succeeded in just barely deflecting the path of the demon's assault. The impact was breathtaking.

Our weapons sent off sparks as they scraped, and the giant blade smashed into the floor just inches from where Asuna lay, gouging a deep furrow with the sound of an explosion.

"Get back!" I shouted, preparing for the demon's next blow. The swings came fast and furious, each individual swipe powerful enough to be fatal. There was no time for me to mount a counterattack.

The Gleameyes used double-handed greatsword skills, but the perfect craft of its combinations left me totally unable to guess what was coming next. All my nerves were on edge, my every instinct dedicated to parrying or sidestepping each blow. The force of them was so overwhelming, however, that I couldn't avoid everything, and my HP dwindled bit by bit with each deflection.

Out of the corner of my eye, I saw Klein's party lifting up the fallen Army soldiers to drag them out of the room. As the demon and I were fighting smack in the middle of the chamber, their progress was limited.

"Urgh!!"

The demon finally connected on a powerful stroke. I went numb with the rattling shock, and my HP dropped precipitously. My equipment and skill loadout weren't designed for tanking. I couldn't last much longer. Fear of death spread through my limbs like a chill. I couldn't even coordinate well enough to escape.

There was only one course of action remaining. I had to put all of my damage-dealing expertise to the test and fight back.

"Asuna! Klein! Just hold out for ten seconds!"

I gave a hardy swing of my sword and deflected the beast's next attack, taking advantage of the brief pause that ensued to drop into a roll. Klein filled the gap with his katana just in time.

Unfortunately, Klein's katana and Asuna's rapier were both selected for their speed in battle, not their weight. They wouldn't stand up to the demon's tremendous horse cleaver. I swiped my left hand while on the floor, calling up the menu.

There was no time for a single mistake. My fingers flew over the buttons, my heart racing. I quickly shuffled through my inventory list, found what I wanted, and materialized it. I set the item in a blank slot on my equipment mannequin, opened my skill window, and switched my currently selected weapon skill.

When all the steps were complete, I hit the OK button to close the window, felt a new weight on my back, and looked up.

"All ready!"

Klein was pulling back and his HP bar was lower—he must have taken a hit. Normally, he'd be using a healing crystal, but that wouldn't work in here. Asuna was occupying the demon's attention now, and in a few seconds, she'd be down under half of her health, into the yellow zone.

When she heard me give the signal from behind her, Asuna nodded and unleashed a thrust attack with a piercing cry.

"Yaaaah!!"

Her sword left white tracers behind as it flew forward and collided with the Gleameyes's blade, sparks flying in every direction. Both of them were knocked backward by the force of the impact, leaving a space in between.

"Switch!"

I leaped in to face the enemy without missing a beat. The demon recovered from its momentary paralysis and swung hard.

The zanbato trailed fire until it came into contact with the trusty sword in my right hand, while my left hand reached for the new sword slung over my back. It pulled free and connected with the demon's torso. It was the first clean hit we'd scored, and for the first time, I actually saw its HP bar diminish.

"Groaaah!!"

It erupted with rage and attempted another downward swipe. This time I absorbed the blow fully with both swords crossed in front of me, and pushed back. It lost balance with the reflection of force, and I leaped onto the offensive for the first time.

A mid-level slash with the right sword. A momentary thrust with the left. Right, left, right again. My swords flashed so quickly, they seemed to burn my brain cells. High-pitched slashing sound effects popped off in quick succession, and beams of light shot out of the fray like stardust.

I was using my hidden specialty, the Extra Skill "Dual Blades." This was Starburst Stream, a high-level, sixteen-part combination.

"Raaaahhh!!"

Paying no mind to the few blows that the demon blocked, I roared as my assault continued, left and right. My eyesight began scorching—I could barely even see the enemy anymore. Even the occasional shock of the monster's sword striking my body felt like it was coming from another world entirely. Adrenaline coursed through my veins, and my nerves sparked with every swing of the swords.

Faster, faster. My mind was accelerated to the breaking point, even the double-speed of swinging twice the swords feeling inadequate. I swung faster and faster, attempting to outdo even the speed-assist of the game system.

"...Aaaaahhh!!"

The sixteenth and final blow caught the Gleameyes directly in the middle of the chest.

"Groaaahhh!!"

Suddenly I realized I wasn't the only one bellowing. The demon was roaring up at the ceiling, white exhaust pouring from its mouth and nostrils.

It seemed to freeze for just an instant.

And the Gleameyes exploded into a vast cloud of tiny pieces. Glittering particles of light showered the room.

Is it...over...?

My eyes swam with the aftereffects of the battle, and I unconsciously swiped both swords and returned them to the scabbards crossed over my back. I checked my HP bar—a few pixels of red remained. I stared at them as though they didn't belong to me, then felt all the strength leave my body. I slid to the floor without a word.

Blackness.

12

"...to! Kirito!"

Asuna's near screaming woke me from the darkness. I slowly sat upright, grimacing at the splitting pain in my head.

"Owww..."

I was in the boss's chamber. Motes of blue light still danced in the air—I hadn't lost consciousness for more than a few seconds, it seemed.

Asuna's face hovered over mine. She appeared to be on the verge of tears, biting her lip, her eyebrows knitted.

"You idiot! That was so reckless!" she cried, squeezing me around the neck. I was so shocked that I momentarily forgot the throbbing pain in my head.

"...Don't strangle me too hard, or you'll wipe out the rest of my HP," I joked lamely, but she looked furious. A moment later, she plugged a small bottle into my lips. The liquid, which tasted like a mix of green tea and lemon juice, was a restorative hi-potion. The potion would finish restoring all of my health in just five minutes, but the feeling of weakness would last for quite a bit longer.

Asuna checked to ensure that I'd finished the entire bottle, then placed her forehead on my shoulder so I couldn't see her face crinkling into tears.

Footsteps approached, and I heard Klein speak up hesitantly.

"We've healed the rest of the survivors, but Corvatz and two others are dead…"

"I see…We haven't lost anyone to a boss since the sixty-seventh floor."

"Can you even call this 'winning' the battle? The idiot…What good does it do to challenge the boss if it gets you killed?" Klein spat angrily. He shook his head and sighed, then changed the subject. "But on the other hand, what the hell did you just do?"

"…Do I have to tell you?"

"Bet your ass you do! I've never seen anything like that before!"

I suddenly realized that every person in the room aside from Asuna was staring at me, waiting on my answer.

"It's an extra skill: Dual Blades."

There was a murmur among the Army survivors and Klein's guildmates.

SAO's weapon skills were normally arranged into several major schools, with new categories unlocking in stages. Take swords, for example: After enough proficiency with the basic One-Handed Sword skill, other options such as Rapiers or Two-Handed Swords would become available in your skill list.

Klein pushed me for details, clearly interested.

"H-how do you unlock it?"

"If I knew that, I'd have announced it publicly." He grunted in understanding.

There were a few weapon categories known as Extra Skills, whose requirements were unknown, possibly even random. Klein's Katana skill was an example of this. It was one of the easier Extra Skills to obtain—most received it from relentlessly upgrading their Curved Swords skill.

Most of the dozen or so Extra Skills known throughout the game had been earned by a good ten people, at least. But my Extra Skill Dual Blades and another skill wielded by a well-known figure were the only exceptions to that rule.

Those two might as well be called "Unique Skills," because only one person in all of Aincrad possessed them. I'd kept my dual-wield capability under wraps until now, but there was no avoiding the inevitable—by tomorrow the rest of the game would be buzzing with the second instance of a Unique Skill. There was no hiding it anymore, not after so many had just seen it in action.

"How could you keep such a crazy ability from me, Kirito?"

"If I knew how I got it, I wouldn't be hiding it. I seriously have no idea." I shrugged.

I wasn't lying. One day about a year ago, I noticed that "Dual Blades" had simply popped into my skill window. There was no way of knowing what caused it to appear.

Since then, I'd been diligently working on the skill where there was no danger of being seen. Even after I'd nearly mastered it, I only ever used it while adventuring if I was in true danger—partially because I wanted it to be my safety net, partially because I didn't want to attract extra attention if I could help it. I'd been hoping that someone else would emerge with the skill at some point, but that moment never came.

I scratched nervously behind my ear, mumbling my defense. "If people find out I've got this rare skill, they might bug me about it…I just don't really want the trouble and attention…"

Klein nodded. "Online gamers are nothing if not jealous. I won't give you grief 'cos I'm a stand-up guy, but there will always be haters out there. Besides…"

He paused, cast a glance at Asuna, who was still clamped tight to my side, and grinned widely.

"Well, consider suffering to be just another part of your training. Good luck, youngster!"

"Easy for you to say…"

Klein bent over to pat my shoulder, then turned and walked to the Army survivors. "Can you make it back to your headquarters?"

One of them nodded. He had to be a teenager still.

"Good. Tell them exactly what happened here. Convince them never to do something so reckless again."

"Yes, sir. Um…thank you."

"Thank *him*." He jabbed a thumb at me. The Army men struggled to their feet and bowed deeply to Asuna and me, then left the room. Once they'd stepped out into the hallway, they each used a crystal to teleport out of the labyrinth.

Once the light of their travel had died out, Klein turned back to us with his hands on his hips, satisfied.

"We're going to go activate the seventy-fifth-floor teleport gate. What's your plan? You're the man of the hour—want to do the honor?"

"Nah, you go ahead. I'm all tuckered out."

"All right. Take care, then."

Klein nodded and signaled to his friends. The group of six made its way to the large door at the back of the chamber, beyond which would be the staircase to the next floor. The lanky leader stopped at the door and turned around.

"Hey, Kirito...when I saw you leap to the Army's rescue like that..."

"What?"

"It did my heart good. That's all. Until next time!"

I had no idea what that meant. Klein threw me a thumbs-up over his shoulder, then opened the door and disappeared through it.

Asuna and I were all alone in the cavernous chamber. The flames emitting from the floor had died down. The previous uneasy eeriness of the room might as well never have been. It was filled with the same soft light as the hallway now, and no traces remained of the carnage that had ensued there.

I spoke to Asuna, her head still on my shoulder.

"Hey...Asuna..."

"...I was so scared...I didn't know what I'd do if you died..."

It was as timid and trembling a voice as I'd ever heard out of her.

"Don't be silly. Besides, you were the one who leaped in first."

I placed a hand on Asuna's shoulder. If I made my touch a little too obvious, the system's harassment detection might kick in, but this wasn't the time to be worrying about that. I pulled her gently toward me and heard her speak right near my ear, barely a whisper.

"I'm going to take a break from the guild for a while."

"T-take a break...? What are you going to do?"

"Did you forget that I said I'd be teaming up with you?"

The instant I heard those words, I was startled to discover a powerful sensation that could only be longing welling up deep in my chest. I was Kirito the solo player. I'd cut off all ties with other human beings in order to survive. I'd turned my back on the only friend I had on the day it all began. I was a coward.

How could I seek the company of a friend—or something even greater?

I'd already learned in the most painful way possible what could happen. I'd sworn to myself that I would never make that mistake again, never open my heart to another.

And yet...

My hand was frozen. It wouldn't leave Asuna's shoulder. I couldn't pull myself away from the virtual warmth that she represented.

I grappled with that massive contradiction, and enveloped by a single, unspeakable emotion, I gave her the simplest of answers.

"...All right."

Asuna nodded over my shoulder.

The next day, I spent all morning moping in the second floor of Agil's general store. I sat back in a rocking chair with my legs crossed, unhappily sipping a cup of oddly scented tea that was probably there because no one would buy it.

All of Algade—all of Aincrad, most likely—was buzzing with yesterday's incident.

The completion of a floor and the opening of a new town were always cause for excitement, but there was more than usual to discuss this time around. You had the "Army battalion wiped out by a demon," you had "a guy wielding two swords who took it down on his own with a fifty-hit combo"... I knew stories grew legs, but this was ridiculous.

Early in the morning, I was even set upon by swordsmen and intel brokers outside my home—how did they find me?—and had to use a teleport crystal just to get away from them.

"I've got to move out. I'll find a real secluded, out-of-the-way floor where no one will find me," I muttered, as Agil grinned from ear to ear.

"C'mon, big shot, don't be like that. Everyone deserves his fifteen minutes of fame. Give them a live demonstration! I'll just handle the ticket sales and—"

"In your dreams!"

I playfully tossed the teacup in the direction of Agil's head, aiming a foot or two to the right, but the motion was so familiar that my Throwing Blade skill kicked in. The cup flashed brilliantly and shot across the room, exploding against the wall with a deafening crash.

Fortunately, the building itself was indestructible—all that happened was the usual system warning that popped up reading IMMORTAL OBJECT—but if I'd hit any of the furniture, it probably would have been blasted to splinters.

"Whoa! Are you trying to kill me?" the shopkeeper screamed. I apologized, my hand raised, and sat back down sheepishly.

Agil was appraising the treasure I'd brought back from yesterday's battle. Judging from the occasional yelps of surprise, it must have contained some pretty rare loot.

Once I'd sold the goods, I was going to split the money with Asuna, but she didn't show up when we were due to meet. I sent her an in-game message through my friends list so she knew where to find me.

We'd gone our separate ways at the seventy-fourth-floor teleport gate yesterday. Asuna said she'd submit a notice of leave from the KoB and headed to their headquarters in Grandzam on the fifty-fifth floor. There was the matter with Kuradeel to report as well, so I offered to come along and corroborate her story, but she smiled and said she was fine alone.

It was already two hours after our meeting time. Something must have happened to make her so late. Should I have insisted on going with her after all? I drank down the rest of the tea, trying to keep my anxiety from rising.

By the time the teapot was entirely empty and Agil was mostly finished appraising my items, I finally heard the tapping of quick footsteps coming up the stairs. The door flew open.

"Yo, Asuna..."

But I swallowed my lighthearted tease before it could leave my throat. Asuna was in her usual uniform, but her face was pale and her eyes were wide with concern. She clenched her hands in front of her chest and bit her lip several times before finally saying, "What'll we do, Kirito?" Her voice verged on tears. "There's been...some trouble."

Once we'd made some fresh tea and Asuna regained some color in her cheeks, she began to explain. Agil was considerate enough to tend to the storefront downstairs.

"After everything that happened yesterday, I went to guild HQ in Grandzam to report to the commander. I told him that I wanted to take some time away from the guild, then went home for the night...and I was expecting that decision to be accepted at this morning's meeting, but..."

Asuna looked down at the cup of tea she held in both hands.

"The commander claimed that he'd only agree to my temporary leave on one condition. He wants to have...a one-on-one with you...

"What...?"

For an instant, I didn't understand. One-on-one? Like a duel? How did Asuna's leave of absence turn into *that*? I asked her.

"I don't know, either," she murmured, hanging her head. "I tried to convince him it was pointless, but...he just wouldn't listen."

"That's strange. I didn't think he was the type of man to put forth a condition like that," I said, picturing the image of the fellow as I knew him.

"Exactly. Normally, he entrusts the guild affairs and even the labyrinth strategy to us. He doesn't give a single order of his own. This seems to be an exception..."

The commander of the Knights of the Blood was such a compelling figure that he roused the hearts of not just his own guild, but virtually all the high-level players active in clearing the game. Yet he hardly ever issued orders. I'd been in his presence during boss battles on multiple occasions, and his silent support for all involved was worthy of admiration.

So it was extremely odd that he chose *this* moment, of all moments, to cast a contrary vote and challenge me to a duel. I was puzzled, but I also wanted to put Asuna at ease.

"Well, anyway...I'll go to Grandzam and see if I can help straighten this out."

"Sorry about this. I didn't mean to cause you so much trouble."

"I'll do anything. You mean a lot to..."

I stopped to search for the right words. Asuna watched me closely.

"You're a valuable ally in beating the game after all."

Her mouth twisted in slight disappointment, but then she gave me a smile at last.

The strongest man in Aincrad. The living legend. The paladin. The leader of the Knights of the Blood was a man of many monikers.

His name was Heathcliff. Before the stories about my Dual Blades made the rounds, he was the only player out of six thousand known to possess a Unique Skill.

Heathcliff's ability was Holy Sword, a skill that balanced offense and defense, and he appropriately wore a sword and shield fashioned into the shape of a cross. When I'd seen him use it in battle, it was the defense that floored me. Rumor held that no one had ever seen his HP bar fall into the yellow zone. His single-handed, ten-minute command of the ravaged front line in the catastrophic battle with the fiftieth-floor boss was the stuff of legend.

It was one of the unshakeable truths of Aincrad: No blade could break Heathcliff's cruciform shield.

Now, standing on the fifty-fifth floor with Asuna, I was gripped with nerves. I had no intention of crossing swords with Heathcliff, of course. I was simply going to ask him to consider granting Asuna temporary leave from the guild.

Grandzam was the main city of the fifty-fifth floor, known as the "City of Iron." Most of the towns of Aincrad were built of stone, but the countless minarets of Grandzam were gleaming steel. It was full of blacksmiths and engravers, and while the town boasted a considerable population, there was nothing in the way of greenery within. When the deepening autumn winds blew, Grandzam was undeniably cold, and it wasn't just the temperature.

We crossed the teleport gate square and walked down a main street made of polished steel plates riveted into place. Asuna's pace was slow—she feared what was about to happen.

After nearly ten minutes of winding through the towers, one came into view that was much larger than the others. A number of silver spears jutted out from above the large front door, and a banner bearing a red cross on a white field hung rippling in the chill breeze. It was the headquarters of the Knights of the Blood.

Asuna stopped in front of the building and looked up at the tower.

"Before this, our base was just a tiny little house in a remote town on the thirty-ninth floor. We used to complain about how cramped it was. I'm not saying that it's a bad thing we've come a long way since then...but I hate this town. It's so cold..."

"Let's get this over with and find something hot to eat, then."

"Is eating all you think about?"

She laughed, swinging her hand over and lightly squeezing the tips of my fingers. She held it there for several seconds, not seeing the panic on my face, then released her grip and said, "All recharged!" She began striding toward the tower, and I hurried to keep up.

We climbed a wide staircase to a large, open doorway, flanked by soldiers in heavy armor with frighteningly long spears. As the clicking of Asuna's boots drew nearer, they raised their weapons and saluted with a *clank*.

"Keep up the good work."

She returned a crisp salute with one hand, walking briskly. It was hard to imagine that this was the same person who'd been moping in Agil's shop just an hour earlier. I hurriedly followed Asuna past the guards and into the tower.

The first-floor lobby of the tower was made of the same black steel as the rest of the city, and it served as a giant stairwell. There was no one inside.

I crossed the floor, a finely crafted mosaic of different kinds of metal, feeling that the building was somehow even colder than the rest of the town. The spiral staircase started at the far end of the lobby.

We climbed the stairs, our clanging footsteps echoing throughout. The tower was tall enough that a person with a weaker strength stat would give up halfway. We passed many doorways, and just when I began to wonder how much farther we could possibly go, Asuna stopped. We were in front of a nondescript metal door.

"Is this it?"

"Yep." Asuna nodded hesitantly. But she eventually steeled her nerves, gave the door a high-pitched knock, and then opened it without waiting for an answer. I had to squint at the overwhelming light that poured through the doorway.

It was a large, circular room that took up the entire floor of the tower. All the walls were made of clear glass. The gray light that streamed inside painted the entire room in a drab monotone.

A large, semicircular desk was placed in the middle of the

room, surrounded by five chairs, each of which seated a man. I didn't recognize the four on the sides, but there was no way to mistake the man sitting in the middle. It was Heathcliff the paladin.

There was nothing imposing about his appearance. He looked to be a man in his twenties, rather scholarly, with a pointed face, as if filed down. Grayish bangs flowed over his high forehead. His tall and slender body was draped in a crimson robe that made him look less like a swordsman than the magicians that this game notably lacked.

But it was his eyes that were most notable. Those brass-colored irises seemed to throw a magnetic field over whatever they met. I'd been around him before, but I felt as intimidated as if it were our first meeting.

Asuna strode over to the table, her boots clicking, and gave a brief bow.

"I've come to say my farewell."

Heathcliff gave a wry smile. "There's no need to rush to that conclusion. Let me talk with him first."

And he cast his gaze upon me. I lowered my hood and walked up next to Asuna.

"I don't believe we've met outside of the boss battles, Kirito."

"Not quite. We did speak briefly at the planning meeting for the sixty-seventh floor," I answered politely. Heathcliff gave a slight nod, then clasped his angular hands together on top of the table.

"That was a painful battle. We nearly lost some good people in that one. They call us the top guild, but our abilities are constantly stretched to the breaking point. And yet, you want to remove one of our core members, a pillar of our guild."

"If she's that important, you should put more care into picking her guards."

The burly man in the rightmost chair bolted out of his seat at my curt reply, his face a dark mask. But Heathcliff held up a hand calmly.

"Kuradeel is serving a period of house arrest. I apologize for his transgression. But I'm afraid we cannot watch our vice commander leave without so much as a comment, Kirito..."

He stared me down. I could sense a powerful will behind the metallic glimmer of those eyes.

"If you want her, you must take her by sword—your Dual Blades, in fact. Fight me, and if you win, you may take Asuna with you. Lose, and you must join the Knights of the Blood."

"..."

I finally felt as though I was beginning to understand the mysterious man.

He was drawn to the allure of battle. And he had absolute faith in his abilities. Even trapped prisoner inside this game of death, he still couldn't cast off his gamer's ego. Just like me.

Asuna had been silently listening to everything Heathcliff said, but she couldn't hold back any longer.

"Commander, I'm not saying I want to quit the guild. I just need a bit of personal time to think about my situation."

I placed a hand on Asuna's shoulder as she tried to plead her case and took a step forward. I walked directly into Heathcliff's gaze. My mouth seemed to move on its own.

"I accept. Speaking with my sword is my preference anyway. Let's settle this with a duel."

"You jerk! You stupid, stupid jerk!"

We were back upstairs at Agil's store in Algade. I kicked the owner back down the stairs when he tried to peek in and observe, and now I was desperately trying to calm Asuna down.

"I was going to try and convince him myself! Why did you have to say that?"

She was sitting on the armrest of my rocking chair, bopping me with her little fists.

"Sorry, I said I was sorry! I just couldn't help it..."

I grabbed her wrists and held them lightly to make her stop. With this method of venting denied her, she settled on puffing out her cheeks instead. It was hard not to laugh at the difference between this Asuna and the one who was all business at the guild.

"Don't worry about it. We'll be safe—it'll be under the one-hit-victory rule. Besides, it's not like I'm guaranteed to lose…"

"Arrrgh…"

Asuna groaned and crossed her slender legs, still sitting on the armrest.

"When I saw your Dual Blades in action, it seemed like you were on another dimension entirely in terms of power. But that goes for the commander's Holy Sword ability, too… His aura of invincibility practically destroys the game balance. I honestly don't know which of you will win. Besides, what happens if you lose? Not only will I not get a break, but you'll be forced to join the KoB!"

"Depending on how you think of it, that might satisfy my goal as well."

"Huh? Why?"

I had to force myself to continue.

"I mean, as long as I'm with you…that's all I need."

Previously, you couldn't have held me upside down and shaken those words out of me. Asuna's eyes went wide with surprise, and her face blushed red so fast it was practically audible. As the pause stretched on, she got up from her chair and went to stand by the window. Over her shoulder, Algade buzzed with its usual activity in the evening light.

I'd told her the honest truth, but I still didn't want to join a guild. I thought about the guild I'd been in before, the guild that no longer existed, and a dagger of pain jabbed into my chest.

I won't go down that easily, I told myself. I got up and joined Asuna at the window. After a few moments, I felt her head rest lightly against my shoulder.

13

The main town of the newly opened seventy-fifth floor was built like an ancient Roman city. According to the map, its name was Collinia. Between the warriors, the traders, and the tourists who weren't going to spend time at the front line but still wanted to see the new city, it was a madhouse of activity. On top of all that, the grand event unfolding today meant that the teleport gate square had been bustling since sunrise.

The town was built of massive, chalky-white blocks of stone. In addition to the temple-like buildings and canals, there was one other significant feature of Collinia—an enormous coliseum looming over the teleport gate. Coincidentally, it was the perfect place for the duel between Heathcliff and me. And yet...

"Fire-breathing corn, just ten col!"

"Nice cold black ale here!"

The entrance to the coliseum was buzzing with merchants hawking suspicious food to the lengthy lines of visitors hoping to see the event.

"Wh-what's going on here?" I asked Asuna, completely stunned.

"I...don't know..."

"Hey, are those KoB members selling tickets over there?! Why has this turned into a huge event?!"

"I...don't know..."

"This wasn't what Heathcliff was planning all along, was it...?"

"I'm guessing this is Daizen's handiwork. I tell you, those accountants know their business." She chuckled. My shoulders slumped.

"Let's run away, Asuna. We'll find a nice secluded little village down around the twenties and tend to some fields."

"I wouldn't mind," she said, straight-faced. "But I have a feeling that if you run away from all of *this*, you'll be absolutely infamous."

"Damn..."

"Well, you made your bed, and now you have to sleep in it. Oh, Daizen!"

I raised my head and saw a very portly man with a rippling belly approaching, proving definitively that it was, in fact, possible for the red-and-white KoB uniform to look bad on someone.

"Thank ye kindly, thank ye kindly!" he called out, a wide grin plastered across his round face. "We're doin' a brisk business on account o' you, Kirito! The only thing that'd make this better is if ya decided to hold it every month!"

"In your dreams!"

"Come, the changin' room is right this way. Go on, my friend!"

I dejectedly followed after the plodding man. My mood was quickly growing fatalistic.

The changing room was a small chamber that bordered the arena grounds. Daizen showed me to the door, then said something about adjusting odds and disappeared. I couldn't even muster up a snappy reply. The stadium must have been full, since I could hear the crowd from there.

Once we were alone, Asuna squeezed my wrist in both hands and looked me straight in the face.

"Even in a one-hit match, you have to watch out for the critical hit on a heavy attack. There are aspects to his sword skills that even I don't know about. If you feel endangered at any time, just resign. And if you push yourself like the last time, I'm holding it against you!"

"Worry about Heathcliff, not me."

I gave her a wry grin and patted her shoulders.

On top of the distant thunder of the crowd, an amplified voice was announcing the start of the match. I pulled my swords just a sliver out of the scabbards crossed over my back and then pushed them back in with a satisfying *ching*. The square of light leading out of the waiting room beckoned.

The circular arena was surrounded by fully packed stands arranged in steps. There had to be at least a thousand people gathered. I could see Agil and Klein in the front row, shouting rather unsavory suggestions like "Cut him down!" and "Kill him!"

I stopped when I reached the center of the coliseum. As soon as I did, a red silhouette appeared from the waiting room on the other side. The cheers grew louder.

Heathcliff wasn't wearing the usual KoB pattern of red on a white background; this time it was a full crimson surcoat. Like me, he chose a minimum of armor, but it was hard to ignore the enormous white crucifix shield on his left hand. His sword must have been equipped behind the shield, as I could see the hilt protruding over the top.

He strode up matter-of-factly, paused to glance around at the crowd, and gave me a pained grin.

"I'm sorry about this, Kirito. I didn't realize it'd turned into such a production."

"I should collect appearance fees."

"...No. You'll be a member of the guild at the end of this duel. I'll treat it as a regular assignment."

He stopped smiling, and I felt the overwhelming force of his brass-colored eyes again. They were so overpowering that I stumbled back a step. We were lying on beds far, far apart in the real world, everything between us a mere exchange of digital data, but I felt something powerfully ethereal from him—a palpable, murderous intent.

With a mental flick of my brain, I was in battle mode. The roar of the crowd died away as I focused solely on Heathcliff's gaze. Even the colors around me began to shift, as though my mind was already accelerating.

Heathcliff looked away, backed up to a distance of about ten yards, and raised his hand. He manipulated the game window that appeared without looking at it, and a duel message appeared in front of me. I accepted. The victory condition: first strike.

A countdown began. The roar of the crowd was muted down to a dull murmur.

All the blood in my body pulsed faster. I gripped the reins around my instinct to fight and stifled a slight hesitation. Reaching over my back with both hands, I pulled both swords out at once. This was not an opponent that I could afford to give anything but my best.

Heathcliff drew a slender longsword from behind his shield and held it out.

His form as he pointed the shield toward me was easy and natural—no imbalance, no awkward force. I suspected that attempting to guess his first move would only confuse me, and I prepared to strike with everything I had.

Neither of us gave our countdown windows even the briefest glance. Yet we both leaped forward at the exact instant that the word DUEL appeared in midair.

I darted in low, gliding just over the ground. As I reached Heathcliff, I twisted, striking down-left with my right sword. The cross shield blocked it, sending up a burst of sparks. But my attack was twofold. A tenth of a second later, my left blade slipped around the side of the shield: a dual-blade charging attack, Double Circular.

Just before the latter swing could hit his side, he met it with his own sword. A circular visual effect bounced off harmlessly. It was a good attack that he blocked, but this was just my initial greeting. The attack's momentum allowed me to maintain distance and regroup.

This time, Heathcliff responded by charging with his shield. It was hard to see what his right hand was doing behind that massive cover.

"Tsk!" I clicked my tongue, dashing right to avoid it. I figured that if I circled in the direction of the shield, I might not see the attack's initial location, but at least it'd be easier to avoid it.

Instead, Heathcliff pulled his shield up parallel to the ground and—

"Mmf!"

With a heavy grunt, he thrust the pointed end of the shield at me. The massive cross darted in close, trailing white light.

"Whoa!"

I had to cross both swords in front of me to block the blow. The powerful shock wave rattled throughout my body, and I was knocked back several feet. I jabbed my right sword into the ground to keep from falling over, did a flip in midair, and landed on my feet.

So the game recognized his shield as being capable of an attack. He might as well have been double wielding himself. I'd figured that having more chances to attack was my key to victory in a one-hit battle, but this was coming out of left field.

Heathcliff came rushing up in an attempt to deprive me of time to recover. His cross-hilt longsword blazed forth at a speed worthy of Asuna the Flash.

Now that he was in the midst of a combination attack, I had to keep using both swords to my utmost just to block him. Asuna had given me as much information as she possibly could about Heathcliff's Holy Sword skill, but secondhand knowledge was a far cry from actual experience. My momentary reflexes were all that protected me from his onslaught.

As soon as my left sword had blocked the last upward slash of his eight-part combo, I immediately unleashed the Vorpal Strike heavy attack with my right.

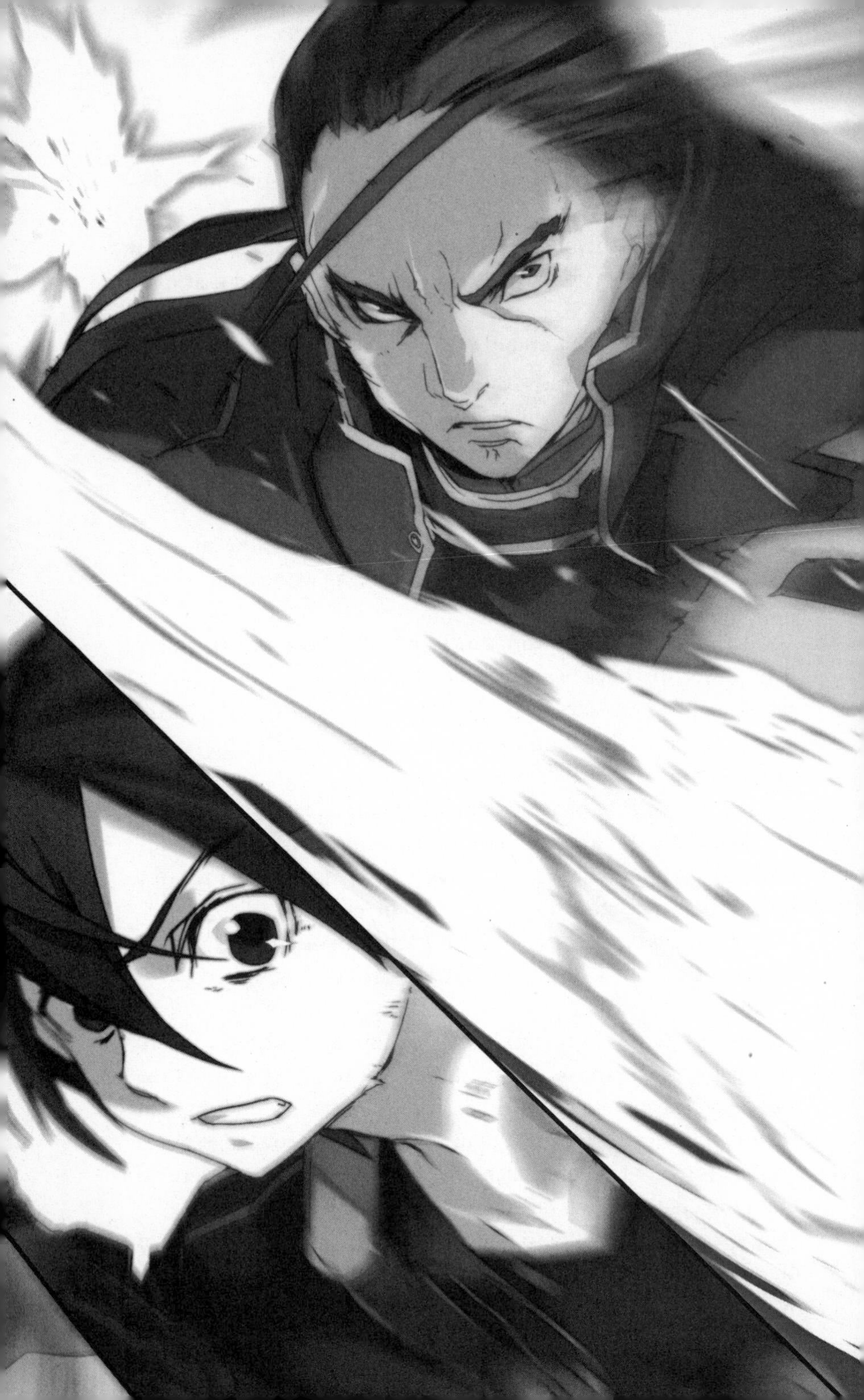

"R...raah!!"

With a metallic sound like a jet engine, my glowing red thrust hit the shield right in the middle of its crucifix. It felt like hitting a brick wall, but I didn't let that stop me.

The collision was explosive, and it was Heathcliff's turn to be tossed backward. I didn't break through the shield, but I'd felt a little bit of give. His HP bar was ever so slightly smaller, but not enough to be a decisive blow.

Heathcliff landed lightly on his feet and pulled back.

"Your reaction speed is admirable."

"And your defense is beyond tough!"

I darted forward again. Heathcliff raised his sword and closed the distance.

We traded furious combinations at high speed. His shield blocked my swords; my swords blocked his. Effects and trails of various colors fizzled around us, and the shock waves echoed off the stones of the arena floor. Occasionally, a quick strike would glance weakly off of one of us, and our HP bars slowly but steadily shrank. Even if neither of us landed a powerful blow, as soon as someone had fewer than 50 percent, the match would be over.

But there wasn't a single cell in my brain considering that as a means of victory. I was facing a true rival, a worthy foe, for the first time since I fell into SAO, and all of my senses were racing like never before. Every time I thought it couldn't get more intense, the attacks kicked into a higher gear.

Again. And again. *Follow me if you can, Heathcliff!*

I was experiencing the ecstasy of battle, the sensation of my abilities unleashed to their fullest extent. If I had to guess, I was probably smiling. As the heat of our combat reached new heights, his health fell faster and faster, and that halfway point was coming into sight.

In an instant, I finally saw something like emotion flash across Heathcliff's mask of a face. What was it, panic? I felt the slightest hesitation, a tiny delay in my foe's attack tempo.

"Raaaah!!"

Seizing upon the moment, I abandoned all defense and went on the offensive with both swords: Starburst Stream, a double-bladed assault named for the blazing arms of a solar prominence. It bore down on Heathcliff.

"Hrrg…!"

He held up his shield to guard. I continued raining down blows, above and below, left and right. His responses grew slower and slower.

I was getting through!

It was clear that my final barrage was going to break through his defense. I saw his shield stray too far to the right, and my glowing strike from the left disappeared into Heathcliff's body. If it hit, his HP would easily fall below 50 percent, and I'd win the duel. But—

—The world shifted.

"…?!"

How else could I describe it? A moment of time stolen from me, perhaps.

I sensed my body and everything else freeze for less than a tenth of a second. Everything except for Heathcliff. His shield, which should have been on the right, had blinked over to the left like a transition between two frames of film. It easily deflected my perfect attack, my certain victory.

"Wha—?"

Any time a major attack is blocked, the attacker is left fatally frozen for an instant. Heathcliff did not miss his chance.

I fell with a simple thrust of his sword, a miniscule attack delivering just enough damage to bring the duel to an end. Out of the corner of my eye, I could see the purple system text announcing the winner.

Battle mode disengaged. The roar of the crowd rushed back into my ears, but I was still dumbfounded.

"Kirito!" Asuna ran over and helped me up.

"Y…yeah…I'm all right."

She looked pensively into my slackened face.

I'd lost...

I still couldn't believe it. That incredible reaction that Heathcliff managed at the end was beyond the ability of any player—of any human being. It was as though his impossible speed actually broke his polygonal model for an instant.

I looked up at Heathcliff, who was standing at a slight remove. Despite his victory, his face was sharp. Those metallic eyes fixed upon me for a moment, then the red paladin spun around without a word, striding through the storm of cheers to his waiting room.

14

"Wh-what's up with this outfit?"

"Seems pretty self-explanatory to me. Now stand up!"

Asuna had forced me into a new set of clothes. It was the same shape as my comfy, tattered old coat, but this one was pure, eye-watering white. There were two small red crosses on both sides of the collar to go with the large one on the back. It was my new Knights of the Blood uniform, as if that needed any explanation.

"I thought I asked for something a little less…striking."

"Trust me, that's one of our plainest designs. It looks good on you!"

I sank into the rocking chair, defeated. We were upstairs at Agil's, as usual. I'd claimed the space for my emergency shelter, and the poor shopkeeper was forced to sleep in a simple bed downstairs. The only reason he didn't kick me out was that Asuna had come to help with the shop for the last two days. She made for an effective marketing tool.

As I groaned in the rocking chair, Asuna sat upon her familiar perch, the armrest. She rocked the chair back and forth, smiling at my stupid new outfit. After a few moments, she clasped her hands together as if remembering something.

"Oh, I guess I never gave you my official greeting. Welcome to our guild, recruit." She gave me a nod, and I straightened up in a hurry.

"Nice to 'meet' you, I guess. The only problem is…I'm just a rookie, and you're the vice commander." I extended my hand and traced a finger along her back. "So I won't be able to do that anymore."

"Hyack!"

She leaped up with a shriek, smacked her new recruit on the head, then sat in the chair on the other side of the room, her cheeks puffed out.

It was early afternoon in late fall. A calm silence fell upon the lazy sunlight.

Two days had passed since my defeat at Heathcliff's hands. Just as he had demanded, I was now a member of the KoB. It wasn't to my liking to raise a fuss at this point. They gave me two days to prepare, and the next day I would report to guild HQ and begin my duty clearing the seventy-fifth-floor labyrinth.

A guild…

Asuna detected my brief sigh and glanced at me.

"Looks like you're stuck with us…"

"It was good timing for me. I was hitting the limit of what I could do solo."

"Well, it's good of you to say so…Hey, Kirito."

Her hazel eyes looked straight into mine.

"Tell me, why do you avoid guilds…and people in general? It's not just because you were a beta tester or that you have a Unique Skill. You're too nice to do this."

I looked away and rocked the chair slowly.

"…Once, a long while back—more than a year ago, I think—I was actually in another guild…"

It surprised me how easily the words came. I had a feeling that Asuna's kind gaze would heal the pain that surfaced every time I let that memory rise to the surface.

"I happened across some folks in a labyrinth and rescued them from trouble, which earned me an invitation to their guild. It was really small—just six members, including me. Their name was brilliant: the Moonlit Black Cats."

She giggled.

"The leader was a really good guy. He always thought of the members first, and we all trusted him. He was Keita, a staff-wielder. Most of the others used two-handed, longer-range weapons, so they needed someone to take the forward position and keep enemies occupied."

To be honest, their levels were considerably lower than mine. That was more a reflection of how obsessively I'd been working at it than a knock on their abilities.

If I'd told them my actual level, Keita would likely have revoked his offer. But at the time I'd been growing weary of solo dungeon-delving, and the comfortable atmosphere of the Moonlit Black Cats was welcoming. They were all friends in real life, and I couldn't help but be drawn in by the way they interacted without any of the distance that was often endemic to net games.

When I chose to ignore everyone else and focus on improving my own level, I lost the right to seek the warmth of companionship, whispered the little voice in my ear. I had to suppress that dark voice and accept their offer, hiding my level and my beta experience.

Keita wanted to convert one of the guild's two lancers to a sword-and-shield fighter, and he asked me to help coach that process. That way, we'd have three people at forward, including me, which would balance our party.

I was put in charge of Sachi, a gentle girl with black hair falling to her shoulders. When we first met, she laughed shyly and said that she'd been playing online games for a while but had a hard time making friends. Most days that the guild wasn't doing activities together, I was giving her one-on-one sword lessons.

Sachi and I were alike in many ways. We had the tendency to create walls around ourselves, but despite our reticence, we both craved the presence of others.

One day, out of the blue, she spilled her innermost secrets

to me. She was afraid to die. She was terrified of the game. She didn't want to venture out into the wilderness at all.

All I could do was tell her that she wouldn't die. I'd been hiding my true level from her the entire time—I didn't have the right to say anything more. But when Sachi heard those words, she cried, and then smiled.

Some time later, the five of us, aside from Keita, decided to venture into a labyrinth. He was back in town, negotiating with the money we'd earned to buy a house that would serve as our headquarters.

The labyrinth had already been beaten, but there were still unmapped areas for us to explore. Just as we were preparing to leave, someone found a treasure chest. I recommended that we leave it behind. It was a high-level area on a floor close to the front line, and the party's Disarm skill wasn't up to snuff. But only Sachi and I were dissenting voices, and the other three over-ruled us.

The chest was trapped: an alarm trap, one of the worst of the wide variety that existed in SAO. A shrill alarm sounded from the chest, and countless monsters poured through every doorway into the room. Naturally, we chose the safe option and attempted to make an emergency teleportation.

But the trap was twofold. It was an anti-crystal zone—we couldn't teleport out.

There were too many monsters for me to protect everyone. The other members panicked and started to run. I used my best skills, the ones I'd been keeping secret, desperate to find us a way out. But the others were in a state of sheer terror and couldn't take advantage of my diversion. One by one, they ran out of health and shattered into pieces and screams. I kept swinging desperately, trying to keep Sachi alive, if nothing else.

But I was too late. A monster's blade cut her down mercilessly as she lunged for my help, her hand outstretched. Up until the very instant she disintegrated like a delicate glass sculpture, her eyes were full of nothing but faith in me. She trusted me and clung to me. To my words—groundless, meaningless, proven false at the very end.

Keita was standing in front of our old headquarters, key to our new residence in hand, waiting for the group to return. When I came back alone and explained what had happened, he listened in silence. When I finished, he asked, "Why were you the only survivor?"

I had to tell him the truth: that I was a much higher level and had been a beta tester.

Keita gave me the emotionless look that one gives something alien and said just one thing.

You're a beater. You didn't have the right to get involved with us.

Those words cut me deeper than any steely sword.

"And what...happened to him...?"

"He killed himself."

Her body jolted still in the chair.

"Threw himself off the outer edge. Probably cursed my name to the very...end..."

My voice caught. I'd tried to seal that memory away in a place where I could never revisit it again, but speaking it aloud brought the pain back as fresh as when it happened. I clenched my teeth. Asuna reached out a hand. I wanted to seek her salvation, but a voice in my heart told me I didn't deserve it. My hands balled into fists.

"I was responsible for murdering all of them. If I hadn't hid the fact that I was a beater, they would have believed me when I warned them about the trap. I killed Keita...I killed Sachi..."

I forced my eyes open and squeezed the words out through gritted teeth.

Asuna rose, came two steps forward, then took my face in her hands. She bore a gentle smile and leaned in very close.

"I'm not going to die." It was like a whisper, but her voice was clear. All the tension drained out of my body. "After all...I'm the one protecting you."

And she held my head to her chest. I was enveloped in soft, warm darkness.

I closed my eyelids and saw, beyond the black veil of memory, the members of the Moonlit Black Cats looking at me, seated at the counter of the old bar, the room brimming with orange light.

My day of forgiveness would never come. I could never repay what I had done.

But in my memory, their faces seemed to be smiling at me.

The next morning, I slipped my arms through my fancy new white coat and left for Grandzam with Asuna.

Today was my first day of activity as a Knight of the Blood. But while they normally worked in parties of five, Asuna had pulled some strings as vice commander and gotten us the privilege of making our own two-man party, so it was really no different from what we'd been doing before.

But when we reached guild headquarters, the orders I got were not what I was expecting.

"Training…?"

"Correct. We will form a party of four, including me, and clear the labyrinth of the fifty-fifth floor, finishing up in the town on the fifty-sixth."

This was one of the four men I'd seen seated at the table during my last visit to this building. He was a large, curly-haired man who was apparently an ax warrior.

"But Godfrey! Kirito-kun's working with me…"

Asuna tried to butt in, but he simply raised an eyebrow and proceeded imperiously.

"You might be the vice commander, but you cannot simply run roughshod over the regulations of the guild. If that's the party you desire when we are actually performing game-clearing duties, so be it. But as the leader of the forward line, I need to assess his ability. Just because he has a Unique Skill does not necessarily mean he will be useful."

"W-well, Kirito-kun's strong enough that he wouldn't have any trouble dealing with you..."

I spoke up before Asuna could completely blow her cool. "If you want to see what I can do, that's fine with me. I just don't want to waste my time on such a low-level labyrinth. I trust you don't mind if we blaze through it in no time?"

The man named Godfrey frowned with displeasure, told me to be at the west gate of the town in thirty minutes, then plodded off.

"What was that all about?!" Asuna stormed, kicking a nearby pole. "I'm sorry, Kirito-kun...I knew we should have just run off on our own."

"Yeah, but then your guildmates would have cursed me to the ends of the earth." I smiled and patted her on top of the head.

"Aww...I thought we'd actually be together today. Maybe I should tag along..."

"Don't worry, I'll be back in a jiffy. Just wait for me here."

"Okay. Be careful out there..."

I waved to her as she looked on solemnly, then I left the building.

But for as much as the day's activity caught me by surprise, nothing prepared me for what I saw at the west gate of Grandzam.

There, waiting right next to Godfrey, was the last man in Aincrad I wanted to see—Kuradeel.

15

"...What's going on here?" I muttered to Godfrey.

"I'm well aware of what transpired between the two of you. But now you're guildmates. So let's let bygones be bygones, eh?"

He roared with laughter. Meanwhile, Kuradeel slunk forward.

"..."

I tensed up, ready to act whatever came. We were inside the town zone, but there was no telling what he'd do.

Instead, Kuradeel surprised me by bowing his head. He spoke in a murmur that was barely audible through his long bangs.

"I'm sorry...about what happened the other day..."

Now I was truly shocked. My mouth fell open.

"I won't treat you with such disrespect again...I beg your forgiveness."

I couldn't see his face behind the greasy locks.

"Uh...sure..." I brought myself to nod. What could have happened? Had he gotten brain surgery?

"That settles it, then!" Godfrey bellowed with laughter again. I wasn't just being paranoid—there was clearly something going on here. But I couldn't read Kuradeel's expression with his head tilted down. SAO simulated emotional expressions, but it tended on the side of exaggeration, and subtle nuances didn't always show. I decided to accept his apology for politeness's sake but made a mental note to stay wary of him.

After a few minutes, one more guild member showed up, and we were ready to leave for the labyrinth. I started to walk, but Godfrey's heavy voice rang out behind me.

"Not so fast. Today's training is meant to be as close a simulation of the real thing as possible. I want to see how you handle dangerous circumstances, so that means I'll need to confiscate all your crystals for the time being."

"Even our teleport crystals?"

He nodded, as if this was obvious. I did not like this turn of events at all. Crystals—particularly teleportation crystals—were the player's last line of defense in a game where the stakes were deadly. At no point in my two years in Aincrad had I ever let my stock run out. I was going to protest, but then thought better of it, as I didn't want to make things worse for Asuna.

When I saw Kuradeel and the other member obediently handing over their items, I reluctantly parted with my own. He meant business, too; I had to turn out my waistpouch before he was satisfied.

"Very good. Let's depart!"

Godfrey barked out the order, and the four of us began walking from the gates of Grandzam to the labyrinth visible far to the west.

The fifty-fifth floor was a dry wasteland nearly devoid of greenery. I just wanted to get this exercise over with and suggested that we run to the labyrinth, but Godfrey vetoed that with a swing of his arm. *Well, he probably dumped all of his points into strength rather than agility, so he can barely run anyway,* I thought, and gave up.

We ran into a few monsters, but I was in no mood to follow Godfrey's orders and dispatched them with a single blow each. Finally, once we'd crested the dozenth rocky hill, the gray stone labyrinth came into full view.

"Let's take a break here!" Godfrey barked out, and the party came to a halt.

"…"

I wanted to keep going straight through the labyrinth, but I figured they wouldn't heed my suggestion anyway, so I sat down on a nearby rock. It was just passing noon.

"I'll distribute rations," Godfrey said, materializing four small leather parcels and handing them out. I caught mine one-handed and looked in, expecting to be disappointed. It contained a bottle of water and a small toasted bread you could buy from any NPC shop.

Inwardly, I cursed my foul luck. *I should be eating Asuna's homemade sandwiches right about now.* I took a swig of the water.

My eye just happened to catch Kuradeel sitting on a rock, slightly removed from the rest of us. He hadn't touched his bag. He was glaring at us from under his drooping bangs, an oddly dark look on his face.

What was he staring at…?

Suddenly, a freezing shiver bolted through my body. He was waiting for something. Waiting…for…

I threw the bottle away, trying to expel every last bit of the liquid from my mouth.

But it was too late. I could feel the strength draining from my body, and I fell to the ground. My HP bar was in the right-hand corner of my vision, surrounded by a blinking green border.

It was paralysis venom.

Godfrey and the other member of our group were rolling on the ground in agony as well. Instinctively, I forced my left hand, still mobile, down to my waistpouch, but another chill ran down my back. Godfrey had my antidote and teleportation crystals. I did have healing potions, but they wouldn't cure the venom.

"Heh…heh-heh-heh…"

I heard a high-pitched chuckle. Above the rock, Kuradeel was holding his sides with laughter, doubled over. Those sunken, beady eyes were glinting with a familiar look of madness.

"Ka-ha! Hya-hya! Hya-ha-ha-ha-ha!"

He burst into crazed, unhinged gales of laughter. Godfrey simply looked on in stunned disbelief.

"Wh...what's going on...? Did you do this...to our water, Kuradeel?"

"Godfrey! Use the antidote crystals!" I called out, and Godfrey finally began to search through his pack, achingly slow.

"Hyaaa!"

Kuradeel gave a triumphant screech, leaped off the rock, and kicked Godfrey's hand away. A green crystal skittered over the dirt. Kuradeel picked it up, then riffled through Godfrey's pack and pulled out several more, which he deposited into his own pouch.

We were out of options.

"What is the meaning of this, Kuradeel? Is this...some kind of trial...?"

"You fools!!"

Godfrey was woefully slow on the uptake, and Kuradeel rewarded him with a kick in the mouth.

"Gaah!!"

Godfrey's HP bar shrank just a bit, and Kuradeel's cursor turned orange to signify a criminal player. But that would have no effect on our plight. This floor was already cleared. No one would be luckily wandering by this exact stretch of wilderness.

"You know, Godfrey, I always thought you were stupid...I just didn't appreciate how much!" His shrill voice echoed off the rocks. "I've got plenty of things I want to say to you, but there's no use stuffing yourself on the hors d'oeuvres..."

Kuradeel drew his greatsword. He tilted his thin body backward and took a huge swing, the thick blade glimmering in the sunlight.

"W-wait, Kuradeel! Wh-what are you talking about...? Isn't this...part of the trial?"

"Shut up and die already," Kuradeel spat.

He swung the sword down without further ado. I heard a dull *thud*, and a huge chunk disappeared from Godfrey's HP bar.

Godfrey had finally realized the severity of the situation and began to scream. It was far too late.

Twice, then thrice, the blade flashed mercilessly. The HP bar lost a chunk each time, and when it reached the red zone, Kuradeel finally stayed his hand.

For an instant, I actually thought he was going to stop short of murder. But Kuradeel only flipped the sword around to a backhand grip, then sank it slowly into Godfrey's body. His health trickled down. Kuradeel shifted his weight into it.

"Gaaahhhh!!"

"Hya-haaaa!!"

Kuradeel's high-pitched squeal of delight practically matched Godfrey's scream. The tip of the sword kept sinking farther, and the HP bar steadily shrank.

As the other member and I watched helplessly, silently, Kuradeel's sword punctured through and hit the ground at the same moment that Godfrey's HP reached zero. I don't think Godfrey ever fully realized what was happening, even up to the moment that he exploded into countless pieces.

Kuradeel slowly pulled his greatsword out of the ground, then swiveled his head at the neck to stare at us like some kind of grotesque automaton.

"Eeeh! Eeeh!!"

The other guildman uttered short shrieks and vainly attempted to escape. Kuradeel hopped over to him with an odd gait.

"I've got nothing against you...but in my story, I've got to be the only survivor," he muttered, swinging his sword again.

"Eeeek!!"

"Got that? Our doomed party..."

He struck, ignoring the other man's screams.

"...was set upon by vagabonds in the wilderness..."

Another blow.

"...and while the other three died valiantly..."

And another.

"...I alone succeeded in breaking the attackers' spirits to return to the guild alive!"

On the fourth strike, the man's HP was empty. The sound sent involuntary chills throughout my body. To Kuradeel, it must have sounded like the voice of a goddess. He was trembling with ecstasy in the midst of the shattering polygons, his face a mask of pure bliss.

This isn't his first time, I realized.

True, before he began this assault, he didn't have the telltale orange criminal cursor, but there are plenty of trickier ways to cause death without tipping off the system. At any rate, it was too late to realize this now.

Kuradeel finally trained his gaze on me. There was unbridled glee in those eyes. He approached slowly, wincingly scraping the tip of his sword along the ground.

"So, hey," he murmured, stooping down to hover over me. "Now I've killed two innocent men, all for the sake of one kid."

"By my reckoning, you got quite a kick out of it."

I talked to keep him busy, but my mind was racing, trying to find a way out of this desperate situation. I could only move my mouth and left hand. Under this paralysis, I couldn't open my menu, couldn't send anyone a message. Knowing that it was probably pointless, I tried to move my hand to a position where Kuradeel couldn't see it, while I kept him occupied with dialogue.

"Why did you join the KoB, anyway? You'd do better in one of the criminal guilds."

"Isn't that obvious? It was her," Kuradeel rasped, licking his lips with a pointed tongue. When I realized he was talking about Asuna, my entire body burned.

"You filthy rat!"

"Oh, don't look at me that way. It's just a game, isn't it? Don't worry. I'll take good care of your beloved vice commander. I've got plenty of handy items just for that purpose."

Kuradeel picked up the bottle of poison nearby and sloshed the liquid inside. He gave me a sloppy wink and went on.

"What you said was quite interesting, about my being suited for a criminal guild, though."

"...It's true, isn't it?"

"I'm paying you a compliment, see? Very sharp of you."

He giggled again, deep in his throat, then suddenly unequipped one of his gauntlets. He pulled back the white sleeve of his robe and showed me the underside of his bare forearm.

"...!!"

I gasped when I saw it.

A tattoo. A caricatured drawing of a black coffin. A leering pair of eyes and mouth were drawn on the shifted lid, and a bony arm was poking out from within the coffin.

"That logo...Is that Laughing Coffin?" I rasped. Kuradeel nodded with an eager grin.

Laughing Coffin was once the largest PK guild in Aincrad. Led by their cruel and clever leader, they devised new and novel ways to kill their targets, and the body count eventually reached triple digits.

Attempts were made to come to a peaceful resolution with them, but the man who volunteered to be the messenger only wound up dead. It was impossible to fathom the motives of those who would kill their fellow players, when that could only diminish the possibility of beating the game. Talking it out was never going to work. Eventually, the clearers arranged a boss-style raiding party and wiped them out in a bloody assault. It wasn't that long ago.

Asuna and I had both taken part in the raid. Somehow, word of our plan had leaked out, and the murderers were ready for us. I went half mad trying to protect the lives of my fellow players, and by the end of the battle, I'd personally killed two members of Laughing Coffin.

"Is this...vengeance? Are you one of the remnants of LC?" I asked hoarsely, but Kuradeel laughed at the question.

"Hah! Hardly. Like I'd be that pathetic. I was only recently inducted into LC. But only mentally. That's when they taught me this handy paralysis trick...oopsy!"

He rose to his feet with a mechanical smoothness and loudly re-gripped his sword.

"Better wrap up the chitchat before your poison wears off. Time for the grand finish, I think. Every single night since our duel...I've dreamed of this moment..."

Fires of delusion burned in the full circles of his gaping eyes, and a long tongue snickered out of his wide-stretched mouth. Kuradeel stood on tiptoes to brandish his blade.

Just before he could start bringing the sword down, I flicked the throwing pick I'd hidden in my left hand. I could only use the wrist, and although I was aiming for his face, the paralysis lowered my accuracy rating. The pick flew off-line, sinking into Kuradeel's left arm. The effect on his HP bar was hopelessly insignificant.

"That...hurt..."

He wrinkled his nose and pulled back his lips. Kuradeel poked the tip of his sword into my arm. He twisted twice, then three times, as though screwing it in.

"...!"

I didn't feel any pain, but I felt the distinctly unpleasant sensation of numbed nerves being directly stimulated. As the sword dug farther into my arm, my HP slowly but surely trickled away.

Isn't it done yet? Isn't the poison wearing off?

I gritted my teeth and waited for the moment I would be free. Paralysis normally lasted about five minutes, though it could vary depending on the strength of the venom.

Kuradeel pulled the sword back and jabbed it into my left foot this time. Again, the nerve-deadening sensation shot through me, and the damage numbers mercilessly piled up.

"Well? What's it like? Knowing that you're just about to die... Tell me, why don't you?" he whispered, staring into my face.

"Why don't you say something, boy? Why don't you cry and wail about how you don't want to die?"

My HP was under half now, the bar yellow. The paralysis would not dispell. I could feel a chill settling into my body. The specter of death snuck up my legs, clad in a robe of pure cold.

I'd witnessed death firsthand multiple times in Sword Art Online. Every single victim, in the moment that they'd burst into countless shards, held the same expression: Am I really going to die right now?

Somewhere within all of us, there was a lack of belief that the game's stated rules could actually be true—that death within the game was death, period.

It was almost a sense of hope, an expectation that once our HP hit zero and we disintegrated, we would simply wake up in the real world, safe and sound. There was no way to determine the truth outside of death. In that sense, dying might just be another means of escape from the game...

"Come on, say something. You're going to die soon, hello?"

Kuradeel pulled the sword out of my foot and stuck it against my belly. My HP sank faster now, reaching into the red danger zone, but even now it still felt like it was happening off in another world. As the agony continued, my thoughts raced down a path without light. A heavy, thick layer of gauze enveloped my mind.

But...suddenly, an unbearable fear seized my heart.

Asuna. I was going to disappear and leave her behind. Asuna would fall into Kuradeel's clutches, and she would suffer the way I had. This possibility burned with a white pain that shot me to my senses.

"Gaah!!"

My eyes opened wide, and with my left hand, I grabbed the sword Kuradeel was plunging into my stomach. I summoned all my strength and slowly pulled it out. I had just under 10 percent of my health left. Kuradeel murmured, surprised.

"Uh...huh? What's this? Afraid to die after all?"

"That's right...I can't...die yet!"

"Ka! Hya-hya! Is that so? Well, that's more like it!!"

Kuradeel cackled like some monstrous bird, then put all of his weight into the sword. I tried to push back with my one hand. The system was weighing my strength stat and Kuradeel's, pitting complex calculations against one another.

The resulting outcome: The tip of the sword slowly but surely began to descend. I was plunged into fear and despair.

Is this really it?

Will I die? Am I leaving Asuna behind in this twisted, insane world?

I fought desperately against the twin perils of the approaching sword point and the fear gripping my heart.

"Now die! Dieeee!!" Kuradeel shrieked.

Inch by inch, my murder approached in the form of a dull gray point of metal. The tip grazed my body...then sank just a bit...

A burst of wind shot through the air.

A wind colored white and red.

"Wha—? Huh...?"

The murderer looked up with a scream of surprise, then went flying through the air with his sword. I stared silently at the figure that had descended in his place.

"...I made it...I made it, God...I made it!"

Her trembling voice was as beautiful as the wing beat of an angel. Asuna nearly crumpled over me, her lips quivering, her eyes wide.

"He's alive...You're alive, right, Kirito?"

"Yeah...I'm alive..."

I was surprised to hear how weak and faded my voice was. Asuna gave a big nod, pulled a pink crystal out of her pocket, placed a hand on my chest, and said, "Heal!" The crystal crumbled and my HP immediately shot all the way to full.

"Hang on a sec. I'll finish this up real quickly," she said after confirming that I was properly healed. She gracefully unsheathed her rapier and began walking.

Ahead, Kuradeel was finally getting to his feet. When he saw the figure approaching him, his eyes grew wide.

"Ah! L-Lady Asuna…why are you here…? I-I mean, this is just a trial, yes, a trial that went wrong—"

He sprang to his feet and attempted to squeak out an excuse, but he never finished. Asuna's hand flashed, and the tip of her rapier slashed Kuradeel's mouth. Because he was already labeled a criminal player, Asuna had free rein to attack him without being branded the same.

"Bwaah!"

He stumbled backward, a hand to his mouth. After a momentary pause, he rose again, a familiar loathing splotched across his face.

"That's enough from you, bitch…Hah! This is perfect. You'll be joining them soon enou—"

But this was cut short as well. Asuna readied her weapon and struck again.

"Hrrg…Aaagh!"

He desperately tried to parry with his two-handed sword, but it was woefully slow. Asuna's sword point slashed back and forth with countless streams of light, tearing across and through Kuradeel's body with frightful speed. Even being several levels above Asuna, I couldn't follow her attacks in the slightest. I was entranced by a vision of an angel, dancing with her sword.

It was beautiful. The sight of Asuna, her chestnut hair bouncing, silently devastating her foe while wreathed in righteous anger, was a thing of sheer beauty.

"Aagh! Gaaaah!!"

Fear had finally set in, and Kuradeel's wild swings weren't even coming close to landing. His HP bar dropped lower and lower, and when it was about to shift from yellow to red, he finally dropped his sword and raised his hands in surrender.

"A-all right, all right! I'm sorry; it was all my fault!" He cowered on the ground. "I'll leave the guild! You'll never see me again, I swear! Just don't—"

Asuna silently listened to his piteous wails.

Slowly, she raised her rapier, then spun it in the palm of her hand to point downward.

Her slender arm clenched and rose several inches, preparing to thrust it directly into the small of Kuradeel's back as he hunched prostrate on the ground. The murderer emitted an even, high-pitched scream.

"Eeeek! I don't wanna die!"

The point stopped as though it had hit an invisible wall. Her body was visibly trembling. Even from here, I could feel the internal battle of Asuna's hesitation, rage, and fear.

As far as I knew, she had never taken the life of another player. Killing a player in Sword Art Online meant the death of that player in real life, too. PK was a familiar term to online gamers, but it obfuscated the truth—here, it was actual murder.

That's right, Asuna. Stop. You can't do this.

But at the same time, a part of me screamed the opposite.

No, don't hesitate. He's hoping you'll stay your hand.

An instant later, my fears came true.

"Hyaaaa!!"

Kuradeel sprang up from his begging position, his sword flashing as he screamed.

With a metallic *clang*, the rapier flew out of Asuna's hand.

"Wha—?"

Asuna yelped and lost her balance. The sword glinted over her head.

"Not very smart, Vice Commander!" he screamed, unhinged. Kuradeel swung the sword downward without hesitation, trailing deep red light.

"Raaagh!"

This time the roar was mine. The paralysis finally undone, I leaped up, crossing several yards in an instant, pushing Asuna out of the way, and taking Kuradeel's sword full on my left arm.

Chunk, it rang unpleasantly. My left forearm flew off, severed at the elbow. Below my HP bar, a limb-damage icon flashed.

Crimson particles meant to resemble blood spurted out of the cut, but I straightened the fingers of my right hand...

And thrust it straight into the gap in his heavy armor. My arm flashed yellow and sank wetly into Kuradeel's stomach.

I'd hit him with Embracer, a point-blank Martial Arts skill. It took every last bit of Kuradeel's remaining HP. The skinny body shook violently, then slumped over, powerless.

I heard the greatsword clatter to the ground, then a hoarse whisper in my ear.

"Why... you... murderer."

A chuckle.

And Kuradeel's entire existence turned to glass shards. With a cold burst, the polygons exploded outward, knocking me to the ground.

For a while, my consciousness numb, the only sound was the wind blowing across the field.

Eventually, I heard uneven footsteps over the gravel. I looked up and saw a frail figure stumbling toward me, her face empty.

Asuna plodded several steps closer, face downward, then slumped to her knees like a puppet whose strings had been cut. She extended her hand toward me, then shrank back just before it touched.

"...I'm sorry... It's my fault... This is all my fault..."

The look on her face was heartbreaking. Tears filled her large eyes, sparkling like jewels, then fell. Finally, I managed to rasp one word out of my parched throat.

"Asuna..."

"I'm sorry. I... I don't have the right... to even... see you anym..."

I desperately raised myself from the ground, finally in control of my body again. The damage I'd suffered still left an unpleasant numbness, but I could at least extend my right and severed left arm to Asuna. I plugged her beautiful pink lips with my own.

"...!"

She stiffened and tried to use her hands to push me away, but

I held tightly to her slender body with all my strength. It was certainly enough to set off the anti-harassment code. At this moment, she would be seeing a system message warning of my actions, and with the push of a button, she could have me instantly teleported to the prison in Blackiron Palace.

But I didn't let my arms slack an inch, moving from her lips to nuzzle her cheek. I buried my face into her neck and murmured, "My life belongs to you, Asuna. I'm all yours. We'll be together until the final moment."

My left arm was still in a severed state and wouldn't return for three minutes, but I held it around her back anyway. Asuna let out a trembling breath and then whispered back to me.

"I promise... I promise I'll protect you, too. I'll be here for you forever. Just don't leave me..."

She didn't need to say any more. I held Asuna tightly, listening to her breathing.

Bit by bit, the warmth of her body thawed the ice within me.

16

The entire time that Asuna had waited back in Grandzam, she had been following my location on her map.

According to her, she'd started running out of town when she saw Godfrey's marker disappear, which meant that in barely five minutes, she had covered the three miles it took us an hour to walk. It was an impossible number, faster than the agility stat boost could explain. When I pointed this out, she smiled and said it was "an act of love."

We returned to guild headquarters, reported what had happened to Heathcliff, and applied for temporary leave. Asuna cited her lack of trust in the guild, and after a momentary silence, Heathcliff accepted her request. But at the end, he gave that strange smile again and added cryptically, "You'll be back on the battlefield soon enough."

Outside of the tower, it was already growing dark. We walked to the teleport gate holding hands. Neither of us spoke a word.

With the orange light of the sun hitting our backs, we walked slowly through the black silhouettes of Grandzam's many towers. I absently wondered where Kuradeel's bottomless hate had come from.

It wasn't that rare for players to commit wicked deeds in SAO. It was said that there were several hundred criminals in the game, from thieves and bandits to those like Kuradeel and Laughing Coffin, who brutally slaughtered their victims. At this point, they were considered a natural feature of the game, much like monsters.

But the more I thought about it, the stranger it seemed. It was obvious that anyone who intentionally caused harm to other players was working to the detriment of our shared quest to beat the game. Their actions suggested that they didn't want to leave.

But when I thought about Kuradeel, he didn't seem to fit that definition. His thoughts had nothing to do with escaping the game or preventing others from doing so. He represented an absence of thought—a man who had stopped pondering the past or future, allowed his own desires to rule him, and fostered the will of evil.

What did that make me? I couldn't honestly state that my entire purpose within the game was to defeat it. If anything, I was exploring dungeons and gaining levels out of simple inertia, nothing else. If the only reason I fought was to know the pleasure of being better than others, did I truly wish for the game to be over?

I suddenly sensed that the metal plate under my feet was losing balance and sinking, so I stopped walking. I gripped Asuna's hand harder, as though fighting to stay attached.

"...?"

I glanced at Asuna for an instant and saw her peering quizzically at me, her head tilted. I turned back to the ground and muttered more to myself than to her.

"...No matter what happens...I'm going to send you back...to the real world..."

"..."

This time, she squeezed my hand.

"We'll go back together."

She smiled.

We eventually reached the teleport gate square. Only a few players milled about, hunched over in the chill winds that suggested the coming of winter. I turned straight to Asuna. The warm light that shone from her powerful soul was meant to guide me.

"Asuna...I want to spend the night with you," I said unconsciously.

I didn't want to be apart from her. I'd just faced the threat of death like never before, and that pall was unlikely to leave my spine any time soon.

I would see them in my dreams tonight, if I slept at all: his madness, the stabbing sword, the feeling of my hand sinking into flesh. I was sure of that.

Asuna looked at me wide-eyed, seemingly grasping the meaning of my statement...and eventually gave a small nod, her cheeks flushing.

Asuna's apartment in Selmburg was just as luxurious on my second visit, and it had a welcoming warmth to it. The decorative objects placed here and there spoke highly of the owner's excellent taste, but when Asuna saw them, she stammered.

"O-oh my gosh, it's such a mess. I haven't been home in a while..."

She giggled nervously and started stashing things away.

"I'll get started on dinner. You can read the newspaper or something."

"Um, okay."

She removed her equipment and disappeared into the kitchen with an apron while I sank into the comfortable sofa. I picked up a large bundle of paper on top of the table.

Calling it a newspaper was a bit disingenuous. It was really just a collection of stories cobbled together by players who made a living gathering information and selling it as "news." But with no real form of entertainment in Aincrad, this was a precious bit of media, and more than a few players bought subscriptions. I picked up the four-page paper, gazed absently at the front, then threw it aside in disgust. The front story was my duel with Heathcliff.

DUAL BLADES WIELDER UNVEILED, MERCILESSLY CRUSHED BY HOLY SWORD, the headline screamed, with a helpful picture of me—taken with a special recording crystal—lying prostrate before the triumphant Heathcliff. All I'd done was help add another entry to his legend.

On the other hand, if this cemented the public's opinion that I was no big deal, it would help deflect attention, I told myself. I flipped to the item marketplace listings, and eventually a fragrant smell wafted out of the kitchen.

Dinner was steak from one of Aincrad's cattle-like monsters, topped with Asuna's special soy sauce. The meat itself wasn't a particularly high rank, as such things go, but the sauce did all the work. Asuna smiled as she watched me stuffing my face.

After dinner, we sat facing each other on her sofas, drinking tea. She was being unusually talkative, rattling off her favorite weapon brands and places she'd like to sightsee on various floors of the castle.

I mostly listened absentmindedly, letting her do all the talking, but when Asuna suddenly fell silent, I couldn't help but be concerned. She stared down into her cup, as though looking for something in the tea. Her face was a steely mask, as if she were preparing for battle.

"H...hey, what's wro—"

She set her teacup down on the table with a clatter before I could finish.

"...Okay!"

Asuna braced herself and stood up. She walked over to the window, touched the wall to bring up the room options and then immediately turned out the lanterns in the corners. The room was plunged into darkness. My Search skill automatically blazed into life, switching my eyesight to night-vision mode.

Now the room was colored a faint blue, with Asuna shining brightly at the window, reflecting the lights of the town. I was confused but held my breath at the beauty of the sight.

Her long hair looked dark blue in the gloom, and the slender white of her arms and legs extending from the tunic shone as if they were producing the light by themselves.

Asuna stood silently at the window. She was hunched over, so I couldn't see her face. When she drew her left hand to her chest, she appeared to be grappling with some inner decision.

Just when I was about to say something, to ask what was going on, she moved. With a small *ping*, she traced her finger in the air and drew open her status window. Her hands moved over the glowing purple options in the blue darkness. It seemed from here like she was manipulating her equipment...

And in the next instant, the knee-high socks she was wearing disappeared without a sound, exposing the slender curves of her legs. Her fingers moved again. This time, her entire one-piece tunic was gone. My mouth dropped open and my eyes were wide.

She was wearing nothing but her underwear now. Tiny little slips of white cloth that barely covered her breasts and hips.

"J-just don't...stare, okay?" she stammered, her voice trembling. As if it was that easy to tear my eyes away.

She crossed her arms in front of her body and fidgeted, but eventually looked up and gracefully lowered her arms.

I felt a shock as though my soul had just escaped my body.

Beauty wasn't the right word for it. Her smooth, shining skin was clad in particles of blue light. Her hair was the finest silk. The swelling of her breasts was more ample than it had originally seemed. The flesh of her slender hips and long legs was as tight as a wild animal's. Paradoxically, her curvature was so perfect that it couldn't have been rendered in any graphics engine.

This was not a finely modeled 3-D object. If anything, it was a sculpture that God himself had filled with a soul.

Our bodies in SAO were semi-automatically generated with data the NerveGear gathered when we logged in and ran the calibration process for the very first time. Given that, it was nothing short of a miracle that such a beautiful body should exist in the game.

I stared and stared at her half-naked figure, my mind blank.

If she never got tired, put her hands back up, or spoke to me, I would have stared in silence for an entire hour.

She looked down and blushed so hard that I could see it in the blue darkness.

"G-go on—you, too...Are you g-going to embarrass me?"

Finally, at long last, I understood what Asuna was doing.

When I'd told her that I wanted to spend the night together, she'd interpreted it beyond the literal meaning.

The instant I realized what was happening, my mind fell into a deep panic. I'd just made the biggest mistake of my life.

"Ah! No, that's not what I— I didn't mean it like— I only meant that I w-wanted to sleep in the same room...that's...all..."

"Wha...?"

I spilled my train of thought in an embarrassingly straightforward manner, and now it was Asuna's turn to be blank-faced. Soon enough, it turned into a mixture of absolute shame and rage.

"Why...you..."

I could see the lethal intent she fused into her clenched fist.

"Idiot!!"

Asuna's punch burst forward at my face with the full assistance of her agility stat, but just before it could connect, the system's anti-crime code kicked in, sending deafening echoes and purple sparks around the room.

"Aaah! I'm sorry, I'm sorry, forget that last part!"

I waved my arms desperately and tried to explain before Asuna could ready another blow.

"I'm sorry! It was my fault! I-I mean, besides...can you even do...that? In SAO...?"

She finally dropped out of her fighting stance, but the look of burning rage and exasperation on her face did not change.

"Y-you didn't know?"

"I didn't know..."

She proceeded in a small voice, her face suddenly shifting from anger to embarrassment.

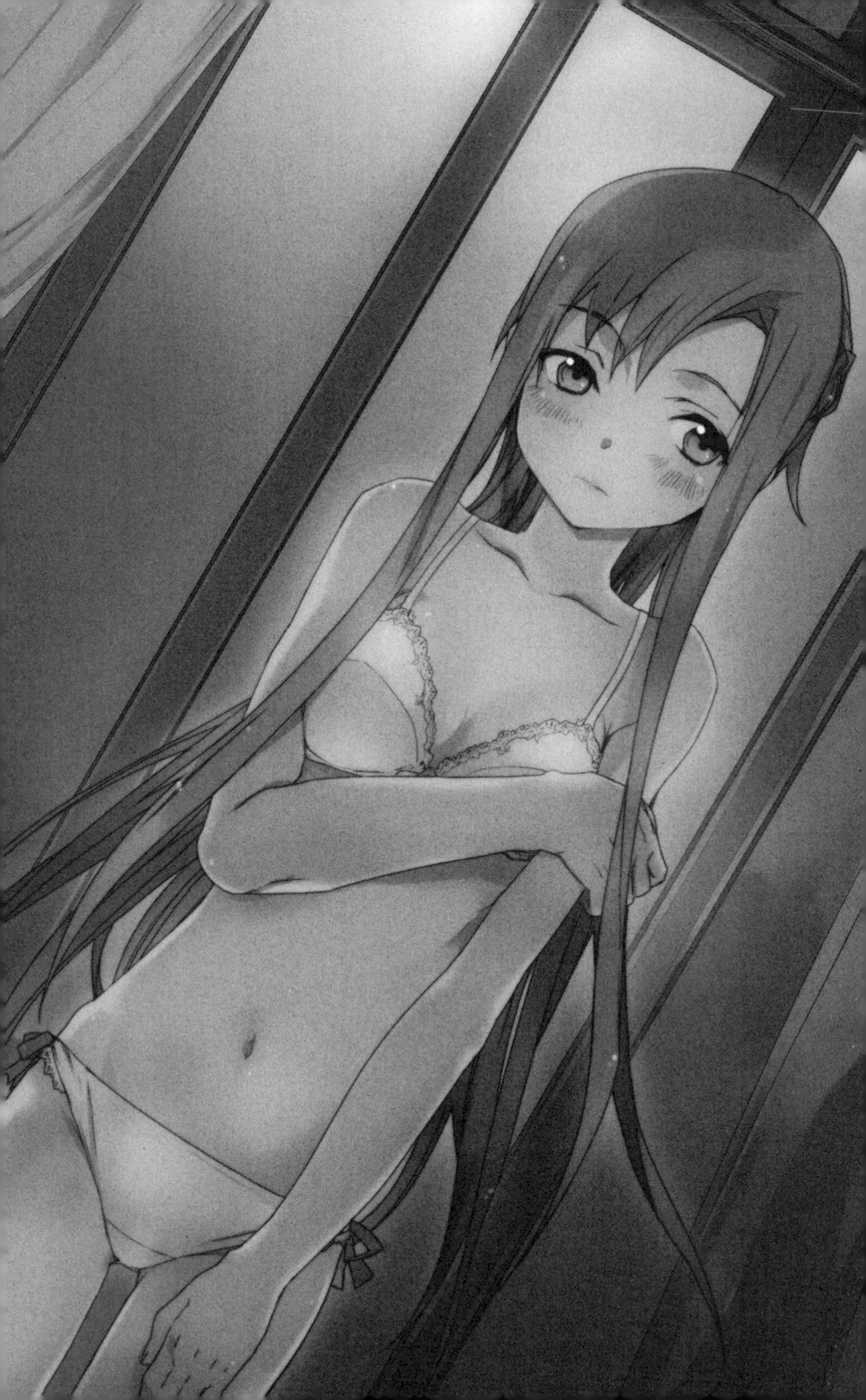

"...If you...dig deep in the options...there's a 'Moral Code Removal' setting."

I had no idea. There certainly wasn't anything like that in the beta, nor in the manual. This was a very unexpected way to pay the price for not caring about anything but fighting while I was in SAO.

But this revelation led to another suspicion. Before my better sense could intervene, I spoke it out loud.

"Does that mean...you've done this befo—"

Her fist exploded in my face again.

"O-of course I haven't! I found out about it from someone in the guild!"

I hastily prostrated myself and apologized over and over. It took several minutes to defuse the situation.

A single tiny candle placed on the table was the only thing that lit Asuna as she lay in my arms. I traced the pale skin of her back with a finger. Just that warm, smooth sensation coming through my fingertips was pure intoxication.

Asuna's eyes opened slightly, batted several times, and she smiled at me.

"Sorry, did I wake you?"

"Mm...I was dreaming. Of the old world...It's weird."

She rested her face against my chest, still smiling.

"In my dream, I got so worried. I was afraid that everything about Aincrad, and the fact that I met you here, was a dream of its own. I'm glad it didn't turn out to be that way."

"That's weird. Don't you want to leave?"

"I do, I do. But I don't want to lose the time I've spent here. We've come a really long way...but these two years are very important to me. I realize that now."

She looked serious for a moment, then took my hand off her shoulder and held it to her chest.

"I'm sorry, Kirito...It should have been me who finished that fight."

I sucked in a quick breath, then let it out slowly.

"No...Kuradeel went after me, and I was the one who drove him to do what he did. That was my battle."

I stared into Asuna's eyes and gave a slow nod.

Her hazel eyes were faintly brimming with tears. She raised my hand to her lips. I could feel their gentle touch.

"I'll be there to help bear what you bear. We'll carry it together. I promise. No matter what happens, I'll be there to protect you."

Those were the words.

The words that I'd never been able to utter up to this point. And now, my lips trembling, the words came tumbling out of my throat—out of my soul.

"...And I..."

The faint sounds barely pushed the air.

"...will be there to protect you."

It was so tiny, so doubtful, so unconvincing. I couldn't help but grimace, and then I squeezed her hand back.

"You're strong, Asuna. Much stronger than me..."

She blinked at this, then smiled.

"That's not true. In the other world, I was always the type to hide behind someone else. I didn't even buy this game for myself."

She giggled, remembering something.

"My brother bought it and had to go on a work trip, so I got to try it out on the very first day. It was so hard for him to leave without it, and now I've been hogging it for two years. I bet he's so angry."

It seemed to me like she'd gotten the worse side of that deal, but I nodded in agreement.

"You need to get back and say you're sorry."

"Yeah...I've got my work cut out for me."

But those brave words came mumbled, and she looked away nervously. Asuna squeezed her entire body against me.

"Hey...Kirito. I realize this contradicts what I just said, but... do you think maybe we should leave the front lines for a bit?"

"Huh...?"

"I'm just scared…We've finally connected in this powerful way, and I can't help but feel like going back into battle will lead to some terrible thing happening…Maybe I'm just tired of this."

I brushed her hair with my fingers and was surprised to find myself agreeing with her.

"Good point…I'm tired, too."

You didn't need dwindling stat numbers to notice that day after day of stressful combat took its toll. Especially when it involved extreme shock like today. Even the strongest bowstring will snap if you keep pulling on it. A little rest was necessary sometimes.

I could feel the impulse that drove me to battle, something that felt a bit like peril, drifting further away. All I wanted to do right now was be with this girl, to grow closer together.

I put both arms around her and buried my face in her silken hair.

"There's a nice place down in the southwest region of floor twenty-two. Lots of forests and lakes, no monsters. There's a tranquil little village there. Couple of log cabins available to buy. Let's move down there. And then…"

When I paused to find the right words, Asuna turned her sparkling eyes to me.

"And then…?"

I forced my stubborn tongue to continue.

"L…let's get married."

I'll never forget the smile she gave me then.

"…Okay."

One large tear rolled down her cheek as she nodded.

17

There are four kinds of system-defined player relationships within Sword Art Online.

First, complete strangers. Second is "friends." Friends registered on the friend list are able to send simple text messages to each other, as well as search for their locations on the map.

The third category is guild members. In addition to the previous functions, teaming up with guildmates in battle gives each member a slight experience bonus. The downside of that is that a certain percentage of all col earned must be subtracted for the guild's coffers.

Asuna and I already met the friend and guildmate criteria, but by temporarily leaving the guild, we filled its place with the fourth and final category.

That was marriage—though it's a far simpler and less ceremonial step than you might think. One person sends a proposal message to the other, and if it is accepted, boom: You're married. The consequences, however, are far greater than a simple friend or guild request.

At the most basic level, marriage in SAO means the sharing of all information and items. You can observe your spouse's status screen at any time, and all items are pooled into a shared inventory. It exposes one's most potent vulnerabilities to another person, which means that in Aincrad, where betrayal and deception are rife, very few couples reach marriage. The abysmal gender ratio doesn't help, either.

The twenty-second floor of Aincrad was one of the most sparsely populated in the castle. As it was closer to the bottom of the egg-like structure, it had a wide area, but the majority of it was covered with thick forests and countless lakes. The largest form of civilization to be found was a tiny village. There were no monsters in the wilderness, and the labyrinth was easy, so the entire floor had been cleared in just three days, and few players bothered to remember it.

Asuna and I bought a little log cabin in the middle of the forest and settled in. Even a small house in SAO was no simple matter to purchase, however. Asuna offered to sell her apartment in Selmburg, but I strongly objected—it would have been an incredible waste to get rid of such a perfect place—so we raised the funds by selling off all of our rare valuables with Agil's help.

Agil looked disappointed that we were leaving. He offered us the use of his upstairs at any time, but a general store was a rather unromantic place for a honeymoon. Plus, just the thought of the uproar that would ensue if word got out that a celebrity like Asuna was married gave me the chills. A lonely place like the twenty-second floor would buy us plenty of time to relax in peace.

"Ooh, the view is nice!"

Asuna leaned out of the south-facing window in the bedroom—for what it was worth, the cabin only had two rooms.

She was right about the view. Because we were close to the outer perimeter, we had an expansive slice of the sky hanging over the leafy trees and sparkling lakes. Given that most of the time, life in Aincrad meant having a lid of stone looming a few hundred feet above your head, the sense of liberation that came with being so close to the sky was breathtaking.

"Just because we have a nice view doesn't mean you should get too close to the edge and fall over."

I stopped sorting our household items for a moment and put my arms around Asuna from behind. The thought that she was now my wife filled me with the warmth of the winter sun, as well as an unfamiliar sensation much like surprise—the knowledge that I'd come so far in my time here.

Until I became a prisoner of this world, I was a mere child, living a circular route of home and school with no great ambitions. But the real world was a long-lost relic of the distant past now.

Beating this game and getting back to the real world should be my goal, Asuna's goal, *every* player's goal...but the thought of it actually happening made me worry. I clenched Asuna tighter.

"That hurts, Kirito...What's wrong?"

"S-sorry. Hey, Asuna..."

I clammed up for a moment, but I had to ask.

"Is this...just inside the game? Us, I mean...Is it something that's going to vanish when we return to the real world?"

"Are you trying to get me angry?" She spun around, pure emotion burning in her eyes. "Even if this were a normal game and we weren't stuck inside it, I don't fall in love for fun."

She squished my face in her hands.

"There's one thing I've learned here: Never give up until the end. If we get back to the real world, I'll find you again, and I'll fall in love with you again."

How many times had I been amazed at Asuna's strength? Or was it just a sign of how weak I was in comparison? In any case, I'd forgotten how good it could feel to rely on someone else, to let them be your support. I didn't know how long we'd be here, but hopefully, as long as we were away from battle...

I let my mind wander, my arms full of gentle warmth and a sweet scent.

18

The float sitting on the surface of the lake didn't even twitch. The more I watched the gentle light reflect off the still surface, the sleepier I felt.

I yawned wide and pulled in the rod. The only thing at the end of the line was a sad silver hook. No sign of the bait that I'd placed on it.

We'd been living on the twenty-second floor for ten days. I'd removed my Two-Handed Sword skill from its slot—I hadn't touched it since a long-past period of experimentation—and set Fishing in its place to catch our food. So much for being an angler and living off the land: I'd barely caught a thing. My proficiency was more than 600, so while I wouldn't be catching any whopping tuna, you'd figure *something* would bite. Instead, I watched the pail of bait I'd bought at the village slowly run empty.

"This is a waste of time," I muttered, tossing the rod aside and rolling over. The breeze off the lake was chilly, but the thick overcoat Asuna knitted me with her Tailoring skill was nice and warm. She was working on her skill just as I was, so it wasn't up to store-bought quality, but it got the job done.

It was the Month of Cypress in Aincrad, November in the real world. Winter was close at hand, but the season shouldn't have an effect on fishing here. I supposed that I'd used up all my luck snagging my lovely wife.

I rolled over, unable to hide the shameless grin this train of thought produced, when I suddenly heard a voice from overhead.

"Are they biting?"

I lurched upward with a start to see a man standing over me.

He was wearing a heavy coat and a cap with earflaps, and he carried a fishing rod, just like me. The real surprise was the man's age. He had to be in his fifties, at least. The lines of old age were carved into the face behind the wire-rim glasses. It was extremely rare to find such an elderly person in the midst of a game populated by hardcore players. In fact, I'd never seen anyone as old as him. Unless...

"I'm not an NPC," he said, reading my mind. He made his way down the embankment.

"I-I'm sorry, I was just really surprised..."

"No, I don't blame you. I've got to be the oldest person in this thing, by a long shot."

He laughed heartily, his solid body shaking. The man sat down next to me and pulled a bait box out of his waistpouch, fumbled with the pop-up menu, and attached the bait to his rod.

"Name's Nishida. I'm a fisherman here. Before this, I was head of network security for a company called Tohto Broadband. Sorry I can't give you my card."

He laughed again.

"Ahh..."

I had a feeling I knew why he was here. Tohto Broadband was a network management company partnered with Argus. They were responsible for the network lines leading to SAO's servers.

"My name's Kirito. I just moved down here from up above. Mr. Nishida, are you...involved in maintaining SAO's connections...?"

"I was the man in charge of that, yes." He nodded. I felt conflicted about this. He must have gotten trapped in this world just by doing his job.

"The bosses told me I didn't actually have to log in, but I'm the type who can't be satisfied unless I see my work with my own two eyes. Well, I sure paid a price for that one."

He laughed again and cast his rod with magnificent expertise. This was a man who knew how to fish. Apparently he liked to talk, as he continued without waiting for a response.

"I believe there's about twenty or thirty other older fellas like me who got caught in something they shouldn't have. Most of them are biding their time down in that first town, but I just can't keep myself from a good day of fishing."

He tugged on the rod.

"I've been on the search for good rivers and lakes, and that's what brought me all the way up here."

"I see...And there are no monsters on this floor."

Nishida simply grinned at that statement.

"What's the word? Are there any good spots up higher?"

"Hmm...the sixty-first floor is all lake—more like a sea, really—so I imagine there are big fish to catch there."

"Aha! I'll have to pay it a visit."

Suddenly, his line jolted downward. Without missing a beat, Nishida tugged the rod up. Not only was he probably an adept fisherman in real life, but his Fishing skill was likely through the roof.

"Whoa, it's a big 'un!"

I leaped to my feet in a hurry, but Nishida calmly spun his rod and yanked a large, sparkling blue fish out of the water. It flopped around at his feet, then disappeared as it was automatically transferred to his inventory.

"Nicely done!"

Nishida smiled shyly.

"Nah, it's all just a numbers game here," he said, scratching his head. "The problem is, I can catch 'em, but not cook 'em. I'd love to have some good sashimi, but there's no point without any soy sauce."

"Ahh...well..."

I hesitated. We'd moved down here to avoid attention, but I had a feeling this fellow was not interested in gossip.

"I feel like...I might have something that'll get the job done..."

"You don't say!"

Nishida's eyes flashed behind the lenses as he leaned forward.

Asuna was initially alarmed when I came home with a guest, but she soon recovered and gave him a smile.

"Welcome home. Who is this?"

"Ah, this is Mr. Nishida, a fisherman. And..."

I turned to Nishida, unsure of how to introduce Asuna. She stepped right in and gave the elderly man another smile.

"I'm Asuna, Kirito's wife. Welcome to our home." She gave him a crisp bow.

Nishida's mouth dropped as he stared at her. She was wearing a plain skirt, hemp shirt, an apron, and a scarf—a far cry from her gallant KoB uniform, but beautiful all the same.

He snapped back to his senses after several blinks.

"Oh, pardon me, I got lost for a moment there. My name is Nishida, and your hospitality is appreciated..."

He laughed and scratched his head.

Asuna easily transformed Nishida's catch into dishes of sashimi and simmered fish. The scent of her fragrant soy sauce filled the room, and Nishida's nostrils flared widely as he sucked in the air.

It tasted less like freshwater fish than a fatty, seasonal yellowtail. According to Nishida, this type of fish required a skill of more than 950 to catch, and we forewent conversation for a few minutes, choosing to savor the meal instead.

Eventually all the dishes were picked clean, and Nishida gave a deep sigh of satisfaction, cup of hot tea in hand.

"Ahh...I needed that. Thank you for the meal. Never thought I'd see soy sauce in this place..."

"Oh, it's homemade. Please, take some."

Asuna brought a small bottle out of the kitchen and handed it to Nishida. She wisely did not mention the ingredients. She smiled and thanked him in return for the fish.

"Kirito's hardly brought me anything from the lake."

I sipped my tea unhappily, the conversation's whipping boy. "The lakes around here are too hard to fish in."

"Oh, I disagree. The only really tough spot is the big one, the one you were trying this afternoon."

"Wha..."

Nishida had stunned me into silence. Asuna grabbed her stomach, chuckling softly.

"Why would they have programmed it that way...?"

"Well, the thing about that lake is," Nishida whispered conspiratorially. We leaned closer. "That's where you'll find the Big One."

"Big One?" we repeated simultaneously. Nishida pushed his glasses up and flashed us a confident grin.

"At the tool shop in town, there's one type of bait that costs head and shoulders above the rest. I was curious, so I had the idea to try it out for myself."

I swallowed.

"But I couldn't catch a thing with it. Tried it out all over the place, then it occurred to me that it was probably for the one lake tougher than all the others."

"And...did you catch something?"

"I got a bite." He nodded, then looked disappointed. "But I couldn't haul it in. Took my rod with him. I caught a glimpse of it, and it was bigger than big. No doubt about it; that thing is a monster in its own right."

He extended his arms to indicate its size. Now I understood why Nishida had simply grinned at me when I told him there were no monsters on this floor.

"Wow, I want to see it!" Asuna said, her eyes sparkling. Nishida turned to give me an inquisitive look.

"You confident in your Strength stat, Kirito...?"

"Uh, well, confident enough..."

"Then why not join me? I'll do everything to get a bite, and you can handle the heavy lifting."

"Ahh, you want to use the switch tactic with the fishing rod? Is that even possible...?" I wondered.

"Let's do it, Kirito! This sounds fun!" Asuna bubbled, excitement in her eyes. She was always ready to try something new. I couldn't deny that my curiosity was piqued as well.

"...Shall we?" I asked. Nishida beamed widely and laughed.

"That's the spirit!"

That night, Asuna wriggled into my bed, complaining about the cold. Once we were fully nestled together, she finally gave a contented sigh. My wife blinked her eyes sleepily, then smiled, remembering something.

"...I guess there really are all types here..."

"He was a jolly guy, wasn't he?"

"Yeah."

We giggled for a few moments, then stifled it.

"I've been fighting up above for so long, I completely forgot that there are still people trying to lead normal lives," I muttered.

"I'm not saying that we're special or anything, but I think being a high-enough level to fight on the frontier means that we have a responsibility to them."

"I've never thought of it that way...I always prioritized getting stronger for my own personal survival, nothing more."

"I think there are plenty of people putting their hope in you, Kirito. Including me."

"Hearing that just makes me want to run away."

"Oh, jeez."

I brushed her hair as she pouted, and inwardly prayed that this life would continue just a bit longer. Sooner or later, we'd have to return to the front line, for the sake of Nishida and all the other players. But just for now...

Agil and Klein had sent messages warning us of the difficulties in clearing the seventy-fifth floor. But in all honesty, my life here with Asuna was the most important thing to me.

19

Three days later, Nishida sent me a morning notice that he was ready to catch the Big One. Apparently he went around to rally up all of his fishing buddies, and we'd have an audience of about thirty for the attempt.

"Yikes. What do you want to do, Asuna...?"

"Hmm..."

Frankly speaking, his arrangement wasn't exactly welcome. I'd chosen this place specifically to avoid intel dealers and Asuna's crazed fans, so appearing in front of a small crowd was the last thing I wanted.

"How about this?"

She tied up her long chestnut hair and wrapped her long scarf up high around her face. After a bit of menu manipulation, she was covered in a big, frumpy overcoat as well.

"Ooh, nice. You look like a tired old farmer's wife."

"...Was that meant to be a compliment?"

"Of course. I'll probably be fine as long as I don't bring my equipment."

Asuna and I left the house before lunch, lugging a picnic basket. We could have just left the stuff in our inventory and materialized it when we got there, but this seemed to make for a better disguise.

It was a warm day for the season. After a lengthy walk through the towering pine trees of the forest, the glistening lake surface could be seen through the branches. There was already a crowd at the shore. As I approached, feeling nervous, I soon recognized the squat figure and distinctive laugh of one of the men.

"Wa-ha-ha! Nice, clear day!"

"Nice to see you, Mr. Nishida."

Asuna and I bowed. The crowd, a gathering with a wide range of ages, was Nishida's fishing guild. We hesitantly greeted the group, but fortunately no one seemed to recognize Asuna.

What surprised me was how proactive the old man was; he must have been an excellent boss. They'd apparently been doing an impromptu fishing competition before we got there, and the group was in an excited mood.

"Well then, I think it's time for today's main event!" Nishida announced in a loud voice, a long fishing pole in one hand. I gazed at the large rod and its thick line, following it until I realized, with a start, what was hanging on the end.

It was a lizard. An extremely large one, about the size of an adult's forearm. Venomous-looking red and black patterns crossed its hide, and its wet surface suggested freshness.

"*Eugh…*"

Asuna was late to notice the creature and stumbled back several steps, a grimace on her face. If this was the bait, there could be only one thing to catch.

But before I could even interject a comment, Nishida turned to the lake and held the fishing rod high. He swung it forward with an audible *whoosh*, his form impeccable, and the lizard flew through the air to land out in the lake with an admirable splash.

Fishing in SAO involved virtually no waiting. Once you'd cast your line into the water, it was only a number of seconds until you either had a bite or the bait was lost. We held our breaths and watched the water.

Eventually the line twitched a few times. Nishida didn't budge an inch.

"I-I think it's coming, Mr. Nishida!"

"Nope, not yet!"

The normally pleasant old man was staring intensely at the line, his eyes burning behind the glasses. He took in every minute vibration at the end of his rod.

The end suddenly bowed much harder.

"Now!"

Nishida bent backward sharply, pulling the rod with his entire body. Even from the side, it was clear the line was absolutely taut, a loud *twang* for all to hear.

"I've got a bite! It's all up to you now!"

He handed me the rod, and I gave it a hesitant yank. It didn't budge. I might as well have been pulling on solid ground. Just as I began wondering if this was an actual bite and turned to look at Nishida—

The line tugged downward with incredible force.

"Whoa!"

I dug both feet in hurriedly and pulled the rod back up. The physical force feedback the game ordinarily used was far weaker than what I was feeling now.

"I-is it safe to pull with all I've got?" I asked Nishida, concerned for the durability of the rod and line.

"They're the finest you can buy! Let 'er rip!"

His face was red with excitement. I re-gripped the handle and pulled with all my strength. The rod contorted into an upside-down *U* shape.

After a level-up, players are given the choice to spend their points on either strength or agility. An ax warrior like Agil might choose strength every time, while Asuna would get better use out of her rapier with more agility. I split my points down the middle as an orthodox swordsman, but when it came to personal preference, I leaned on the side of agility.

Despite the lack of focus on strength, my level was apparently high enough to give me the advantage in this particular test. I dug my feet in and slowly backed up, steadily pulling the unseen quarry closer and closer to the surface.

"Oh! I saw it!"

Asuna jumped up and pointed over the water. I was well clear of the shoreline and leaning backward, so I was in no position to take a closer look. The other onlookers murmured and rushed to the water's edge, peering down into the water, which grew exponentially deeper away from the shore. I finally gave in to my curiosity and summoned all my strength to yank the rod upward.

"...?"

Suddenly, all the figures crowding around the water in front of me flinched. They all began to back up.

"What does it look li—"

Before I could finish, they all turned around and ran, full speed. Asuna passed me on the left, Nishida on the right, their faces pale. When I turned back to call to them, the weight suddenly lifted from my hands, and I fell backward onto my rear end.

Damn, the line snapped, I thought. I tossed the pole aside and leaped to my feet to run to the water. The next moment, I saw the surface of the lake bulging upward, an enormous silver circle.

"Wha—?"

I stood there, eyes and mouth gaping, until I heard Asuna's voice calling out from a distance.

"Kirito, watch ouuut!"

I turned and saw that Asuna, Nishida, and all the others had retreated to the bank above the shore a considerable length away. I heard an enormous splash behind me and finally realized the gravity of the situation. An unpleasant foreboding itching at my skin, I turned around to the water again.

The fish was standing.

To be more accurate, the creature appeared to be more like a reptilian coelacanth, somewhere on the evolutionary link between fish and crocodile. Little waterfalls spilled over its scales, and six massive legs crushed the grass on the shoreline as it peered down at me.

Peered down. The full height of the thing was well over six feet.

Its mouth was located just taller than my head, and it seemed made for swallowing cows whole. A familiar lizard leg poked out of the corner.

There was a basketball-size eye on either side of the ancient fish's head, and they looked into mine. A yellow cursor automatically appeared over the beast.

Nishida had said that the Big One in this lake was a monster "in its own right."

There were no rights about it—this *was* a monster, through and through.

I took several steps backward, my smile twitching. Then I spun around and took off like a rabbit. The beast let out an earthshaking roar, then barreled after me. I was practically flying through the air, every last point of my agility in use, and in a few seconds I had reached the others and was ready to argue.

"Th-th-that's not fair! You can't run off without me!"

"I don't think this is the right time for the blame game, Kirito!"

I turned back to see the giant fish charging after us, its movement clumsy but fast enough.

"It's running over the land…Does it have lungs?"

"Kirito, this is no time for idle contemplation! We gotta scram!"

Now Nishida was the one yelping in panic. Most of the crowd had frozen stock-still, several of them collapsed on the ground.

"Do you have your weapons?" Asuna asked close to my ear. She had a point—it would be incredibly difficult to lead all these people to safety.

"Sorry, I don't…"

"Oh, fine, then."

Asuna shook her head, then turned to the giant legged fish, which was nearly upon us. She opened her window with familiar ease.

As Nishida and the other fishermen watched helplessly, Asuna ripped off her thick scarf and overcoat, her glimmering chestnut hair rippling in the breeze. Underneath the coat were a long green skirt and a plain hemp shirt, but her silver rapier sheath sparkled in the sun. Asuna drew her sword, proudly facing the oncoming monster.

Next to me, Nishida finally realized what she was planning to do, and he grabbed my arm.

"Kirito! Your wife is in terrible danger!"

"It's fine; let her handle this."

"Have you lost your senses? If you won't help her, I will."

He snatched a fishing rod from one of his friends and was preparing to rush to her aid when I hurriedly stepped in to stop the elderly man.

The giant fish maintained its speed and opened its gaping mouth to reveal countless fangs. As it bore down on Asuna, she turned to her side and thrust with her right hand like a fencer.

The inside of the giant fish's mouth flashed with an explosive shock wave. The monster flew high up into the air, but Asuna's feet had barely budged.

The sight of the monster itself was certainly intimidating, but my expectation was that its actual level was not very high. They wouldn't place a truly deadly monster down on such a low floor, and as part of an event dependent solely on your Fishing skill, no less. If nothing else, SAO maintained a proper difficulty curve.

Asuna's single blow had devastated the fish monster's HP bar. When it fell to earth with a deafening crash, she followed up with a speedy combination that lived up to her moniker.

Nishida and the other fishermen could only stare in amazement as Asuna unleashed attack after deadly attack, her footwork almost a dance. But were they impressed by her strength or her beauty? Probably both.

Asuna continued to dazzle the onlookers with her utter power until she noticed the creature's HP bar was in the red. Now she leaped gracefully backward and darted as she landed. She plunged directly into the creature, her entire body blazing like a comet—the top-level rapier skill, Flashing Penetrator.

The comet burst through the fish from mouth to tail with a

sonic boom, and as Asuna finally came to a stop well past the end of the monster, it separated into a mass of glowing pieces. A split second later, an ear-wrenching explosion sent waves across the lake.

Asuna returned the rapier to its sheath with a *ting*, then began walking back toward us. Nishida and company were still frozen, mouths agape.

"Hey, nice job."

"It's no fair leaving the heavy work up to me. You owe me a nice dinner or something."

"Uh, we share funds now, remember?"

"Oh...right."

We continued teasing each other until Nishida finally regained his senses, blinking rapidly.

"Well...that was a surprise...Your wife is, ah, quite powerful. Do you mind if I ask her level...?"

Asuna and I faced each other. This conversation could lead down a dangerous path.

"F-forget about that. Look, we got an item from the fish!"

Asuna manipulated the window, and a shining silver fishing rod appeared. Given that it came from a unique boss monster, it was bound to be a rare prize not available for purchase elsewhere.

"Oh? What's this?"

Nishida took it, his eyes sparkling. All the others around him murmured in amazement. Just when I thought we might have distracted them...

"A-are you...Miss Asuna from the Knights of the Blood?"

A younger fellow came forward a few steps and stared closely at Asuna. Recognition flooded his features.

"Yes, I knew it! I've got a picture of you!"

"Uh..."

Asuna gave him an uncomfortable smile and backed away. Now the murmuring in the crowd doubled in volume.

"This is fantastic! I never thought I'd get to see you fight in person...C-can I have an autogra—"

He stopped suddenly, looking back and forth between Asuna and me. Then he murmured, his face stoic, "Y-you're…married…"

Now it was my turn to give him a stiff smile. We stood there awkwardly while the man gave a wail of grief. Nishida simply blinked uncomprehendingly.

That was how, after two weeks of blissful peace, our secret honeymoon ended. I suppose that ultimately, I should consider myself lucky to have participated in such a silly event.

That night, a message arrived from Heathcliff, calling members to a planning meeting for the boss monster of the seventy-fifth floor.

Next morning, I sat slumped over on the side of the bed as Asuna, already dressed, clicked her boots on the floor and chided me.

"C'mon, no moping around!"

"But it's only been two weeks," I groaned childishly. Despite my foul mood, I couldn't deny that Asuna looked very smart in her familiar white-and-red knight's uniform again.

Given the circumstances that led to our leave of absence from the guild, we certainly could have refused the summons. But the line at the end of the message—which said, *We have already suffered casualties*—weighed heavily on our consciences.

"I think we should at least hear him out. C'mon, it's time!"

She patted my back, and I finally got to my feet and opened my equipment screen. Since I was on temporary leave from the guild, I put on my familiar old black leather coat and minimal armor, topping it off with my two swords crossed over my back. The fresh and unfamiliar weight seemed like my punishment for leaving them to rot in my inventory for so long. I drew them out of their scabbards and slid them back to make them feel better. The sound was crisp in the cozy room.

"I always thought you looked better like that."

Asuna hopped to grab my arm, grinning. I craned my neck around to gaze a silent farewell at our new house.

"...Let's get this over with and come back home."

"Yeah!"

We nodded to each other, opened the door, and stepped out into the cold morning air, heavy with hints of winter.

The familiar sight of Nishida and his fishing rod greeted us at the twenty-second-floor teleport-gate square. We'd told him when we were leaving, but no one else.

He'd said he wanted to talk, so the three of us sat down on a bench to the side of the square. Nishida gazed up at the bottom of the floor above as he began to speak.

"I'll be honest... I've been keepin' everyone who's on the upper floors, fighting to beat this game, out of sight and out of mind. It might as well have been happenin' in a different world altogether. Perhaps I gave up on ever getting out of here."

We listened in silence.

"As you know, in the electronics business, things evolve a mile a minute. I've been a tinkerer since I was just a boy, so I managed to keep up until now, but two years away from the business is too long. If getting home means I'll just be a useless bump on a log feelin' sorry for myself, maybe I'm better off staying here and enjoying a good fish, I figured..."

He trailed off, a small smile on his lined face. I didn't know what to say to him. There was no way I could imagine what a man in his position had lost, being trapped in Sword Art Online.

"Me, too," Asuna mumbled. "I thought the same thing until about six months ago. I cried myself to sleep every night. Every day, my family, my friends, my school, my entire reality seemed to break down a little bit more. I felt like I was going crazy. When I slept, all my dreams were of the real world... I did nothing but work on my skills, trying to beat the game as quickly as I possibly could."

Surprised, I turned to look at her. I would never have guessed that based on my first meeting with her. Of course, I was never known for being particularly observant of others...

Asuna shot a glance at me, then smiled.

"But one day about half a year ago, I teleported to the front line to tackle the latest labyrinth, and I saw someone napping on the grass in the square. He seemed to be pretty high-level, which made me angry. I told him, 'If you're just going to waste your time around here, could you please assist us in clearing the labyrinth instead?'"

She put a hand to her mouth and giggled.

"So he says, 'This is the day with the best weather settings in the best season of Aincrad. It'd be a waste to spend it in a dungeon.' Then he points to the grass next to him and says, 'C'mon, relax a little.' I mean, how rude can you get?"

She stifled another giggle, then looked to the horizon.

"But that brought me to my senses. This guy is just living his life here, I thought. He isn't losing another day in the real world; he's gaining another day in this world. I never realized anyone saw it that way. So I sent my guildmates ahead, and I lay down in the grass next to him. The next thing I knew, the breeze was so nice, and the air so warm and comfortable, I dozed right off. No bad dreams—it was probably the deepest sleep I'd had since coming here. When I woke up, it was evening, but he was still there with me, looking exasperated. That was him."

Asuna squeezed my hand. Though I didn't say it, I was incredibly confused. It sounded like a familiar enough story, but…

"…Sorry, Asuna, I don't think I meant it to be that profound. I think I just wanted to take a nap."

"I realize that! You don't have to spell it out."

She pouted for a moment, then turned back to Nishida, who was smiling as he listened to us.

"Ever since that day, I would think about him as I got into bed. And I stopped having the nightmares. I figured out where he lived, and I'd tried to make time when I could go see him… Eventually, I began looking forward to each new morning. When I realized I was in love with him, I was filled with such joy. I wanted to treasure that feeling. For the first time, I felt glad that I was here…"

Asuna looked down, rubbed her eyes with her white gloves, then took a deep breath.

"To me, Kirito is the reason that I've spent two years here, the proof that I've lived, and the hope for tomorrow. I put on the NerveGear that day just to find him. Mr. Nishida, it might not be my place to say this, but I think you must have found something here as well. This might be a virtual world, where everything we see is just artificial data, but our hearts are real. Which means that everything we've experienced and gained here is real, too."

Nishida blinked and nodded his head vigorously. I could see his eyes flashing behind his glasses. I had to blink the heat out of my eyes, myself.

It was me. I was the one who was saved. There was no meaning to my life, whether in the real world or trapped in this world, until I met her.

"Indeed…indeed," Nishida murmured, looking up at the sky. "Just listening to your story was a valuable experience for me, Asuna. Same goes for catching the Big One back there. It's not worth giving up on life. It's not worth it."

He gave one big nod and stood.

"Well, I've taken enough of your time. You've taught me what I needed to know—that as long as folks like you are fighting above, it's only a matter of time until we make it back to the real world. I can't do anything for you, but…give it everything you've got. Everything."

He clasped my hand and shook it vigorously.

"We'll be back. You'll visit us, won't you?"

I made a fishing motion and he gave a big nod, his face crinkling. We shook hands once again, then headed for the teleport gate. Asuna and I walked into the shimmering heat mirage, faced each other, and spoke together.

"Teleport: Grandzam!"

The blue light expanded and eventually blotted out Nishida, eternally waving.

20

"The recon squad was wiped out?!"

The news that awaited us upon our return to the Knights of the Blood HQ in Grandzam was shocking.

We were in the glass-encased meeting room near the top of the iron tower, the place I'd met Heathcliff before our duel. Heathcliff sat at the center of the semicircular table, sage-like in his robe, while his guild officers sat on either side. This time, Godfrey was nowhere to be seen.

Heathcliff steepled his bony hands in front of his face, deep furrows etched into his brow. "It happened yesterday. We succeeded in mapping the entire seventy-fifth-floor labyrinth without suffering any damage, though it took quite some time. We were expecting a significant challenge with the boss battle, however..."

I could imagine that. Out of all the floors we'd conquered, the twenty-fifth and fiftieth featured bosses that were easily more dangerous than what had come before or after. In both cases, we suffered major losses beating them.

On the twenty-fifth floor, the two-headed giant monster wiped out the Army's best and brightest, one of the biggest factors in their shift away from pushing the front line. On the fiftieth floor, the many-armed metal statue boss's onslaught was so fierce, many of the fighters teleported out to safety, devastating the strength of the remaining forces. If the backup squad had been any later to arrive, we'd likely all have been wiped out. It was the man in front of me who kept our flagging front line upright.

If all the quarter-points of the game featured such a powerful boss, we were bound to be facing a nightmare.

"So we sent a twenty-man reconnaissance team from five guilds in," Heathcliff continued, his voice flat. I couldn't read the expression from his half-closed brass eyes.

"They took every precaution. Ten stayed back at the entrance to the boss lair, and when the other ten reached the center of the room, right as the boss was about to appear, the door closed. What we know after that comes from the ten in the rear guard. The door stayed shut for five minutes; lock-picking skills and direct force had no effect. When it finally opened…"

Heathcliff's mouth tightened. He closed his eyes and continued.

"…There was nothing inside the room. The ten players and boss were gone. No signs of teleportation, no return…I had someone check the monument in Blackiron Palace, just to be sure…"

He shook his head rather than say the rest. Asuna sucked in a breath next to me, then let it out in a murmur.

"Ten…people…How did that happen?"

"Was it an anti-crystal zone?"

Heathcliff nodded at my question. "That is my only conclusion. Asuna had reported that the seventy-fourth floor's chamber was the same way. We should assume that all boss lairs will be similarly equipped from now on."

"This is crazy." I sighed. If emergency escape was impossible, the number of players likely to die of unforeseen accidents would skyrocket. The entire point of clearing the game was to prevent people from dying. But beating the bosses was a necessary step…

"It's really starting to live up to that 'game of death' billing…"

"But that doesn't mean we can simply abandon our attempts to conquer it."

Heathcliff closed his eyes and spoke softly but clearly.

"It would appear that this battle will make the use of crystals impossible, as well as remove the option of a simple retreat. That means we must bring as large a party as can be effectively controlled. I hope you understand that I did not wish to summon you from your honeymoon, but the circumstances require it."

I shrugged. "You'll have our help. But Asuna's safety is my very top priority. If the situation turns dangerous, I will put her well-being before the party's."

A slight smile played over Heathcliff's lips.

"Those who work to protect something are strong in spirit and fiber. I look forward to your valor. The operation begins in three hours. Our planned party is thirty-two strong, including you. We meet at the seventy-fifth-floor gate. Dismissed."

The red-clad paladin and his officers rose as one and left the room.

"Three hours. What should we do?" Asuna asked, resting on the side of the long metal table. I stared back at her, silent. Her slender limbs in that red-and-white battle outfit; her long, shining chestnut hair; her sparkling hazel eyes—she was a beautiful, priceless jewel.

I kept staring at her until finally her pale cheeks took on a shade of red.

"Wh-what is it?" She laughed shyly. I spoke hesitantly.

"...Asuna..."

"What?"

"Hear me out, and don't be mad. I don't want you... to participate in this boss battle. Will you wait here instead?"

She stared at me closely, then looked down sadly.

"Why would you say that...?"

"I know I gave Heathcliff my word, but you don't know what might happen in a place where crystals won't work. I'm scared. When I think about the possibility that something might happen to you..."

"So you're going to venture into danger like that and expect me to wait where it's safe?"

She stood up and briskly strode over to me, twin fires blazing within her eyes.

"If you don't come back from this, I'll kill myself. There won't be any reason for me to live any longer, and I'll hate myself for waiting around doing nothing. If you want to run, let's do it together. If you want to do it, Kirito, so do I."

She stopped, then jabbed a finger against my chest. Her eyes softened, and a slight smile appeared on her lips.

"But... I bet everyone taking part in this battle is scared. Everyone wishes they could run away. But they still got a few dozen to come. And I think it's because of the commander and you—the two strongest men in SAO—standing at the head of the party. I know it's not the kind of thing you're comfortable with. But I want you to do it for us, not for others. Let's do this together... so we can get back to the real world and meet again."

I reached up and held the finger Asuna was pointing at my chest. All I could feel was a terrified desire not to lose her.

"Sorry... I'm being a coward. My heart says it wants the two of us to run off together. I don't want you to die, and I don't want to die, either. I don't care..."

I stared into Asuna's eyes and continued.

"I don't care if we never get back to reality. I want to live with you in that little cottage. Forever... just the two of us..."

With her other hand, Asuna clutched something invisible to her heart. She closed her eyes, her brows knitted, as though bearing something excruciating. When she spoke, it was a painful whisper of longing.

"I know... It sounds like a dream... Wouldn't it be nice? Together every day... forever..."

But she stopped, then bit her lip, cutting off that frail hope. She opened her eyes and looked at me, her face serious.

"Kirito, have you ever thought... about what's happening to our real bodies?"

I was taken aback. It was something that every player wondered at times. But with no way to contact the real world, it was pointless to worry about. It hung over all of us like a vaguely looming cloud—we just chose not to stare it down.

"Do you remember when this whole game started? When he... When Akihiko Kayaba gave his little tutorial. He said the Nerve-Gear was designed to give you a two-hour window without power. The purpose being..."

"...to provide enough time for our bodies to be taken to a proper hospital."

She nodded at my answer.

"So after a few days, pretty much everyone experienced an hour-long period of disconnection."

I remembered that. I'd stared at the warning blaring in front of my eyes and wondered if my brain would be fried in just two hours' time.

"I think that was the point that every player was transferred to a hospital. I mean, few families can support a human being in a vegetative state at home for years at a time. I think we were taken to actual hospitals and then reconnected..."

"Yeah, you might be right."

"If our bodies are just lying in hospital beds, hooked up to various cables, forcing us to live...I can't imagine that can last forever."

I was suddenly hit with anxiety that my body was getting weaker and weaker. I hugged Asuna close, as though we could confirm our existence by simply touching.

"Meaning that whether we clear the game or not...there *is* a time limit that we'll all reach at some point..."

"Yes, and it'll be different for everyone... It's taboo to talk about your old life here, so I've never said this to anyone, but you're different. I want...to be with you for the rest of my life in the real world. I want to have a proper relationship, so we can really get married and grow old together. So...so..."

She couldn't finish. Asuna buried her face in my chest, sobbing uncontrollably. I rubbed her back slowly and finished her thought.

"So...we have to fight now."

The fear wasn't gone. But when Asuna was fighting against our fate, trying to keep herself together, I couldn't let fear cloud my judgment.

It's okay. It's going to be okay. If we fight together...

I squeezed Asuna harder, as though brushing away the chill I felt sneak into my chest.

21

The gate square in Collinia, the city on the seventy-fifth floor, was already full of high-level players who were likely in the raiding party. When Asuna and I stepped out of the gate and toward them, they all stopped talking and turned concerned gazes to us. Some of them even gave us the guild's special salute.

I stopped and hesitated, but Asuna returned the salute with familiarity. She jabbed me in the ribs.

"C'mon, Kirito. You're one of the leaders, so greet the team!"

"Wha…"

I gave an awkward salute. I'd taken part in several boss battle parties before, but this was the first time I'd attracted so much attention.

"Yo!"

I felt a pat on my shoulder and turned around to see Klein with his familiar katana and ugly bandanna. More surprising was the figure next to him: large, heavy Agil, ax at the ready.

"You guys are doing this, too?"

"Don't act so surprised!" Agil called out, aggrieved. "I heard this battle was supposed to be a tough one, so I nobly set my business aside to participate. If you can't appreciate my selfless gesture…"

He rattled on exaggeratedly. I patted Agil on the arm.

"Trust me, I know all about your self-sacrifice. It's why you elected not to take a share of the loot, right?"

This time, he placed a hand to his bald head and grimaced. "W-well, I don't know if I'd go *that* far," he whined. Klein and Asuna laughed together. The laughter spread to the other players, and suddenly the group's nerves had eased a bit.

At one o'clock on the dot, a number of new players emerged from the gate. Heathcliff was outfitted with his red cape and crucifix shield, joined by the other KoB elite. Upon their appearance, the tension returned to the rest of the group.

In terms of level alone, Heathcliff was probably the only one who outranked Asuna and me, but it was hard not to be impressed by the guild's sense of unity. Outside of the red-and-white colors, their equipment was varied, but the group aura they exuded was far stronger than the Army's.

The paladin and his four followers crossed through the group and walked toward us. Klein and Agil took several steps back, as though rebuffed by their personal force, but Asuna returned the salute coolly.

Heathcliff stopped and gave us a nod, then turned to address the entire gathering. "It seems we're all here. Thank you for coming. I believe you are all aware of the stakes. It will be a terrible battle, but I believe in your ability to emerge victorious. For the day of liberation!"

With a powerful cry, the entire group echoed his enthusiasm. His magnetic charisma left me speechless. Hard-core gamers typically trended toward the antisocial and uncooperative, so it was a surprise to see one display such leadership. Or was it this world that brought that quality out of him?

Heathcliff turned to me, as though sensing my gaze, and gave me a slight grin.

"I need your help today, Kirito. Put your Dual Blades to the test."

I didn't sense a hint of desperation or tension in his soft voice.

Only a man with nerves of steel could face the upcoming battle with such confidence.

I nodded silently. Heathcliff turned back to the group again and raised a hand.

"Let's get going. I'm opening a corridor to the spot right in front of the enemy's lair."

He pulled a dark blue crystal out of his waistpouch, and a murmur ran through the crowd. Normal teleport crystals transported the user to the floor of his or her choosing, but Heathcliff's corridor crystal was an exceedingly useful version that temporarily opened an entire teleport gate, offering access to the specified location to anyone who wanted to use it.

The downside to that utility was its rarity, and the crystal wasn't available to buy at NPC shops. It had to be found in labyrinth treasure chests or looted from powerful monsters, so few players even wanted to use them, if they were lucky enough to get their hands on one. In fact, the murmuring of the players was not so much excitement over the glimpse of such a rare item, but rather surprise that he'd actually use one.

Seemingly unaware of the stir he'd raised, Heathcliff raised the crystal high and called out, "Corridor open." The exceedingly valuable crystal crumbled instantly, and a flickering portal of blue light appeared before him.

"Follow me, everyone."

He turned to look over the group, then whirled his red cape and stepped into the light. For an instant he flashed blindingly, then disappeared. Seconds later, the four KoB members followed him.

Over time, the gathering in the square had grown to a considerable number. Perhaps they'd arrived to see us off, knowing that we were about to tackle a boss. Cheers of encouragement rose as the swordsmen trickled through the new teleport gate, one after the other.

Finally, only Asuna and I were left. We nodded to each other, held hands, then stepped into the vortex of light together.

*   *   *

Teleporting always left me a bit dizzy. When I was able to open my eyes, I was inside the labyrinth, in a wide hallway. Thick pillars lined the walls, and a giant door was visible at the end.

The seventy-fifth-floor labyrinth was made of a material like obsidian, but with a very faint hint of translucence. Unlike the rough-hewn nature of the lower-level labyrinths, the black stone here was polished like a mirror and placed at perfectly straight angles. The air was chilly and damp, and a faint mist trailed over the floor.

Next to me, Asuna wrapped her arms around herself, feeling the chill.

"...I don't like the look of this..."

"Nope."

I nodded.

In the two years leading up to today, we'd conquered seventy-four bosses. With that much experience, you learned to gauge the strength of the foes by the look of their lairs.

Around us, the thirty other players were bunched into groups of two or three, their windows open. They were checking their equipment and items, but they all looked tense.

I walked Asuna over to one of the pillars and put an arm around her frail body. I could feel my nerves working before the battle. My body trembled with anxiety.

"...It's going to be okay," Asuna whispered into my ear. "I'm going to watch over you."

"That's not what I'm—"

"Hee hee." She gave a little smile and continued. "And you can watch over me."

"Yeah...you bet."

I squeezed harder for an instant, then released my grip. In the middle of the corridor, Heathcliff let his armor clank loudly and spoke to the group.

"Is everyone ready? We have no information about this boss's attack patterns. The Knights of the Blood will take forward position to absorb its attacks. Observe its patterns as best you can and strike back, being as flexible as you can manage."

The group nodded silently.

"Well, best of luck," Heathcliff murmured, then strode over to the obsidian door and placed a hand upon it. We tensed up.

I patted Agil and Klein on the shoulders from behind, speaking as they turned to me.

"Don't die on me."

"Just worry about yourself."

"I'm not getting knocked out while there are spoils to be had."

After the bravado of their replies, the door slowly slid open, creaking heavily. All present drew their weapons. I pulled both of mine over my back. I looked over at Asuna and her rapier and nodded.

Finally, Heathcliff drew his longsword from behind his cross-shaped shield, raised it high, and shouted, "Let the battle begin!"

He charged through the open doorway. We followed.

The interior was a large domed space, probably as large as the coliseum that had played host to my duel with Heathcliff. The black curved walls rose high, forming a round ceiling far above our heads. We rushed inside, lined up naturally, then heard the enormous rumble of the door closing behind us. It probably wasn't going to open again—not until the boss was dead or we were.

Several seconds of silence passed. I tried to concentrate on every direction from our position, but the boss showed no signs of appearing. Each second ticking by was torture on my frayed nerves.

"Hey," someone called out, unable to bear the silence any longer.

"Above!" Asuna cried next to me. I looked up with a start.

It was stuck to the top of the dome.

Enormous. Deadly. And long.

· *A centipede?* I thought in the moment. It had to be at least ten meters long. The body was split into several segments, but the

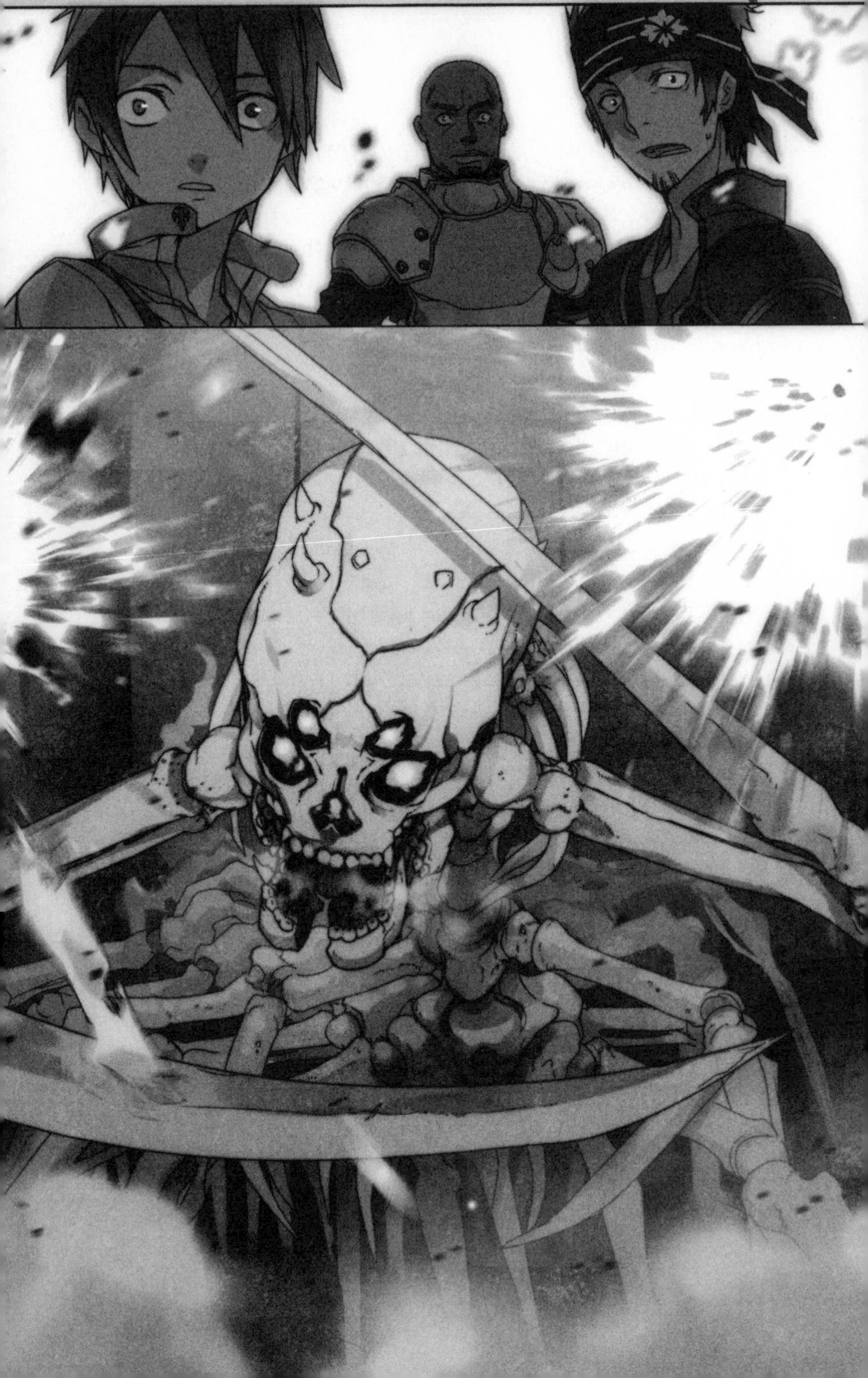

structure was more like a human backbone than the thorax of an insect. Each gray, cylindrical segment had spiny legs that looked like exposed bone. Following the trail, I saw the body widen until it reached a wicked-looking skull. It wasn't human. The cranium was more elongated, with two sets of slanted eye sockets, blue fires burning inside the cavities. The protruding jawbone was lined with sharp fangs, and two scythe-shaped arms of bone extended from the sides of the skull.

As I focused, the system automatically brought up the yellow cursor with the monster's name on it: the Skullreaper.

Its countless legs squirming, the skeletal centipede slowly crawled across the dome as we watched in shocked silence. Suddenly, it released all of its legs and dropped straight on top of the party.

"Don't freeze up! Keep your distance!"

Heathcliff's sharp cry cut the icy air. Everyone moved, regaining his or her senses. We scrambled to avoid the spot where it dropped. But three players couldn't avoid its descent quickly enough. They looked up, momentarily caught unsure of which direction to go.

"This way!" I screamed. They finally snapped into a run, but—

The moment the centipede landed, the colossal impact shook the floor. The three men stumbled and lost their balance. The monster swung out with its right "arm"—more of an elongated scythe of bone, the blade as long as a human being—and swiped all three.

They were tossed into the air from behind. As I watched their flight, their HP bars plummeted with terrifying speed—into the yellow warning zone, then the red danger zone, then...

"...?!"

And just like that, to zero. Their bodies, still in midair, shattered unceremoniously. The explosions echoed throughout the chamber.

"...!!"

Asuna drew a sharp breath next to me. I could feel my body tense up.

Dead in one hit?

Players powered up in SAO through their level and skills. As your level rose, so did your maximum HP, so even if your ability with the sword was average, as long as your level was reasonably high, it was mathematically much less likely that you would die. And today's party was exclusively high-level players, so any one of us should have been able to handle even a full combination attack from a boss. The key word being *should*. But in one simple blow...

"This is insanity," Asuna muttered.

The skeleton centipede raised itself off the ground, let out a deafening roar, then charged into a fresh group of victims.

"Aaaah!!"

Screams of terror issued from that direction. The bone scythe was raised again.

A shadow leaped into the path of its fall: Heathcliff. He raised his massive shield and greeted the scythe. There was an ear-wrenching collision. Sparks flew.

But that was only one of two scythes. The left arm continued attacking Heathcliff, while the right swung upward and darted toward a mass of frozen players.

"Shit!"

I leaped forward without a second thought, flying through the air to close the gap, then maneuvering into the downward path of the scythe with a deafening blast. I crossed my swords to block the blow.

The impact was unfathomable. But the scythe kept coming. Despite the sparks, it kept pushing my swords backward, right under my nose.

Damn, it's so heavy!

Suddenly, a new sword trailing white light sliced upward and caught the scythe from below. Another shock wave. As soon as I felt its force relent, I summoned all of my strength and pushed the bone scythe back.

Asuna turned to look at me for a split second and called out,

"We can manage if we take it at the same time! We can do this together!"

"Great, back me up!" I nodded. Just the thought of her next to me filled me with infinite willpower, it seemed.

The scythe swooped toward us again, sideways this time, but we blocked it with simultaneous diagonal slashes. Our synchronized attacks created a ribbon of light that struck the scythe, sending off another powerful blast. This time, the foe's arm faltered backward.

I raised my voice to shout above the din.

"We'll stop its scythe! You attack it from the flanks!"

That command seemed to snap the group's paralysis. The others raised brave cheers and plunged into the Skullreaper's body, weapons raised. Multiple attacks struck the foe solidly, and for the first time, I saw its HP bar dip slightly.

In just a moment, screams arose. When I had the time between scythe strikes to see, I noticed a long, spear-like bone at the centipede's tail throwing more human figures into the air.

"Damn…"

I gritted my teeth. Asuna and I were trying to hold down the right scythe, Heathcliff the left, but we couldn't last much longer.

"Kirito!"

I turned to look at Asuna.

—Don't look away! Distractions will only get you killed!

—You're right… here it comes!

—Block it on the upper left!

We shared information with just an exchange of glances, then blocked the scythe in perfect rhythm.

We forced ourselves to ignore the occasional screams from players around us, focusing solely on blocking the creature's deadly blows. Somehow, as it went on, not only did we stop needing to share words, but looks as well. It was as though we were plugged directly into each other's minds. We instantly used the exact same moves to block the enemy's breathless attacks.

In the moment, locked in the midst of the most extreme of

battles, I felt a sense of unity I'd never known before. Asuna and I had melded into a single, sword-swinging force of combat—in a way, it was an incredibly sensual experience. The occasional heavy attack from the monster knocked off slight amounts of our HP bit by bit, but it was completely out of mind.

22

The fight lasted for an entire hour.

At the end of that limitless stretch, when the monster finally split into pieces, no one left had enough strength to muster a cheer. We all sat or fell to the obsidian floor, panting heavily.

—*Is it...over?*

—*Yeah, it's over.*

With that final exchange, it seemed the connection between Asuna and me was broken. A powerful fatigue enveloped my entire body, and I sank to my knees. We sat back-to-back, unable to move.

We had both survived, though these were not circumstances for open celebration. A dear price had been paid this day. Starting with the three deaths on that first blow, our forces had suffered steady losses, the horrible shattering sounds popping off left and right. I'd counted six before I gave up.

"How many did we lose?" Klein asked in a hoarse voice, slumped over to my left. Next to him, Agil lay flat on his back, his limbs spread apart. He could only turn his head to look at us.

I waved my right hand to bring up my map, counting the green dots. I subtracted the total from our original number.

"Fourteen are dead."

Even as I totaled the number, I couldn't believe it.

These were all experienced, top-level players. Even without an escape route or instantaneous healing, careful combat that prioritized survival should have kept the number of fatalities lower. And yet...

"You can't be serious..."

There was none of the usual edge to Agil's voice. A dark pall hung heavily over the survivors.

We were at the three-quarters mark—there were a full twenty-five floors ahead of us. Even with several thousand players remaining, there were only a few hundred capable of truly tackling the endgame. If we lost this number on every floor from now on, there might only be one player left to fight the final boss.

And if it's going to be anyone, it'll be him...

I turned to look to the back of the chamber. While everyone else slumped on the ground, one man clad in red stood straight and tall: Heathcliff.

He wasn't totally unharmed, of course. I focused on him to bring up his cursor, which showed that his HP bar was significantly lowered. It'd taken everything Asuna and I had to continue blocking one of those giant scythes, and he'd managed the other all on his own. Numerical damage aside, the mental fatigue alone should have been enough to knock him down.

But his proud, calm bearing showed not the slightest hint of exhaustion. He was unbelievably tough. Like a machine—a battle machine with a perpetual engine...

I continued gazing blearily at Heathcliff's profile, my mind hazy with fatigue. The living legend's face stayed calm. He silently stared down at the KoB members and others who lay on the floor. His gaze was full of warmth and compassion...just like...

Just like he was watching little mice, playing in a cleverly constructed cage.

I felt a tremendous chill race through my entire body.

My mind raised into motion. Everything froze, from my fingertips to the center of my brain. A premonition had awoken inside of me. The tiny seed of possibility grew and grew, sending out roots of doubt.

Heathcliff's gaze, his implacability—it was not the face of a man congratulating his fellows. It was the expression of a merciful God, gazing down from a great height...

I suddenly remembered the incredible reaction time he'd exhibited during our duel. It surpassed the speed of humanity. No, let me rephrase—it surpassed the maximum speed SAO allowed its players to move.

Not to mention his regular attitude. He was the leader of the strongest guild in the game, but he never gave orders. He let other players handle all matters and chose to observe. What if that wasn't a sign of trust in his subordinates... but the self-control not to act on things that other players could not know?

Someone unbound by the rules of this game of death, but not an NPC. No program could create that merciful expression.

If he wasn't an NPC or an ordinary player, that left only one possibility. But how could I confirm it? There was no way.

Except there was. One available right now, and only now.

I checked Heathcliff's HP. It was quite diminished after the excruciating battle, but still not to the halfway point. In fact, it was just barely still in the blue.

This was a man who had never once fallen into the yellow zone. He possessed an insurmountable defense.

The only time I'd seen Heathcliff's expression change during our duel was when I was about to knock his HP under 50 percent. But it wasn't being knocked into the yellow zone that he was afraid of.

No, it was more likely...

I slowly gripped my right sword. Gradually, ever so gradually, I drew my right foot back. I lowered my waist, assuming the position for a low-altitude dash. Heathcliff hadn't noticed me. His calm gaze was trained only on his battered guildmates.

If my guess was completely wrong, I would instantly be labeled a criminal player and suffer extreme punishment.

Sorry if it comes to that...

I looked at Asuna, crouched next to me. She looked up at the same time and our eyes met.

"Kirito...?"

She looked startled, but she only mouthed the words. It was too late—my right leg was already pouncing.

I crossed the thirty feet to Heathcliff in an instant, low to the ground, then burst upward, twisting my right thrust: Rage Spike, a basic one-handed charge attack. It was weak, and wouldn't come close to killing Heathcliff if it hit, but it would serve to prove my suspicions...

Heathcliff didn't fail to notice the sweep of pale blue that approached from his left, and I saw his eyes widen with shock. He abruptly raised his left hand, trying to block with his shield.

But I'd seen that habit several times during our duel. My blazing sword angled sharply in midair, clipping the hilt of the shield and striking—

—An invisible wall, just before it hit Heathcliff's chest. I felt a powerful impact travel up my arm. Purple sparks shot everywhere, and the space between was similarly purple—the color of all system messages.

IMMORTAL OBJECT. A system designation that was not afforded to human players, frail and limited that we were. This is what Heathcliff was afraid of during our duel—the possibility that his so-called divine protection would be exposed for what it really was.

"Kirito, what in the—?"

Asuna started to shout in surprise as she chased after me, then stopped short when she saw the message. Heathcliff, Klein, the other players—no one moved. The system message blinked out in the silence.

I removed my sword and leaped backward to maintain distance. Asuna took several steps to reach my side.

"He's designated as a system-level immortal object? Wh... what does this mean, Commander?"

Heathcliff did not answer her confused query. He simply looked at me, a severe frown on his face. I spoke, my swords lowered.

"This is the truth behind the legend. The system is designed to prevent his HP from ever falling into the yellow zone. The only things that can be labeled immortal objects are the environment, NPCs, and system managers, not players. But there aren't any more GMs in the game—except for one."

I cut off and glanced upward.

"There's something that has stuck in the back of my mind ever since I came here. I figured he had to be watching us from somewhere, managing and fine-tuning the world. But I forgot a basic psychological fact, something that even a kid knows."

I trained my gaze directly on the crimson paladin.

"There's nothing more boring than watching someone else play an RPG. Isn't that right, Akihiko Kayaba?"

The entire chamber was full of frosty silence.

Heathcliff just looked at me, his face still placid. No one else moved. They couldn't.

Next to me, Asuna took a step forward. Her eyes were devoid of emotion, like two empty voids. When she spoke, it was in a dry whisper.

"Commander...is this...true...?"

Heathcliff did not answer. He tilted his head and finally spoke.

"...Will you at least tell me how you figured it out?"

"I first noticed something was off during our duel. You moved too fast in that final moment."

"I should have known. That was a painful failure for me. I was so overwhelmed by your attack, I had no choice but to use the system's assistance."

He nodded slowly, finally showing his first sign of emotion—a twisted corner of the mouth, the faintest hint of a wry grimace.

"My plan was to not reveal myself until the ninety-fifth floor had been reached. But alas..."

Heathcliff turned to gaze over the group, his grin looking more and more aloof, then he finally announced himself.

"Yes, I am Akihiko Kayaba. And I am this game's final boss, the one who should have awaited you on the top floor."

I felt Asuna swoon slightly. I propped her up with my right hand, my stare never leaving him.

"I don't think much of your taste. The greatest player in the game turns heel and becomes the final boss?"

"But it's a compelling scenario, is it not? We had fun, but I wasn't expecting to be exposed just three-quarters of the way through. I had you pegged as the biggest wild-card element in the game, but even my estimates were off."

Akihiko Kayaba, the developer of the game and jailer of all ten thousand prisoners, gave off his recognizable dry smile and shrugged. Heathcliff's physical appearance was a far cry from the real Kayaba. But that mechanical nature, his metallic disposition, was the same as that of the faceless avatar that had descended from the ceiling on that fateful day. Kayaba continued, the smile still playing over his lips.

"I'd always expected that you would be the one to confront me in the end. Out of the ten unique skills in the game, Dual Blades is the one given to the player with the quickest response time. That player should have been the one to stand before the final villain, whether triumphant or beaten. But you exhibited power beyond my expectations. Both in the speed of your attacks and the sharpness of your observation. But...I suppose having one's expectations betrayed is one of the best features of an online RPG."

One of the frozen players had finally risen to his feet. It was one of the Knights of the Blood. His naive, narrow eyes were filled with anguish.

"You...you bastard...We actually swore our loyalty to you... We put our hopes in you! And you betrayed us..."

He lifted a large halberd.

"You evil, twisted—!!"

And the man screamed and charged. There was no time to stop him. He took a huge swing at Kayaba—

But Kayaba was faster. He swung his left hand instead, opening a window and manipulating it instantly. Suddenly, his attacker's body froze in midair, then fell with a clatter. A blinking green border surrounded the man's HP bar—paralysis. Kayaba kept tapping commands into the window.

"Oh...Kirito!"

I turned to see Asuna kneeling on the ground. From what I could see, everyone in the chamber aside from Kayaba and me was collapsing unnaturally, groaning.

I put my swords over my back, kneeling to lift Asuna up and hold her hand. Kayaba turned to look at me again.

"What are you doing? Killing everyone here to cover up your evil deeds?"

"Hardly. I would not be so cruel," he said, smiling and shaking his head. "But I am left with no other choice. I must accelerate my plans and await your visit at Ruby Palace on the top floor. I have been building the KoB to handle the powerful foes of the ninetieth floor and above. It is not my first choice to abandon you partway like this, but I think you've shown that you have the strength to make it on your own. However, before then..."

He stopped and trained his gaze on me, twin beams of pure willpower. He stuck the tip of his sword into the obsidian floor. A sharp, clear, metallic tone rent the air.

"I believe you deserve a reward for exposing my true identity, Kirito. I will grant you the opportunity to fight me in a one-on-one duel, right here and now. No immortality, of course. If you beat me, the game will be over, and all players will be able to log out of this world. What do you choose?"

The instant she heard those words, Asuna struggled futilely in my arms, shaking her head. "You can't, Kirito! He's trying to get rid of you...We should pull back and think this through..."

My conscience agreed with her. He was a game manager, able to bend the system to his will. He might claim a fair battle, but there was no telling what he might do. The best choice here was clearly to retreat, share opinions, and come up with a plan.

But...

What did he say? He *built* the KoB? We could make it on our own...?

"You sick bastard," I muttered before I knew what I was doing.

He had kidnapped ten thousand people, fried the brains of two-fifths of them, and watched in person as we struggled, ignorant and helpless, to play along with his own pet narrative. There could be no greater enjoyment for a game master.

I thought back to Asuna's past as described down on the twenty-second floor. I remembered her tears as she clung to me. How could I stand before the man who created this world for his own pleasure, who had ripped Asuna's heart to shreds over and over, and simply back down?

"All right. Let's settle this."

I nodded slowly.

"Kirito!" Asuna screamed. I looked down at her. It felt like I'd been shot through the chest to do this, but I forced a smile all the same.

"I'm sorry. But this has to be it. There's no turning back now..."

Asuna opened her lips, about to say something, then stopped and gave me a desperate smile. Tears trailed down her cheeks.

"You aren't going...to die, are you...?"

"Nope...I'm going to win. I'm going to win, and I'm going to bring an end to this world."

"All right. I believe you."

Even if I lose and turn to nothingness, you have to live on. I thought the words but couldn't say them. Instead, Asuna squeezed my hand, long and hard.

I let go, then laid her body on the obsidian floor. I stood and walked over to Kayaba, loudly drawing my swords.

"Kirito, don't do this!"

"Kirito!"

I turned and saw Agil and Klein desperately trying to push themselves upward. First I met Agil's eyes and nodded to him.

"Thanks for all your support of the swordsmen in the game,

Agil. I know what you've done. You've spent nearly all of your earnings helping to outfit players in the mid-level zones."

I smiled at Agil, whose eyes were wide with surprise.

Klein, ugly bandanna, stubble, and all, was breathing in and out rapidly, trying to find the right words. I stared straight into his sunken eyes and took a deep breath. Try as I might, I couldn't stop my voice from trembling.

"Klein...remember when we first met? I'm sorry for what I did...leaving you behind like that. I always regretted it."

That was all I could scratch out, but the instant I finished, the corners of my old friend's eyes sparkled and began to drip. After several moments of silent tears, he struggled anew to get to his feet, his throat ripping with anger.

"D...don't you dare apologize to me! Now is not the time! You're not going to do this! I'm not gonna forgive you until I've at least had the chance to buy you a dinner back in the real world!!"

He tried to keep shouting, but I silenced him with a nod.

"All right, it's a deal. We'll meet up on the outside."

I flashed him a thumbs-up.

Then I turned to the girl who'd helped me say the words I couldn't say for two years and gave her one last gaze.

One last gaze at Asuna, her face smiling but tearstained...

Inwardly, I told her I was sorry, then spun around. I looked at Kayaba, still imperious and implacable, and opened my mouth.

"...I have just one request."

"And that is?"

"I don't intend to go down easily, but if I do die, ensure that Asuna can't commit suicide right away."

He raised an eyebrow in surprise but nodded assent.

"Very well. I'll see to it that she cannot leave Selmburg."

"Kirito, you can't! No...you can't do this!!"

Asuna's teary cries echoed behind me. I didn't turn around. I drew my right foot back, pushing my left sword to the front and my right sword down.

Kayaba hit a few more commands on his window that

equalized our HP bars just at the edge of the red zone—enough that one clean, heavy hit would finish the battle.

Next, a system message appeared over his head reading, CHANGED INTO MORTAL OBJECT—Kayaba had removed his artificial defense. He closed the window, then pulled his sword out of the ground and hunched behind his giant shield.

My mind was cold and clear. After my inner apologies to Asuna had risen and dissipated like soap bubbles popping, only my instinct to fight was left, freezing and sharp.

To be honest, I didn't have a foolproof plan for victory. In our previous duel, I hadn't gotten the sense that my sword work was clearly inferior to his. But if he chose to use the same system assistance—as he called it—that had caused me to freeze for a second while he reacted, there would be nothing I could do.

It was only Kayaba's pride on the line that would keep him from using it. Based on his statements, I had to conclude that he would try to defeat me within the limits of his Holy Sword ability. My only hope for survival was to catch him off guard and finish the fight quickly.

The tension rose between us. Even the air seemed to tremble with the weight of the situation. This wasn't a duel. It was a fight to kill. That's right—I was going…

"…to kill you!!" I spat, charging forward. I brought my right sword in for a long horizontal swipe. With his left hand on the shield, Kayaba blocked it easily. Sparks flew, illuminating our faces for an instant.

As though the sound of metal clashing was the opening bell of our fight, we instantly accelerated into a full-blown sword battle.

Out of the countless fights I'd experienced in this world, this was the most irregular, the most human. We'd both exposed our secrets to the other before. My Dual Blades skill was Kayaba's design, so I had to assume that he knew all of my combos. It certainly explained how he'd stopped all of my attacks in the previous duel.

I didn't use any of the system's combination attacks—I swung my swords freely, using only my instincts. I wasn't getting any help from the game, but it seemed like my accelerated consciousness made my every move much faster than normal. Even my eyes couldn't keep up with the speed, my swords waving into afterimages: one, five, ten, twenty. But...

Kayaba deflected each of my blows with easy precision. When he had the opening, he would dart in with a sharp stab of his own. Instantaneous reaction speed was the only thing that kept me from being hit. The battle maintained an uneasy stasis. I focused on Kayaba's eyes, trying to read his thoughts, his actions. Our gazes met.

Kayaba's— Heathcliff's brass eyes stayed chilly. That hint of humanity I'd witnessed in our public duel was nowhere to be seen.

I suddenly felt a slight chill run down my back.

I was facing a man who had slaughtered four thousand people. Was that even humanly possible? Four thousand deaths, four thousand voices of vengeance. No man who can live with that much weight over his head can be human—he's a monster.

"Raaahh!!"

I roared, trying to banish the tiny inkling of fear blooming in my heart. I whipped my arms around even faster, striking multiple times a second, but Kayaba never blinked. He wielded his shield and longsword faster than the eye could follow, perfectly blocking each and every blow.

Is he just toying with me?

The fear soon turned to panic. If Kayaba was able to defend every single blow, he must have the ability to strike back and deliver a critical hit at any moment.

Doubt clouded my heart. He didn't even need the system's assistance.

"Shit!"

In that case... how about this?

I switched tactics, unleashing the Dual Blades' highest skill, the Eclipse. My sword edges bore down on Kayaba with ultra

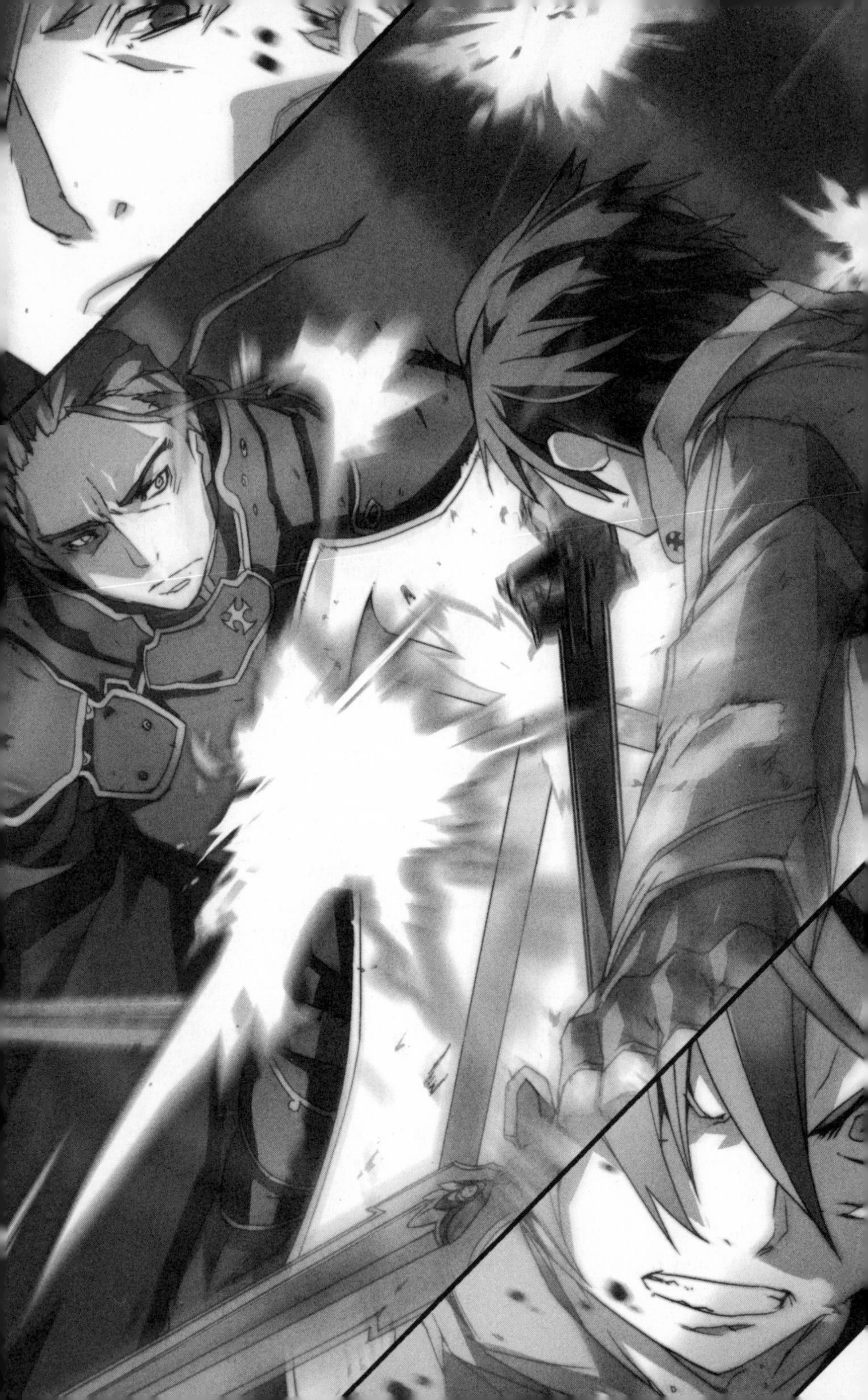

speed, flashing in all directions like a solar corona. Twenty-seven consecutive strikes—

—But Kayaba was simply waiting for me to fall into the system's preprogrammed combination. For the first time, his mouth displayed signs of emotion. But unlike our last fight, this was a smile of certain victory.

After the first few swings of the combo, I realized my mistake. At the very end, I'd relied on the system for help, rather than my own instincts. I couldn't break out of the combo partway—it would freeze me momentarily. But Kayaba knew each and every attack in this string.

As blow after blow was parried easily by Kayaba's crucifix shield, the only thing I could do was breathe a silent apology.

I'm sorry, Asuna...At least I know you'll still be alive...

The twenty-seventh and final left thrust struck the center of the shield in a shower of sparks. The next instant, the sword in my left hand gave a metallic screech and shattered into pieces.

"Farewell, Kirito."

Kayaba's longsword was held high over my head, glowing crimson. It swung downward, a blur the color of blood—

In that instant, a voice, loud and fierce, echoed inside my head.

I'm going...to watch over you!!

With incredible speed, a human blur darted between Kayaba's glowing blade and me. Chestnut hair flipped through the air.

Asuna...why?!

She should have been paralyzed by the game system itself. But she stood before me, her chest held high, both arms extended.

I could see surprise on Kayaba's face. But no one could stop his attack now. It all moved in horrifying slow motion, the sword slicing Asuna from shoulder to breast.

I lurched forward desperately, reaching out for her as she fell. She crumpled into my arms, soundless.

Our eyes met. She smiled faintly. Her HP bar was gone.

*   *   *

Time stood still.

Evening. Meadow. Breeze. A slight chill.

We sat on the hill side by side, gazing out on the lake, the reddish-gold setting sun melting into deep blue.

Leaves rustled. Birds called as they returned to their nests.

She slipped her hand into mine, leaned her head on my shoulder.

The clouds trailed past. Stars began to twinkle, one, then two.

We silently observed the colors of the world shift and blur.

Eventually, she spoke up.

"I'm a little sleepy. Mind if I use your legs as a pillow?"

I smiled and answered, "Go right ahead. Good night..."

Just like then, Asuna looked up at me from my arms, her face beaming, her eyes full of love. But the weight and the warmth of that previous time were gone.

Her body slowly took on a golden glow. Motes of light separated and scattered.

"This can't be... Asuna... why...? Why did you...?"

My voice trembled. But the light mercilessly glowed brighter.

A single tear fell from her eye, sparkled momentarily, then vanished. Her lips moved, faintly, carving the sounds.

I'm sorry.

Good-bye.

Swish...

The light in my arms flashed, then burst, countless golden feathers floating through the air.

And then she was gone.

I scrambled to regain the floating lights, a voiceless scream ripping my throat. But the golden feathers blew away as though on a gust of wind, spreading out, evaporating. Disappearing. Forever.

This can never happen. It should not. It can't. It can't—
I crumpled to my knees. The final feather floated downward to rest on my hand, then blinked out.

23

The ends of Kayaba's mouth twisted, and he gave an exaggerated shrug, hands wide.

"That was a surprise. Almost like a story event in a single-player RPG, isn't it? She shouldn't have been able to recover from that paralysis... As I said, quite unexpected."

But I couldn't even hear him. My every emotion was aflame, burning out, plunging into deep, black despair.

I had lost my reason to do anything.

Fighting in this virtual world, returning to the real world, continuing on with my life—it was all meaningless. When my lack of strength led to my guildmates dying those many months ago, I should have joined them in death. I'd never have met Asuna. I'd never have made the same mistake again.

And I didn't want her to commit suicide? How could I have been so foolish, so shallow? I didn't understand a thing. How could anyone live with such utter emptiness...?

I gazed down absently at Asuna's rapier, gleaming on the ground. I reached out and picked it up.

I stared at the frail, thin blade, hoping to find some trace, some record of her existence there, but there was nothing. Not a single fragment of its owner was present in that shining reflection. I slowly climbed to my feet, one of my swords in one hand, Asuna's rapier in the other.

Enough. I would take my memories of the few days I'd been able to spend with her and then go to the same place.

I felt as though someone called my name from behind me.

But I didn't stop. I pulled back the sword in my right hand and struck at Kayaba. I took two or three ungainly steps forward, then thrust the blade.

It wasn't a skill, not even a proper attack. Kayaba swung his shield and easily deflected the attempt with a pitying look, then buried his longsword in my chest.

I looked down passively at the metal glimmer sunk deep into my body. There was nothing to think. Just the objective resignation of my end.

In the right corner of my vision, my HP bar slowly drained. Perhaps my accelerated senses had not worn down yet, because I could see the bar diminishing, dot by dot. I closed my eyes. In the moment that my mind ceased to exist, I wanted to see nothing but Asuna's smile.

Even with my eyes closed, the HP bar was still there. The strip of red surely and steadily shrank. It felt as though the system itself, the god that had granted me life for so long, was silently licking its chops, waiting for the moment it would claim me forever. Ten more pixels. Five. Then...

I suddenly felt a rage the likes of which I'd never experienced.

It was *this*. This was what had killed Asuna. Even Kayaba, its creator, was only a part of it now. This was what had ripped apart Asuna's body, blasted her mind, enveloped me—the will of the system itself. The digital god, mocking its players' ignorance, swinging its merciless scythe.

What are we? Foolish puppets, dancing on the unreachable strings of the SAO system? If the system says yes, we survive, and if it says no, we perish. Is that all we are?

My HP bar ran out, as if to laugh at my helpless rage. A small purple message appeared front and center: YOU ARE DEAD. God had spoken.

A powerful chill ran through my body. Sensation faded. I could feel countless lines of code setting me free, slicing me into pieces, preparing to feast. The chill rose from my spine to my neck, then flooded into my head. The nerves of my skin, sound, light—everything grew further away. My body was dissolving—turning into polygonal shards—dispersing...

But I wasn't going to play along.

I opened my eyes. I could see. I could *still* see. In fact, I could see the look of shock on Kayaba's face, his hand still gripping the sword in my chest.

Perhaps my senses had accelerated again, and the instantaneous process of my avatar exploding was happening in extreme slow motion. The contours of my body were already softening, dots of light spilling off and blinking out here and there, but I still existed. I was still alive.

"Raaaahh!"

I screamed. I screamed and resisted. Against the system. Against the Absolute.

Asuna, spoiled and lonely Asuna, had wrung out every last ounce of willpower to beat that irreversible paralysis and thrown herself before a strike that couldn't be blocked. Just to save me. I couldn't let her sacrifice go to waste. It wasn't an option. Even if death was ultimately inescapable...there was one thing...left to do...

I squeezed hard, knitting the sensation back as if it were a fine thread. The texture of what I held—Asuna's rapier—flooded back into my hand. *Now* I could feel her will exuding from it. I could hear her voice, urging me on.

My left arm began to move, achingly slow. As it rose bit by bit, the contours shuddered, visual artifacts peeling off. But I never stopped moving. Inch by inch, I raised my arm, my soul flaking away.

Unbelievable pain shot through my body, the apparent price

for my heresy, but I gritted my teeth and kept moving. The distance, just inches, was unbearably long. I was freezing cold. Only my left arm had any sensation left, and the chill was quickly eating through it. My body was crumbling, spilling like a delicate ice sculpture.

But finally, at long last, the shining silver tip of the sword touched the center of Kayaba's chest. He did not move. The shock on his face had worn off—only a peaceful smile was left on his slightly opened lips.

Half by my own will, half driven by some mysterious unknown force, my arm closed the final distance. Kayaba shut his eyes and accepted the rapier piercing his chest. His HP bar emptied.

For an instant we both stood there, each with his sword stuck through the other. All of my willpower spent, I gazed into space.

Is this...what you wanted...?

I never heard her response, but there was a momentary *thump*, a pulse of warmth gripping my left hand. I released the strength that was keeping my body from shattering entirely.

As my consciousness slid into nothingness, I could feel my body disintegrating into a thousand pieces and Kayaba's doing the same. Two familiar bursts of sound overlapped. Now it all really was drifting away, separating faster and faster. Was that Agil and Klein calling my name? And beyond that, the artificial tone of the system's voice...

The game has been cleared. The game has been cleared. The game has been...

24

The entire sky was ablaze with the setting sun.

I suddenly realized I was in a very strange place.

A thick crystal slab was under my feet. Beneath that transparent floor, strings of crimson-splashed clouds flowed past. I looked up and saw nothing but infinite evening sky. An endless expanse, sprayed with gradient colors from brilliant orange to bloodred to deep purple. I could hear the sound of a slight breeze.

Aside from the red and gold clouds floating by, there was nothing in the air but this small circle of crystal, and I was standing at its edge.

Where am I? I remembered my body shattering into countless pieces and dissipating into nothing. Was I still somewhere inside SAO...or had I actually gone to the afterlife?

I looked down at my body. The leather coat and long gloves were the same equipment I had been wearing when I died, but everything was ever-so-slightly translucent now. And it wasn't just my clothes. Even my body itself had turned into a partially see-through material like colored glass, and it was sparkling red with the light of the sunset.

I stretched out my hand and waved the fingers. The game window popped open with the same sound as ever. I was still stuck in SAO.

But there was no equipment mannequin or menu readout on the window. It was simply a featureless box that read [EXECUTING FINAL PHASE: CURRENTLY 54%] in small letters. The number ticked up to 55 percent as I watched. I'd thought that dying and disintegrating happened at the same time that the device fried the brain. What was happening here?

I shrugged and closed the window, then jumped as someone called out to me.

"...Kirito."

It was like the song of angels. A shock ran through me.

Please let it be real; please don't let it be an illusion, I prayed, and turned.

She was standing there, set against the burning sky.

Her long hair was rippling in the breeze. Her smiling face was close enough that I could cup her cheek if I reached out, but I couldn't move.

If I take my eyes off of her for just an instant, she'll disappear, I thought. Instead, I stared silently. Like me, her body seemed made of a delicate crystal. As it sparkled and gleamed with the light of the sunset behind it, it seemed to me that the sight was more beautiful than anything in the world.

I desperately tried to hold back the tears, and finally I cracked a smile. When my voice came out, it was barely a whisper.

"Sorry...I guess I died."

"...Dummy."

A large tear rolled down her cheek as she smiled. I opened my arms and called her name.

"...Asuna."

She jumped to embrace me, tears sparkling, and I held her tightly. I'd never let her go. No matter what happened, I would never release my grip.

After a long, long kiss, we finally extricated our faces and looked at each other. There were so many things to say about that final battle, so many things to apologize for. But words were no longer necessary. Instead, I turned to look at the endless sunset and asked, "So...where are we?"

Asuna silently looked down and pointed. I followed her finger.

Far, far away from our little floating crystal platform was a point in the sky—and there it floated. It was like a cone with the tip chopped off. The entire structure was made of countless thin layers. If I squinted, I could see little mountains, forests, lakes, and even towns in the spaces between the layers.

"Aincrad..."

Asuna nodded. That had to be Aincrad. A giant castle, floating in an endless expanse of sky. The world of swords and battle that had played host to our painful two-year struggle. And now it was below us.

Before I came here, I'd seen pictures of the structure in promotional material for Sword Art Online. But this was the first time I'd ever actually seen it like this in person. My breath caught in my throat; I felt something like awe.

The floating fortress of steel...was collapsing.

As we watched, a chunk of the lowest floor broke off, spilling away into countless smaller pieces. If I trained my ears, I could hear the heavy crumbling sounds beneath the wind.

"Ah..."

Asuna murmured. A larger piece of the bottom broke away, and this time there were trees and cascades of lake water among the structural rock as it plummeted through the red sea of clouds. That was where our little log cabin used to be. Floor by floor, the place that had consumed two years of our memories peeled apart like tiny membranes, and I felt grief well up in my heart.

I slowly sat down on the edge of the crystal platform, still holding Asuna.

My heart was oddly calm. I didn't know what had happened to us, what would happen to us, or why, but I felt no fear. I'd done what I needed to do, lost the life I had been given, and now sat with the girl I loved, watching the end of the world. Nothing mattered anymore. I felt fulfilled.

Asuna must have felt the same. She hugged me close, watching Aincrad fall to pieces, her lids half lowered. I slowly stroked her hair.

"That's a fine sight."

The voice from my right took me by surprise. Asuna and I looked over to see that a man was now standing at the edge with us.

Akihiko Kayaba.

The developer of Sword Art Online, not the paladin Heathcliff. He wore a white shirt and tie underneath a long white lab coat. The contours of his face were fine and sharp, but the metallic eyes and the way he placidly observed the disappearing castle were the same as his prior incarnation. Like us, he was partially transparent.

Less than an hour ago, I had been locked in a battle to the death with this man, but I felt at peace now. It was as if I had to leave all my rage and hatred behind to reach this world of endless sunset. I pulled my eyes away from Kayaba and back to the castle, then spoke.

"What's happening to Aincrad?"

"You might call it a visual metaphor." His voice was quiet. "At this moment, the SAO mainframe, stored five levels underground at the Argus building, is deleting all data saved on its server. In another ten minutes, nothing will remain of this world."

"What happened to all the people who were there?" Asuna murmured.

"Don't worry about them. Just moments ago..."

He waved a hand, then glanced at the window that popped up.

"...all 6,174 surviving players were logged out and regained consciousness."

So Klein, Agil, and all the other people we'd met there, the ones who had lived through those two years with us, were all back in the real world, safe and sound.

I shut my eyes tightly, warding off the emotion that threatened to seep out.

"...And those who died? We both 'died,' and we're here right now, so isn't it possible that you could bring the other four thousand back to consciousness?"

He closed the window, his face unchanging, then placed his hands in the pockets of his coat.

"Life is not meant to be treated so lightly. They will not come back. In every world, the dead must disappear. You two are a special exception. I wanted a bit more time to speak with you."

That is what a man who killed four thousand people has to say for himself? But for some reason, the anger did not come. Instead, I had another question. A very simple question that every player in the game—every person who was aware of what happened here—wanted to know.

"So why...did you do this?"

I thought I detected a pained smile cross his face. He was silent for a while.

"Why, you ask? For a long time, even I had forgotten. Why did I do this? When I learned about the development of the full-dive system—in fact, long before that moment—I dreamed of creating that castle. Creating a world that surpassed all the rules and laws of reality. And finally...I even saw the laws of my own world eclipsed."

He turned the serene light of his eyes upon me, then back again.

A slight gust picked up, rustling Kayaba's lab coat and Asuna's hair. The castle was more than half gone by now. Even memorable Algade had crumbled into nothingness, swallowed by the clouds. Kayaba continued.

"Children experience a great variety of dreams and fantasies. At a young age, I was gripped with a vision of a castle of iron floating in the sky...Even after I grew older, that vision never left my mind. In fact, with every year the picture grew larger and more real. For years, my one and only desire was to leave the surface and travel to that castle. You see, Kirito, a part of me still believes that castle really exists...in some world, somewhere..."

Suddenly, I felt the illusion that I had been born there, too, a boy who dreamed of being a swordsman someday. One day, that boy would meet a girl with hazel eyes. They would fall in love, be bound as one, and live out their days in a little cottage in the woods...

"Yeah...I hope it does," I murmured. Asuna nodded softly in my arms.

The silence returned. As I gazed far away, I noticed that the process of entropy was now affecting more than just the castle. In the far distance, the supposedly infinite sea of clouds and red sky were being visibly swallowed by white light. The light was bleeding through here and there, slowly approaching.

"One last thing. Congratulations on beating the game, Kirito and Asuna."

We both turned to look up at him. He was gazing down at us, a beatific smile on his face.

"And now, I should be going."

The wind blew, and suddenly he was gone, as if erased from existence. The crimson sunset was sparkling subtly through the crystal platform. We were alone again.

Where had he gone? Back to the real world?

No—that was unlikely. He must have deleted his own mind and traveled off in search of the real Aincrad.

Only the tip of the virtual fortress was left now. We were seeing the seventy-sixth floor and above for the very first time, but only in a state of rapid self-destruction. The curtain of light that swallowed the world was growing close. As the rippling aurora touched everything in its path, even the clouds and sky itself shattered into those familiar, fragile shards.

An enormous red palace with a fragile spire sat atop the very tip of Aincrad. If the game had proceeded according to plan, we would likely have crossed swords with the wicked overlord Heathcliff there.

Even as the top floor fell, the master-less castle continued to float, as if defying its fate. The deep red gleam of the structure stood out against the red backdrop, like the heart of the castle, left behind after all its flesh had fallen away.

Eventually, the wave of destruction swallowed it as well. It disintegrated into countless rubies from the bottom up, spilling down into the clouds. The tallest tip of the castle burst into pieces just as the curtain of light swallowed all of it. Aincrad ceased to exist, and the only things left in the world were clouds, the little floating platform, and Asuna and me.

There wasn't much time left. We were in the midst of a brief stay of execution, courtesy of Kayaba. When the world was completely gone, the NerveGear would execute its final procedure, and then it would truly be over.

I cupped her cheek with my hand and slowly met her lips. It was our final kiss. I took my time, trying to etch her entire existence into my soul.

"Well, this is good-bye."

She shook her head.

"No. It's not good-bye. We'll disappear as one. So we'll always be together."

It was almost a whisper, but firm. She turned in my arms to face me head-on, tilted her head slightly, and gave me a gentle smile.

"Hey, tell me your name. Your real name."

I was momentarily stunned. Then I realized that she was talking about my name in the life I'd left behind two years ago. The fact that I'd led a different life under a different name seemed like a story from the distant past, a world long lost. I spoke the name that floated up from the depths of my memory, grappling with the strange sensation.

"Kirigaya...Kazuto Kirigaya. I lost count, but I probably turned sixteen last month."

In that instant, I felt like the life that had paused so long ago started ticking once again. Kazuto slowly began to surface from deep within Kirito the swordsman. The heavy armor I'd gained in this world began to fall off, piece by piece.

"Kazuto...Kirigaya..."

She sounded out each syllable, then gave me a conflicted laugh.

"So you're younger than me...As for me, I'm Asuna Yuuki. Age seventeen."

Asuna...Yuuki. Asuna Yuuki. I repeated the most beautiful sounds I'd ever heard, committing them to my heart.

Suddenly, I felt something hot spilling out of my eyes.

The emotions that had been frozen in the endless twilight churned into motion. Incredible pain that ripped my heart in pieces. The first tears I'd shed since being taken prisoner in this world came flooding out of me. Sobs caught in my throat like a little child, my hands balled into fists.

"I'm sorry...I'm sorry I said...I would bring you back...I promised to do it...but..."

I couldn't finish the rest. In the end, I couldn't save the most important person in the world to me. The regret that I had let her shining future come to a premature end turned to tears that flowed out of me without cease.

"No...it's okay..."

Asuna was crying, too. Her tears were like glistening jewels in all the colors of the rainbow, particles of light that dripped and evaporated.

"I was so happy to have met you and lived with you, Kazuto. It was the happiest time of my life. Thank you...I love you..."

The end of the world was at hand. The giant fortress of metal and the endless expanse of sky had vanished into the light, and only the two of us remained. The air around us was sucked into the vacuum, fragmenting into dots of light.

Asuna and I embraced, waiting for the end.

In the midst of the incandescent light, it felt like even our emotions were being burned away. Only my yearning for Asuna was left. Everything disintegrated and evaporated, but I kept calling Asuna's name.

My vision was filled with light. Everything was covered in a veil of white, dancing into microscopic motes. Asuna's smile dissolved into the light that filled the world.

I love you... I love you so much...

A voice like a ringing bell sounded in the last bit of my consciousness.

The boundary that made Asuna and me separate beings vanished, and we crossed into each other.

Our souls mingled, became one, scattered.

Disappeared.

25

The air had a smell.

That, more than my continued consciousness, was the first surprise.

There was an enormous amount of information flowing into my olfactory glands. The piercing odor of disinfectant. The sunny scent of dry cotton. Sweet fruit. And my own body.

I slowly opened my eyes. The powerful beam of light seemed to pierce the back of my brain, and I quickly squeezed my eyelids shut.

After a while, I slowly opened them again. There was an interplay of various colors. Belatedly, I realized that it was fluid blocking my sight. I blinked, trying to clear it away, but the fluid kept coming. Tears.

I was crying. Why? There was a sharp pain in my chest that told of deep, agonizing loss. I felt as though I could hear someone calling out from a distance. I squinted against the light and tried to brush away the tears.

It seemed that I was lying on top of something soft. I could see what looked like a ceiling. There was a grid of off-white panels, and some of them were glowing, lit by something behind them. There was a metallic slit in the side of my vision. Probably a respirator. It was emitting air with a low groaning sound.

...A respirator. A machine. That shouldn't be here. Even the most proficient blacksmith couldn't fashion a machine. And even if it really was what it appeared to be, in Aincrad there was no electricity to—

This wasn't Aincrad.

I opened my eyes. That train of thought had finally woken me up. I tried to bolt upward—

But my body wouldn't listen. I had no strength. I raised my shoulder a few inches but immediately sank back down, pathetically weak.

I could move my right hand, though. I drew it out of the light blanket that had been placed over my body, raising it in front of my face.

For a moment, I couldn't believe that the startlingly thin limb in front of me was actually my own. This bony thing could never swing a sword. When I looked closely at the sickly pale skin, I saw countless soft, downy hairs. Purplish veins were visible beneath the surface, and fine wrinkles bunched around the joints. It was so incredibly realistic. In fact, it was so...*biological*...that it didn't feel right.

Some kind of injection catheter was fixed into the inner joint of my elbow. A thin cord ran out and up into a clear packet on the left, hung on a silver mounting rack. The packet was about 70 percent full of an orange liquid, dripping with a steady rhythm through a nozzle into the tube.

I moved my left hand, which was splayed next to my body, trying to find some sensation in it. I seemed to be lying on a bed made of some kind of high-density gel material. It felt slightly cooler than my body temperature, chilly and wet to the touch. I was naked, directly on top of it. A long-lost memory came back to me: a news segment from years ago, describing a product just like this one, a new development for patients who were bedridden for long periods of time. It protected against skin inflammation and broke down bodily waste.

I tried looking around now. The room was small, the walls the same off-white as the ceiling. There was a large window on the right with white curtains. I couldn't see beyond them, but the yellow-tinged light passing through the material seemed to be sunlight. At the left foot of the gel bed was a metal tray cart, on top of which lay a rattan cage. A large bouquet of flowers in subdued colors was placed inside the cage—this must be the source of the sweet scent. Behind the cart was a square door. It was shut.

Based on the information I'd just gleaned, this must be a hospital room. I was lying in it, all alone.

I focused again on my right hand, still in the air. On a whim, I held my index and middle fingers together and swiped downward.

Nothing happened. No sound effects, no menu window. I tried it again, harder this time. And again. Nothing happened.

Which meant this wasn't SAO. Another virtual world perhaps?

But the overwhelming amount of sensory information I was picking up spoke urgently of another possibility: the real world. The one I'd left two years ago, the one I thought I'd never see again.

The real world...It took me quite some time to fathom what that truly meant. For years, the world of swords and battle *was* my reality. It was hard to believe that world was gone, that I was no longer there.

I was back.

But there was no rush of emotion or joy with that realization. Only confusion and a faint sense of loss.

This was my reward for beating Kayaba's game. Even though I'd died, turned to nothingness, accepted my fate, and even felt satisfied with it.

That's right—I was fine with it all ending there. In the midst of that fierce light, I'd disintegrated, evaporated, become one with the world, with her...

"Ah..."

The sound tumbled out. There was a sharp pain in my throat; I hadn't used it in two years. But I wasn't even aware of that. I opened my eyes wide, trying to mouth the word, the name that came to me.

"A...su...na..."

Asuna. The pain that burned deep in my chest came back. Asuna, my beloved, my wife, the woman who had stood at the end of the world with me...

Was it a dream? A beautiful illusion I'd witnessed in an artificial world? For a moment, I wasn't sure.

No, she was real. We'd laughed together, cried together, fallen asleep together—those things weren't a dream. Kayaba had said, "Congratulations on beating the game, Kirito and Asuna." I heard him say her name. If I was included among the players who survived, Asuna must be as well.

The moment I realized this, my love and overwhelming longing for her exploded within me. *I want to see her. I want to touch her hair. I want to kiss her. I want to hear her voice.*

I summoned all the strength I could and tried to sit up. For the first time, I realized that my head was being held in place. I felt under my chin and unlocked a tough harness I found there. There was something heavy on my head. Using both hands, I was able to pull it off.

Once in a full sitting position, I looked at the object in my hands. It was a streamlined helmet in navy blue. Cables the same shade of blue extended from the long pad on the back of the helmet and down to the floor.

It was a NerveGear. This is what kept me connected to that world for two years. The unit was powered off. If memory served, there were gleaming lights that lined the outside when it was running, but now it was dark, the edges of the helmet flaking off and the alloy base exposed.

Inside it was all the memory of that world. I stroked the front of the gear, lost in thought.

I'll probably never wear you again. But you were good to me...

I laid the headgear down on the bed. At this point, my struggles with it were just a memory of the distant past. There were things for me to do here now.

It seemed like there was a commotion in the distance. I focused my ears, and as though my hearing was finally coming back to normal, various sounds jumped out at me.

I could hear a great number of people talking and yelling. Footsteps thumped hastily outside the door, and gurney wheels clattered by.

I didn't know if Asuna was in this hospital. The people playing SAO were from all over Japan, so the probability that she would just so happen to be in this building was slim at best. But this is where I'd start. No matter how long it took, I would find her.

I ripped off the thin blanket. There were countless cords attached all over my gaunt body. The electrodes on my limbs were probably meant to stimulate the muscles to prevent atrophy. I painstakingly removed each one. Orange lights on a bedside panel flashed on, and a high-pitched alarm sounded, but I ignored it.

I pulled out the IV, then swung my legs to the floor, finally free. Slowly and gently, I tried to stand. Quavering, I managed to support my weight at first, but my knees soon gave way. I had to laugh. *I could really use that strength stat again.*

On my second attempt, I was able to stay on my feet by leaning on the IV stand for support. I looked around the room, then spotted a patient's gown on the lower shelf of the cabinet that held the flowers.

Just the act of putting it on left me breathless. My limbs, which had been still for two entire years, were all screaming in protest. But I couldn't give up now.

Faster, faster, I told myself. My entire body needed her. My fight would not end until the moment I could hold Asuna in my arms again.

I gripped the metal stand like my trusty sword, giving it my weight, taking the first step to the door.

(The End — *Sword Art Online*, Volume 1)

AFTERWORD

The volume of *Sword Art Online* you hold in your hands now was my first novel, written for the Dengeki Game Novel Prize in 2002.

Despite my rush to finish it up, the draft was well over the submission limit of 120 pages, but without the skill or the bravery to cut it down to size, I slumped down to my knees in the corner and mumbled, "Forget it..."

But being the cheap type, I couldn't just toss out what I'd written, so in the fall of that year, I set up a website, deciding that I'd just publish it on the Internet. To my very fortunate surprise, I received a great many positive reactions from the start, and I used that as motivation to write a sequel, then a side story, then another sequel, and the next thing I knew, I'd been doing it for six years.

In 2008, I thought, *I'll give this another try.* I had just finished up a different story (well over the page limit again, but this time I was able to cut it to just under 120) that ended up winning the fifteenth Dengeki Novel Prize, as well as a number of other awards, for which I am very grateful. But that wasn't the end of my luck. I'll never forget my exultation when my editor read the scrawling output of my *SAO* series—just a pet project at this point—and said, "Let's publish this, too."

On the other hand, it was also extremely nerve-wracking. For one thing, this work contained so many major problems that it would be impossible to list them all here, most pressing of all being: If we're going to print something that's been available on the 'net, is it right to abruptly take the website down?

As a matter of fact, it was only through a series of lucky coincidences within a window of opportunity the size of the eye of a needle that I got the publisher's approval: the fact that it was happening just after I'd delivered my latest work, the fact that it was around the time that online games were just being recognized by society at large, and the fact that my editor was Kazuma "My Work Is My Girlfriend" Miki. If he hadn't taken the time out of his already packed schedule to read in a week every word of *SAO* I'd written, this would never have seen the light of day. I told myself that I wasn't a true gamer—er, true writer if I didn't take advantage of this once-in-a-lifetime opportunity. And thus, the paperback edition of *Sword Art Online 1: Aincrad* came to be.

This story is my starting point. It's something I've been writing to explore the concept of the online game and the virtual world. If possible, I'd love for you to experience that journey with me, all the way to its end.

It is here that I must thank my tremendous illustrator, abec, who took the tricky setting of "fantasy in a near-future VR game" and produced vivid depictions of the characters who battle against their fates. I should also thank my editor, Mr. Miki, who carefully read over the amateur original work and helped it be reborn in this new form.

And thanks are due to the many people who helped support the web version of *Sword Art Online* over the years. Without your encouragement, not only would this book never have existed, I would not be the Reki Kawahara I am today.

Lastly, my greatest gratitude goes out to you, for picking up this book!

Reki Kawahara — January 28th, 2009